"I absolutely love how wonderful Annika's books make me feel. I start reading and lose track of everything. Funny, sexy and enjoyable!"

~Wickedly Sweet and Synful Book Blog

W0007193

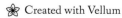

BREAKING THE BILLIONAIRE'S RULES

SECOND EDITION

ANNIKA MARTIN

Surround yourself with interesting people. Get them talking and laughing.

~THE MAX HILTON PLAYBOOK: TEN GOLDEN RULES FOR LANDING THE HOTTEST GIRL IN THE ROOM

Mia

My roommate Kelsey swings open the door to our apartment before I can finish unlocking it. "Oh my god, I nearly dropped my phone when you texted," she says. "I can't even imagine!"

"Right?" I throw my hat and scarf onto the couch. "Don't bother to hide your horror, because it'll be ten times worse than you think."

"Uh!" She pulls me into a quick hug.

"I feel sick every time I imagine how it'll be."

Kelsey lets me go. "Who even does that?" Her fists are balled, her lips pursed into an angry little rosebud. She's a dancer with awesome powers of emoting. "He just wants to crush you! He wants to demolish your dignity like a house of cards!"

"Okay, you can hide your horror a little," I say.

"No, I can't hide it. I hate him so much on your behalf, I want to burst!"

"Thank you."

"Of course," she says.

"You guys, do I need to call the overacting drama police?" My friend and former roomie, Lizzie, comes in from the other room.

"Oh my god, Lizzie!" I give her a big squeeze.

"I called in the cavalry," Kelsey says.

"Maybe it won't be so bad," Lizzie tries.

I raise a brow. "This is a man who woke up one day and thought, 'I'm rich and famous and I can have anything I want, and what I most want is for my old high school nemesis to be forced to deliver sandwiches to me in my office. In a friggin' cat suit.'"

"You can't be sure he requested you *personally*," Lizzie says.

"The office said as much when I tried to switch. It was a specific request for me to be the one to handle that building. It's that or I lose the job. And not just one time—no, no, no. Ongoing deliveries. You know it's him." I unbutton my coat. "It'll be the worst ten-year high school reunion ever."

Confession: I've spent a truly unhealthy amount of time imagining running-into-Max scenarios. They always involve me wearing an amazing gown; possibly a tiara. And our high school hostilities are so insignificant to me, I'm having trouble remembering them. I'm all, *Max who?* But in such a gracious way. My career is going so gangbusters that everything from high school is a dim footnote.

Unfortunately, ten years out from our graduation from The Soho High School for the Performing Arts (aka SHSPA, aka *the Shiz*) I don't have much to show for my career.

"Well, pizza's coming, so there's that," Lizzie says.

"Heart eyes." I peel off my winter coat, stripping down to the Meow Squad cat suit I'm forced to wear on my lunch delivery route.

I look up and catch them staring at it, and I can tell they're imagining it—what it will feel like. What is there to say to that?

Then Kelsey says the one thing you *can* say to that. "You're not alone."

I take a deep breath. My knotted shoulders relax a smidge. These girls are everything to me. Two best friends who are in it with me. "Thank you."

I go to my room to change into my favorite sloth T-shirt and bright pink yoga pants, and then I go back out and curl up on the couch.

Kelsey gives me a beer. Her purple fingernails match perfectly with the purple streaks in her jet-black hair. "CLC," she says. *Carb-loving comfort.*

Lizzie snuggles in next to me on the other side. "Were you just mortified?"

I retell the moment of discovery. One second I'm standing out at the Meow Squad truck, waiting for tomorrow's delivery assignment, feeling pretty happy about my life. Sure, I have a job where I have to dress as a cat and deliver food-truck orders to office workers, but it's a part-time job with insurance, the holy grail for up-and-coming actresses.

And then the next moment, I see Maximillion Plaza on the roster.

And the sun goes behind the clouds.

And shadows move across the land at terrifying speeds.

Giant birds with dinosaur faces screech across the sky.

"And I'm like, no friggin' way! You know he found out. I swear to you, the day I first tried on the outfit, the biggest thing on my mind was not how stupid I looked, or how grateful I got hired and all of that. My first thought was, what are the chances I'll ever have to deliver to Max Hilton? A million-something people in Manhattan, what are the chances Max orders from Meow Squad, and I end up with the delivery? Maximillion Plaza wasn't even in the Meow Squad delivery area when I first started. I thought I'd be safe. I should've known."

Lizzie winces. "Maybe he wants to apologize?"

"No way. Trust me—no apologies will be forthcoming. He's rubbing his hands in sweet anticipation."

"Was it that bad?" Kelsey asks.

"He once baked dirt into a brownie she had to eat on stage," Lizzie says. She's heard all of the stories. "She took a bite and she had to keep chewing—"

"—and it was dry and weird and gritty, and I so wanted to spit it out," I say. "Though to be fair, I did put a remote-control squeaking mouse cat toy in his piano right before his freshman recital. And I made it scrabble around while he played Chopin's Nocturne in E flat. A sweet, quiet piece." I snicker, remembering. "Of course he didn't react. Nothing fazes Max. He has a protective titanium exoskeleton."

Lizzie gets the pizza alert text and runs down to the lobby. Our apartment's official pizza is brie, potato, and caramelized onion. Crazy toppings are firmly against my pizza religion, but once you're out of Jersey, all is lost in the realm of pizza.

"You'll get through it." Kelsey doles out napkins.

"You don't know. Max is my kryptonite. Beyond kryptonite. Kryptonite doesn't live to destroy you. Kryptonite doesn't stare at you with an amused light in its eyes as you die inside."

"Well, you'll be able to quit when we land our parts," Kelsey says. "We'll have jobs for a year. At least."

"Dude, *Phantom of the Opera* has been running since eighty-eight," I say. "If this is successful, who knows how long it runs."

"Jobs for twenty years. Fifty!" Kelsey says. "We'll be old ladies, singing and dancing up there."

"Pinky slap!" I hold out my pinky. Kelsey slaps it with her pinky.

We're both going out for the massive *Anything Goes* revival. Kelsey's trying for one of Reno's Angels, a really demanding singing and dancing part, and I'm trying for the lead, Reno Sweeney. I'm shooting crazy high, but I feel like the part has my name on it. Deep down I feel it.

"We deserve it," I say.

"So deserve it!"

Kelsey especially does. Over winter, she found out her live-in boyfriend was cheating on her with four different women. Hence her presence as my new roomie.

Lizzie arrives with the pizza and sets it out.

Noelle, our shy mail carrier neighbor pops her head in. "I got your text."

"Enter!" I say.

"You sure?"

"Do I need to drag you in?"

She comes in and shuts the door behind her. She was so funny when she first arrived—our timid little mail carrier lost in the big city. Our building kind of adopted her. She lost her family, but she has us.

I scoot over to give her a place to sit, then I grab a piece of steaming, carb-laden yumminess and sink my teeth in, and for one blissful moment, Max is out of my mind.

"You should've switched over to my room when I moved

out," Lizzie says. "You shouldn't have to look at his stupid tower."

"Agreed," Kelsey says. "You know I'll trade rooms with you any day of the week. Just say the word."

I mumble and eat some more pizza. It's true; I can see part of Max's tower, Maximillion Plaza, through the configuration of buildings out my window. I had a lot of feelings when I realized that was his tower. Feelings like dark, hard diamonds in my heart.

"I wonder how he found out you were a Meow Squad delivery girl," Lizzie says. "Is it on Facebook or Instagram?"

"The day I'd post an image of me in that uniform," I say. "He had to find out some other way. God, I can only imagine his glee. He would've been like, *how the mighty have fallen.* But a more clever and witty version of it."

Kelsey groans and grabs another piece. Lizzie explains the drama to Noelle, who looks horrified.

"He is going to rub it in so hard," I tell her. "He'll be laughing the whole time while I set out his sandwich. And then I'll have to say *Meow* at the end. Like a trained monkey."

"Or a trained kitten," Lizzie says.

"Is that supposed to be a helpful comment?"

"Yes?" she squeaks. "No?"

Playfully I punch her arm. "Get with the pity program!"

Even back in high school Max was cool and superior, though if you watched him long enough—like really watched him—you could see that silence was one of his big strategies. And that underneath that aloof silence was the slightest edge of teen awkwardness. That's a little bit of what made me fall for him so hard.

Now he's remote and beautiful in his Manhattan lair, the head of the billion-dollar men's style empire that grew out of his infamous pickup guidebook, the international bestseller that helped catapult him to a level of notoriety to rival the Kardashians.

"Millennial Dean Martin," *Slate* magazine once called him.

I read somewhere that he laughs about that. I don't doubt it for a minute; of course Max would think he's too cool even for suave Rat Pack playboy Dean Martin.

"Will it help if I carry a black magic marker around town and black out one of his teeth whenever I see his face on a bus stop ad?" Kelsey asks.

Noelle widens her eyes at the very suggestion of vandalism.

"Yes," I whisper. "That would be extremely helpful."

"I'll give him a Frankenstein scar," Lizzie offers.

"That might make him look hotter."

"A penis coming out of his nose?" she tries.

"Here's the only thing I'm wondering," I say breezily, trying to come off like it doesn't bother me as much as it does, "is he planning on guffawing and being all *boo-yah* as I set out his sandwich? Or will he go for superior silence with a smirk? Never mind," I decide. "It'll be the smirk."

I sit back and stare at the nearly empty pizza box. I was a lot more excited about the pizza when it was still in the box.

Lizzie grabs her giant purse. "I have treats. First, dessert!"

"Did you frost special anti-Max cookies?" I ask hopefully.

"Something better." She pulls out a three-pack of Peanut Butter Kandy Kakes and tosses it to me.

"Oh my god! Where in the city did you find these?"

"Internet."

I rip open the plastic, press the package to my nose, and suck in the smell of my childhood. It was always a good day when you found Kandy Kakes in your lunch bag. It was about the treat, but it was emotional, too. Finding one of these meant our family was on a good streak. "You guys want one?"

"Not so much." Kelsey wrinkles her nose. "You have to be from Jersey to like those. I think it's a rule."

"Lizzie? Noelle?"

They shake their heads.

"All for you," Lizzie says.

Nobody I know appreciates Kandy Kakes, which is fine by me. I sink my teeth into the sponge cake-y, peanut-buttery goodness, which is of course wrapped in a thick layer of milk chocolate.

When I re-emerge from my dessert bliss, I notice Lizzie's tearing at something, trying to tear the molded plastic wrap off something rectangular. "What is that?"

"Something else I think might help."

"What?"

"Hold on." She claws at the package with her fingernails. "Uhh!"

"Is it a one-woman performance art show depicting wrap rage?" I ask.

She throws the package at me.

I catch it and turn it over. It's a dart set. "Um, thanks?"

Kelsey has scissors. "Gimme that." She cuts open the dart set.

"It goes with this." Lizzie pulls a beat-up paperback from a bag and slaps it onto our coffee table.

Not just any paperback. I grab it. "Excuse me? What is this?"

That would be a rhetorical question. I know exactly what it is. *The Max Hilton Playbook: Ten Golden Rules for Landing the Hottest Girl in the Room*. Most people call it *The Hilton Playbook*. It's Max's "how to get girls by being an arrogant jerk" guide. It sold millions of copies back when it came out, just a year or two after we graduated from high school.

Max launched his men's style empire after that. Shoes.

Watches. Body spray. Instagram stardom. They're saying he has a deal for a Netflix show.

I flip the book over.

The entire back cover is Max's face. It's one of the more iconic pictures of him; he looks devastatingly handsome, but that's not what's special about it—it's the way the shot captures his gaze, his ability to make you feel like he's looking right into you and you alone, all sparkling, knowing humor. Like he knows all of your secrets because you trusted him for a little while, and he stomped all over your heart. And you stupidly still love him.

"Don't worry, I didn't buy it new," Lizzie says, grabbing it from me. "No jerky billionaires were made richer in the getting of this book."

"That's not my question," I say. "It's more like, why is this thing even here?"

Lizzie smiles at Kelsey. "Because *plans*."

"Did you ever actually read this thing?" Lizzie asks.

"Hell no," I say. "Who would read it?"

"Not me." Lizzie rips the back cover off the book and tacks the picture onto the dart board. Kelsey clears the wall of our mementos, my fun cross stitches and even the picture of my dream shoes, Louboutin Solibria pumps in starshine pink.

"You got me a game of darts?" I say.

"On Max Hilton's face," she says, handing me the darts, which Kelsey has finally liberated.

"Oh, yikes!" Noelle exclaims.

"You shouldn't have," I say.

"Go go go!" Kelsey claps. "Kill, pussycat, kill!" Kelsey has the prettiest smile you've ever seen when she's excited.

I don't really want to throw darts, but my friends have gone through all this trouble. I shoot. I hit the wall. My galpals clap.

"I don't know about this, you guys." I sink back down onto

the couch. My friends take their turns with far more luck, then it's time for more beer.

We leave the darts on his face. It was a sweet thought.

"It's a good look on him," Kelsey says.

"Doomed to serve my nemesis every day of my life for the foreseeable future," I say. "Isn't that one of the punishments they give Greek gods? I would honestly rather roll a boulder up a mountain or have birds tear at my flesh."

"It really *is* as if he wants to punish you," Kelsey muses. "And he's found the most stunningly effective way to do it."

"If you're trying to cheer me up, it's not working."

Kelsey snorts and picks up Max's book. "Over a million copies sold," she reads. "A million suckers." She starts flipping through. "Newsflash, losers: Max Hilton picks up girls because he looks like Max Hilton. Not because he has some golden rules."

"I was thinking," Noelle says, "if you were truly insignificant to him, why would he bother making you deliver sandwiches? What if he needs you to do the delivery because you're *not* insignificant?"

Such a weird idea. My chest buzzes with forbidden hope. Always dangerous.

"You never know," Lizzie says. "Noelle might be right."

"Spoken by a woman newly in love," I say.

Lizzie grins. She's enjoying living with her man now. And she owns her own cookie bakery, so to say that she's seeing the bright side of things is an understatement. She's looking through a kaleidoscope of hearts and sugar frosting.

Kelsey's unusually quiet. Her nose is buried in the book.

Lizzie tries to distract me by informing me that today is National Square Dance Day. She describes the extreme difficulty of creating a cookie to commemorate square dancing. Her cookie bakery specializes in cookies that are frosted to ironically commemorate holidays. "I ended up doing a woman with a really big skirt. I thought about an accordion, because chocolate—"

"Wait one minute," Kelsey says. "No. No freaking way."

"What?" I ask.

Her jaw is set hard. "Nathan used one of these pickup techniques on me. He worked Max's system on me, and I fell for it."

Lizzie's eyes widen. She knows all about Kelsey's cheating ex.

"Maybe it's a coincidence," I try.

"You were there!" she says. "It was last fall at the Chiron Club. Remember how he wore the hat? And he told the funny, sweet story about the strange dog that got in his house?"

I sit up, not liking this. "The dog story was fake? The dog story was the only thing I liked about him."

"It's a script from this book! There are all these scripts of funny stories for men to tell in the back."

Lizzie looks stunned. "Who does that? Who picks up a girl with a fake story?"

"Nathan did. And these rules. What the hell? Okay, get this —" Kelsey holds up a finger and begins to read. "'Pick a girl, any girl. Go ahead and pick out a hot one—if you learn my system properly, you can have her. Get everyone laughing, but ignore the hot girl.'" She looks up. "Remember how he was all friendly and funny to all of you and ignoring me? It's a little technique called *reverse-chasing*."

"No," I say, feeling sick on her behalf. Nathan broke her heart into pieces and stomped on it. It was all Max's book?

"Okay, now I'm pissed at him on three levels," Lizzie says. "It's not right."

Kelsey continues to read. "'Act annoyed if she tries to get your attention.'" She looks up. "Remember? Nathan was totally doing that! His story was funny and sweet, and then I asked him a question, just joining in on the fun, and I touched his arm because it seemed like he wasn't hearing me and he's like, 'hey, stop pawing the goods.'"

"Stop *pawing* the *goods*?" Lizzie says. "That's a line from Max's book?"

"And we thought it was so funny that he said that," I say, stunned. "Men flock to you like rabid magpies, and this guy was all, 'stop hitting on me.'"

"It's a technique right from Max's book," Kelsey says. "I can't believe it worked on me. I can't believe I got picked up with a technique!"

I shake my head, remembering how Nathan seemed to defy the laws of dating physics—he was obviously straight and single and open to a hookup, but not interested in pretty Kelsey, the woman every man seems to want.

"*Reverse-chasing*," she reads, "'Act like you think she's hitting on you. Rebuff her imaginary advances, but be playful about it.'"

"And when you asked him to dance, he goes, 'You think I'm easy? Just a piece of meat for you to parade around the dance floor?' And then you're staring at him in shock, and he goes, 'are you mentally undressing me?'"

Through gritted teeth, she says, "A script."

Suddenly we're all three reading the book.

"He used a lot of these techniques to pick up the other women he was sleeping with, too," Kelsey says. "This book was Nathan's bible."

My face feels hot.

"No way," Lizzie says at one point, grabbing it from Kelsey. "This jungle kiss—I think somebody did it on Jada Herberger." Jada's an actress friend from the fourth floor.

Lizzie's on the phone with Jada. "Tell me if this sounds familiar." She begins to read instructions from Max's book.

Basically, the man is supposed to tell the woman that her perfume is intriguing, and then act surprised when she says the name of it, like he can't quite believe it. He's then supposed to gently brush the woman's hair off her shoulder, taking another whiff, just to be sure.

Lizzie continues to read, "'Now memorize this line—*There's something about it. The way it mixes with your body chemistry that's...hard to describe.* Now pull away. Take your time. You're not the pursuer here—she is. Say, *scent is such an afterthought in our society—people don't understand how deeply and intimately it links to the most primal part of our brain. That's why you'll see animals scenting each other before mating...*'"

Screaming on the other end.

Lizzie winces and pulls the phone away from her ear until it stops. "No, I'm reading it in a book! That line is straight out of a book," she says. "The Hilton Playbook. Get this—" She reads another passage where the man is to talk about how wild animals gently bite the scruffs of the animals they're mating with, that this, too, connects to the primal brain. Max's instructions go on to instruct the man to run his hand up the back of her neck and pull gently on her hair and say, *see?*

More screaming from the other end.

Lizzie pulls the phone away from her ear. "Jada's coming up."

"Tell her to bring beer," Kelsey says.

"Bring beer!" Lizzie says.

Jada's up with a six-pack of beer a few minutes later. She has bright blonde hair and pouty lips that are vampiric in a pretty way. She and her roommate Tabitha love all things shiny and sparkly. She's a walking color explosion tonight, right down to her silver sparkle combat boots. "You're telling me the guy was following a script?" she demands. "Is that the book?"

"You want to hear the rest?" Lizzie asks.

"No!" Jada hands over the beer and folds her arms in a huff. Then, "Yes."

Kelsey sets her up with a frosty glass for her beer as Lizzie reads on, this whole sexy thing about mammals and being hard-wired to respond to being smelled and having their hair gently pulled...and even more, being lightly bitten on the neck.

"Noooo." Jada presses her palms to her forehead. "That was all the Hilton Playbook?"

"More?" Lizzie says.

"We've gone this far," Jada says. "May as well."

Lizzie reads on. "'She'll be ready to kiss you, but don't give her what she wants. Say, *that's why it's such an intense sensation to be bitten on the neck. The lightest pressure with the teeth, right on the side of the neck, stimulates the basest of instincts. Not a lot of people understand this.* Now touch the side of your own neck, showing her where you want her to bite you. Look into her eyes and say, *It's okay, you can.* Act as if she's been dying to do it. If you've been doing my system right, she'll reach around and take the back of your hair and gently bite your neck.'"

"This is so messed up," I say. "Did you bite him, Jada?"

"I feel so stupid," Jada says, mortified. "Yes, I bit him."

"Nothing to feel mortified about." I sling an arm around her. "How were you supposed to know?"

"You couldn't know," Noelle agrees.

"Get this—Nathan, my ex? He was following the book, too," Kelsey tells Jada. "And I lived with him for a *year*. While he cheated on me—using more techniques from it!"

"Oh my god," Jada says.

I grit my teeth. I can't believe Max's book played such a huge role in Kelsey's disaster of a relationship. And now Jada?

Lizzie still has her nose in the thing. She raises a finger in the air. "'If she does *not* take the bait, do not smile. She needs a negative consequence. Find something more interesting to look at. Then turn back to her. Now she's ready for your command. Look into her eyes. *Go on. Bite me here.*'"

I shake my head. No words.

The passage goes on. The man is to criticize her bite, and show her how to do it properly. He may give her "mild approval in the form of a lazy smile" when she gets it right. "'Remember, you are the prize she is vying for. Eventually, she'll get the bite right. At this point, finally, you should drop your gaze to her lips. She's won the privilege of your kiss.'"

We all scream.

Jada grabs the book. "I can't believe it was all an act from a book!" She frowns. "Written by that jackass who thinks he's Gandy with his face plastered everywhere? I can't believe I fell for it."

"I would've gone for it," I say, trying to make her feel better. "Who doesn't want a guy with knowledge of erotic animal things? A little crazoo in bed, you know..."

"And base primal instincts," Lizzie says. "Base primal instincts are a plus in a man. Except when he's driving. Or fixing a computer."

"Did he wear a weird hat?" I ask. "Max's book suggests a weird hat."

"No, but he had a lot of cool bracelets and a really shiny shirt under his blazer," Jada says. "And he was not primal or in *any way* crazoo in bed. Because it was all Max Hilton's material. Why am I just finding out about this now? I need to read this whole book!"

"Mia knows Max Hilton," Kelsey says. "They went to the Shiz together."

"Max Hilton went to the Shiz?" Jada says. "What was he studying, utter jackhole-ishness?"

"Yes," I say, heaving myself off the couch. "You could major in theater arts, classical music, or utter jackhole-ishness." I pull the darts off Max's face. "And his name was Maxfield Miller. Not Max Hilton."

Jada just looks mystified. "The Shiz? I'm still hung up on that detail. You can't be a faker and go to the Shiz."

"Classical piano," I add, because I know that's going to be her next question—*what did he study?*

She does a dramatic, almost cartoon-like double take. "Piano? Max Hilton can play...piano?"

"Dude," Kelsey says from the couch. "If Max got into the *Shiz* for piano, he can play piano." She says it like that explains it, and it does explain it. The Shiz is one of the most elite performing arts high schools on the planet. "He comes from a classical music dynasty—didn't you know that? His father is some famous conductor, and his mother is Gloria Perez, the violinist. And he and Mia were high school rivals in a bitter feud."

"You and Max were in a bitter feud?" Jada says.

"Ninety-nine percent of the time." I hand her the darts. "Go for it."

Jada lines up her shot, one eye closed.

I watch her throw, glad none of them thought to ask me to tell about the one percent of the time where Max and I didn't hate each other. That's the part I think about the most, the part that I daydream about the most.

It's the part that hurts the most.

Jada nails his face with scary precision, three times in a row —*whop-whop-whop*—much to Kelsey's delight. Kelsey is acting upbeat, but I can tell she's hurt and angry, and I don't blame her. Finding out that Nathan was following Max's stupid book the entire time has opened old wounds—and even made them worse. Their whole relationship was even more fake than she thought.

Jada turns back to me. "Max Hilton got into the Shiz for

classical *piano?* I'm sorry, I'm still having trouble comprehending that. I thought he was some kind of shallow style guy."

I shrug. He's a shallow style guy now, but for one short summer, he was thoughtful and sensitive and romantic, and I loved him with all my heart. Apparently it was all an illusion.

I plaster on a grin. "His true talent? Really dorky old-timey show tunes."

"No!" Jada says.

"You should hear him sing songs from *Oklahoma!* Playing the aw-shucks lovesick cowpoke, Curly McLain. Goofy comic songs. I'm telling you," I say.

Cue more stunned drama. Theater friends give good reaction to gossip, and this gossip is better than most. Max is the ultimate icon of cynical cool urbanity. He's James Bond and David Gandy's love child on steroids.

"That is the last thing I can imagine out of Max Hilton," Noelle says.

Exactly.

Because Max's brand is all about ordering cocktails by the pool and careless jet-set fun. And high-style shots of him on billboards and the sides of busses and in the pages of magazines. And showing up on the society sites surrounded by beautiful women.

And those women? They become known as Max Hilton girls. That's his power—the women he dates actually lose their names. They lose their identities. They become frivolous accessories for his enchanted life.

"Is this goofy-singing-cowboy thing something we can find on YouTube?" Jada asks. "Pretty please, please say *yes?*"

"Do you think, with all of Max Hilton's money and power, that he would allow a YouTube of him singing goofy to be out there?" I say. "That he and his people wouldn't put the boot down on something like that so hard?"

What I don't say is that I've looked. Like there have been times I go back to it in my mind and I think it maybe never happened, and so I look. And it's never there. And it crushes me anew every time. Maybe it's stupid, but that's the Max I loved. Or thought I loved.

"How did you never tell any of us this bit of gossip?" Kelsey demands.

I shrug again. In truth, I've kept the memory in a little box inside me like a fragile keepsake. Even now, telling it, I feel like I'm betraying him, somehow. Betraying that amazing summer. Even though there's nothing to betray. That role was nothing but a cynical joke to Max.

"You witnessed this?" Jada says.

"I was in the summer production with him," I say. "I sang opposite him. So yeah."

Jada blinks, newly baffled.

I wouldn't believe it either if I hadn't been there.

"And you were enemies," Jada confirms.

"We made careers out of humiliating each other. Max's business partner Parker went there, too," I say. "It's just old Shiz week over there at the Maximillion Plaza."

"And guess which Meow Squad delivery cat is going to have to deliver his lunch from now on? Starting tomorrow?" Kelsey says.

Jada gasps. "No!" Then, "Not that it's *that* bad."

"Don't even," I say. "I have to be a servile minion to my high school rival. Wearing a cat suit. And he's a billionaire in a gleaming tower. And really, what better way to say I'm a *loser* than to wear triangle ears on your head for your foodservice job?"

Lizzie gives me an exaggerated frown.

"Shut it." Kelsey points at me. "You're not a loser. You're an amazing actress. You got such raves on *St. George and the Dragon*. You know you're gonna land *Reno*."

"Would you be fired if you let your friend Jada put toothpaste in his sandwich?" Jada asks.

I smile.

We spend the next hour reading the book to each other. Max's ideas are diabolical. Creative genius. You can say a lot of things about him, but he never was stupid. There are lots of lists of principles and things. *Women are like dogs. They like to know you're in charge.* That one gets major groans.

There's a knock at the door at nine. I think it's a neighbor, coming to complain about the noise, but it's Antonio, my cousin from Italy, script in hand.

"Oh my god!" I say. "Antonio, I completely forgot."

Antonio's a male model who did a lot of runway work in Milan, and now he's here trying to break into acting. He doesn't have a lot of stage experience, which is a nice way of saying he's awful at acting. He's the most loyal guy with the biggest heart ever, and I've been trying to help him, but he has a serious overacting problem that hasn't been improved by his fascination with books on character motivation and method acting.

Antonio's smile is tentative—wary, even; I can't tell whether he's upset that I forgot about our practice date or whether he's overwhelmed by the angry vibe in the room.

"You guys remember my cousin Antonio, right? We were supposed to run lines." I turn back to him. "I'm so sorry."

"We'll all run lines with you." Kelsey pulls him in and shoves the book into his hands. "First you have to tell the truth, though—do you recognize this book? Have you ever used it to pick up women?"

Antonio reads the inside description, which guarantees success picking up nines and tens or you get your money back.

"A pickup book? I'm a male model with an Italian accent, *cara*. What would I need with such a book?"

"True, he doesn't need such a book," I confirm. "Unless it's to drive off women by beating them over the head with it. He could use it for that."

Antonio sighs wistfully, flipping through the book, reading random pages. "Americans." He shakes his head. He reads aloud, "'Never ask a woman what she wants—tell her what she wants. You are a capricious god and she is your subject.'"

We all groan.

He reads more, fascinated. To be fair, the book *is* fascinating.

"Such stuff would work on men, too," Antonio observes, shutting the book. "You could wrap a man around your little finger with these techniques."

"If you're an awful person," I say.

Antonio shrugs in his European way. "But if you wanted to bring a man to his knees. Some of them would perhaps need to be adjusted but..." He lifts the book. "This is what I'm saying."

"Seriously?" Kelsey asks. "You honestly think these techniques could bring a guy to his knees?"

"Of course," he says.

Kelsey stares at him a moment longer, then she's grinning so wide, it squeezes my heart. It's been a long time since she smiled like that, and it makes me want to smile, too.

Then she turns to me. Not just turns to me, points the high beam of her exuberant gaze at me. "Could those techniques maybe even bring Max to his knees?"

I narrow my eyes. I love seeing her happy again. But I'm not sure I like where this is going. "What are you thinking here, Kelsey?"

"I'm thinking about justice," she says.

"Yes!" Jada turns to me, too, now. "Justice. You could show him how it feels, Mia."

"I'm not doing Max Hilton pickup techniques on Max Hilton," I say.

"It's not about pickup techniques, it's about showing him how it feels to have somebody work a system on him," Kelsey says. "He needs to know. It's perfect karma."

"Except he wrote the book," I say. "It probably wouldn't work on him."

"Or maybe it would work on him better than it would work on anyone else," Lizzie says. "He wrote a manual on how to get to a person's heart. How many hearts do you think he knows firsthand? One. He knows exactly *one* heart firsthand. His own."

"You're assuming he has a heart."

My pals laugh. They think I'm being extreme. I'm not. They weren't there when he crushed mine.

I should've known he was heartless. All of the signs were there. For example, Max could play the most demanding pieces with stunning precision...and zero emotion. A wildly impressive robot. I'd call him that sometimes. I'd joke to my friends that he played like the *Terminator*, knowing it would get back to him.

"Anyway," I say. "I think he'd recognize somebody running his own golden rules on him."

"No way. He'd never know. He wrote that book almost ten years ago," Kelsey says. "My sister writes books. She can't remember anything she wrote even one year back. She says her head fills up with a new book and crowds out the old one. And this guy, he's running a billion-dollar business and being all Mister Celeb? Trust me, Max Hilton has no memory of what's in this book."

Jada turns to me. "Do it! Teach him a lesson. Make him crawl on his grovelly knees."

"I don't know if it can be done by a person who's just delivering sandwiches," I say. "And the whole reason he requested my deliveries is to make fun of me."

"You'll see him every day. It's perfect!" Jada says. Antonio and Kelsey agree—they're full of ideas. Even Lizzie is getting into it.

I bite my lip.

I've been dreading tomorrow with every fiber of my being. I even thought about quitting, weighing the pain of going without insurance, without allergy meds, and possibly even without a place to live against being under Max's imperious thumb.

But no. I need that job.

It never occurred to me to fight back. I was preparing just to endure it.

The girl I was in high school would be all *hell no!* to that. The south Jersey girl full of fire and confidence and mile-high plans to conquer Broadway—she'd never buckle under and assume defeat. She'd never quit Meow Squad just because Max may or may not have ordered a sandwich. And she'd raise hell if it helped her friends.

Sometimes I wonder where that girl went.

Admittedly, it's been a demoralizing few years of scrimping and saving, working menial jobs, trying out for every part under the sun, working my ass off in dance lessons and acting lessons and voice lessons and lessons to get the Jersey girl erased from my voice, get my accent smoothed out. I've been out there hustling, but in some ways, I feel like I'm still on square one.

"Use his own system to wrap him around my little finger..." I whisper, trying it out, "and then I bring him to his knees."

"His grovelly knees," Jada clarifies.

Kelsey is beaming at me. She's convinced I can do it.

I wring my hands, thinking back over the endless hours of holding her, comforting her as she sobbed over how bad Nathan screwed her over—using Max's book as his guide. And then there's Jada. And lord knows who else.

My friends need me.

And maybe I need me, too. Max doesn't get to mess with me again.

I stand straight and tall. I jam my fists into my hips with a confidence I don't really feel. "Okay, then," I say. "I'll do it. I'm gonna bring Max Hilton to his grovelly knees."

Kelsey hugs me. Noelle and Jada are clapping. Antonio is insisting it can be done, and Lizzie is finding pens and markers, and then we open more beers.

2

You are the alpha. Adorn yourself with symbols of your superiority.

~THE MAX HILTON PLAYBOOK: TEN
GOLDEN RULES FOR LANDING THE
HOTTEST GIRL IN THE ROOM

Mia

Two hours later, Max's dart-porcupined picture is a distant memory.

There is something new on the wall: a giant chart made up of taped-together sheets of butcher paper that Lizzie borrowed from an artist on the third floor. Across the top, in heavy blue magic marker, Kelsey has written *Operation Bring Max Hilton to his grovelly knees!*

There are ten checkboxes for his ten golden rules, which are more like techniques. The hot-cold move. The power play. Pulling out the praise rug. Every time I do a technique on Max, I get a checkmark.

The idea is that I'm supposed to do at least one technique on him per visit. And at the end of ten visits, he'll be on his knees. I don't know if I can pull it off, but it means something to Kelsey and Jada that I'm fighting for them. And it makes me feel like less of a victim with these visits.

I point to the first box. *Adorn yourself with symbols of your superiority.* "This one is already a problem."

Kelsey turns to the page with the rule and reads, "'Demonstrate your alpha status by wearing standout clothes and otherwise adorning yourself with symbols of your utter superiority.' Seems pretty straightforward."

"I have to wear the cat outfit. You get fired if you cover it up or don't wear it. Seriously, they'd fire me if I showed up in a gown or a tiara or something."

Kelsey wants to see the employee handbook. I grab my laptop and find the PDF of it.

Jada reads over our shoulders. "It says that you can't hide the ears or put other clothes over the cat suit, but what if you became the most fabulous cat? There's nothing here forbidding you from jazzing up the outfit."

"You guys, the fact that I'm a delivery girl who has to wear an embarrassing cat outfit is not a quality I want to play up."

"Unless you work it!" Kelsey says. "You know how to work an outfit better than anyone."

"I'm not working the Meow Squad delivery outfit."

"Let's get Tabitha! She has a glue gun! And sequins and rhinestones!" Jada says.

"The sequins and rhinestones are staying downstairs," I say.

"But we need them!" Lizzie says. "And Tabitha can do your hair. And you'll need fake eyelashes."

"Oh my god, no!"

"I have those silver go-go boots," Kelsey says. "Go get your outfit, Mia. We're going to make you the most fabulous delivery cat of all."

I'm shaking my head.

"Don't you want to bring him to his grovelly knees for all of womankind?" Jada asks. "While turning the tables on him? And then crush him under your sparkly silver heel?"

Lizzie is grinning. "This is going to be perfect!" She reads more from the alpha-signaling chapter.

Meanwhile, Kelsey grabs the magazine picture of the insanely expensive Louboutin Solibria pumps in starshine pink that I've been coveting.

I sigh when I see them, like I always do. They're the ultimate fairy godmother shoes.

She waves it in the air. "If you do all ten of the golden rules to Max over the course of your deliveries, I'm putting one hundred dollars toward your Louboutins." She tapes it at the far-right side of the *Operation Bring Max Hilton to his grovelly knees!* chart.

"I'm in for a hundred," Jada says.

"Two hundred fifty!" Lizzie says.

Antonio shrugs, throws down some twenties. Just like that, we're almost halfway to the shoes.

"Wow," I say.

"As thanks," Kelsey says.

Ten minutes later, expert blinger Tabitha arrives with her glue gun, and we get to work on blinging up my cat delivery outfit while Antonio reads the book aloud. He's discovered a concept called *prize baiting* where you're supposed to go places with a really beautiful woman on your arm, ideally two women. It's all about seeming pursued by others while appearing unavailable to your target.

"I don't know about going around with two beautiful women on my arm," I say.

"What about two beautiful men?" Jada asks. And suddenly everyone is staring at Antonio.

"I do not share," Antonio says. "Please. One of me is enough, no?"

We all groan, but we're joke groaning, because one Antonio is worth two if not three or four normal hot guys.

"I'll do it. I'll be your suitor," Antonio declares. "But I'll need a good backstory."

"No backstory," I say. Backstory is what leads Antonio to overacting. Hidden motivations and all of that. "It wouldn't be a speaking part."

"I follow you in on your delivery," Antonio says, "so jealous am I when you so much as look at another man."

"You can't follow me on my deliveries," I say. "You'd get me fired. This is a small walk-on part. A cameo. No jealousy backstory."

Antonio's bummed, but my outfit is looking kind of wonderful, though that might be the beer talking. Kelsey's calling for me to model it.

I go in my bedroom and put it all on, including the cat ears. I inspect the transformation in the mirror. Jada and Tabitha have edged the V-neck of the cat suit with sequins, which spray outward over the bodice—there's a definite figure skater vibe going on. The apron got the same treatment. I fit the ear headband onto my head; the ears are trimmed with sequins except for crystal jewels at the tops. They did a very creative job.

Somebody's playing Flawless by Beyoncé. I decide to go for it. I shove my feet into Kelsey's silver boots and dance my way out. Everybody *oohs* and *aahs*. I don't know if it's the beer or the fun night or what, but I'm feeling pretty good.

We hang out a bit more after that, me in the outfit. At one point, I pick up the book, looking to see if there are even sex tips.

He's rumored to be amazing in bed, but I tell myself it would be all cold precision, like his piano playing.

Heartless tricks where he amuses himself with you and then casts you aside with your heart in pieces.

Maybe now he'll see how it feels.

3

An agreeable personality is a boring personality; be cocky and challenging.

~THE MAX HILTON PLAYBOOK: TEN GOLDEN RULES FOR LANDING THE HOTTEST GIRL IN THE ROOM

Mia

My blinged-out outfit isn't feeling all that fun in the grim morning light of our cold kitchen. In fact, rather than improving the look of my delivery uniform, the sparkly stuff seems to be saying, *in case you haven't noticed, check it out! I'm wearing a dorky delivery outfit!*

I pull on my winter coat and hat and trudge to the subway station. The closer I get, the more my heart sinks. I'll have to do my entire route in it—not just the delivery to Max Hilton.

But I remind myself that I'm not doing it just for me. I'm doing it for justice. For Kelsey and Jada and all the other women who got worked over by his system.

I reach the Meow Squad truck. I don't see our driver, but my work frenemy, Sienna, is there.

I stroll over with confidence that I don't feel.

Sienna has pretty strawberry blonde hair and a dusting of freckles on her perfect nose, basically, the kind of looks that allow her to come off either beautifully scrappy or beautifully elegant, depending on the needs of whatever part she's competing with me for. She also has amazing fashion sense and cool friends who seem slightly futuristic.

She feels confident about her superiority to all of us, and she's 98 percent right. I like to pretend I don't care about her opinion, but I actually do.

Sienna even has an amazing talent for posing. It helps that she has a really long, willowy body and long limbs, so when she leans against a wall, it's *willowy girl leaning cool*, whereas when I do it with my considerably shorter and less willowy limbs, it just looks like *pasta-fed girl of sturdy Italian stock is sooo weary. Pasta-fed girl needs to work on cardio. Pasta-fed girl shouldn't have gotten bangs, but she's doing the best she can, so give her a break already.*

Sienna is eyeing my sparkly boots. "What's up with the boots?"

"Nothing. Just..." I decide it's now or never. I pull off my hat and take off my coat and shove the stuff in the back of the truck. And then I turn and try to look natural.

Sienna is staring at my uniform with a stunned look. Utterly stunned. Let's just say here that you wouldn't call it stunned admiration.

She devotes extra staring time to my sequined ears, her

pretty features twisted into horrified yet delighted confusion. "You lose a bet or something?"

I'm about to explain the whole thing, but then I decide not to. An actress commits to a part. "No, I've decided that I'm the queen of delivery cats."

Sienna adds a lip twist. "Are you trying to be funny?"

"Do I look like I'm trying to be funny? Do you see the work that went into this? I'm the queen of the delivery cats."

"What? You just...decided that?" she asks.

"That's right," I say, trying to keep the uncertainty out of my voice. "I decided it."

She gapes at me a bit longer.

I smile and pull out my phone.

"Oh-kaaaaaay." She pulls out her phone, too, with an attitude of, *done with the crazy person.*

I scroll through Instagram miserably. I just have to get through this one day. And Max's reaction. What have I done?

It's possible somebody else at Maximillion Plaza specifically requested me as the delivery girl assigned to that tower. I don't know anybody else there, but maybe somebody who saw me in a show or something?

Probably wishful thinking.

"So isn't *queen of the delivery cats* kind of like declaring yourself the *queen of the Port-a-potty?*" Sienna's staring at me again.

"It's not like that at all," I say, pocketing my phone. "I am queen. It's a desirable thing."

She frowns. "So you think you're the manager now?"

"No." I try to look proud. I straighten my spine, suck in a breath. "It's like, the queen of England doesn't actually run the country. I'm queen of the delivery cats like that. I'm queen in spirit, in enthusiasm, in adornment. I'm alpha cat, and these shiny things signify my alpha cat status."

"Well, they signify something, that's for sure," she grumbles.

"They signify my superiority," I say, really going for it, at least on the outside. On the inside, I wish I could rip off the sequins and rhinestones and glam eyelashes and hide in a hole.

"That's not the word I was thinking of," Sienna continues. "The word I was thinking starts with a P and rhymes with *rathetic*."

I shrug, trying to think of something clever to say back to her.

There's this little pep talk in the alpha-signaling section of Max's book where he discusses how difficult it is to stand out from the herd. "When you alpha-signal, it's not just about looking amazing, it's also about communicating that you have enough personal power to pull off a bold look. The more you own your look, the more power you communicate," he writes. "Just keep owning it, and when that doesn't work, own it some more."

Thinking about that passage comforts me, which is ironic on about five different levels.

"I'm the top cat now," I say, trying to keep owning it, repeating it. "I'm the *queen* of the cats."

"What if I decide to be queen?" Sienna asks.

"Too bad," I say. "There can only be one queen."

She laughs, like it's all a big joke. But she actually seems mad. Could superior Sienna honestly be jealous of me suddenly?

This crazy scheme may not work as part of a plan to give Max Hilton a taste of his own medicine, but it's turning out to be an amazing Sienna Carlisle annoyance device.

"Whatever." She goes back to her phone.

Our sector driver, Rollins, comes around to the back of the truck. He gives me a startled look, then starts pulling out carts.

Meow Squad delivers food-truck food to people in office

towers and residential high-rises throughout Manhattan. The stuff gets ordered and paid for through an app. We're a well-oiled network of food dispersal—people in cat costumes whose job it is to wait in line and bring food to drivers like Rollins, who assemble the carts and bring them to the runner cats, and we runner cats do the deliveries.

Our high-style carts are more tall than wide, all the better to fit into crowded elevators. They're made of brushed stainless steel with the orange Meow Squad logo on the sides and hot and cold insulation compartments. We're adding new buildings and new cats all the time.

Rollins lifts my cart out of the back and onto the pavement, turning the handle to me with a nervous smile at my new adornments.

Rollins is a sweet, naïve farm boy who grew up in the rural hinterlands of some western state, and then came to the city as part of a really religious production of *Joseph and the Amazing Technicolor Dreamcoat.*

He thinks tattoos and facial piercings are Satanic and says nerdy things like, *We give 110 percent of ourselves in every rehearsal!* We're all kind of shocked he's lasted this long in the city.

We go through our carts, checking our condiments and chips stash.

"This is going to be great," I say to nobody in particular, trying to exude personal power. "I'm the ultimate delivery cat. And the ending meow? I've got something better."

That gets Sienna's attention. We delivery cats are supposed to say *meow* after each delivery. It's a fire-able offense not to say it. Most of us say it to the tune of *thank you*. It sounds less dorky that way.

"What are you going to do?" she asks.

I mimic putting down a meal, then I put my hands on my

hips and strike a pose, determined to commit. I focus on channeling personal power, on putting style and moxie into the line, even if it makes me sound ridiculous and *rathetic*. "Meowwwwwww!" I emote.

Sienna looks stunned.

Rollins barks out a laugh.

I hold the pose a moment longer and then turn back to my duties, shaking inside.

What a dork I am.

When I turn back to Rollins, he has this odd look on his face. Have I finally put poor, wholesome, wide-eyed Rollins over the edge? Is he wondering how he can switch with another driver? Or just go back home where he's safe from crazy people?

"Cat got your tongue?" I say. Because if Rollins has something to say, I just want it out there.

"It's just that..." Long pause.

"What?" I press.

He starts to say five different things and then stops himself each time, opening and closing his mouth like a fish. Then he says, simply, "You're gonna kill it with tips out there."

I blink. "You think?"

He nods. "Queen of the cats," he says with a note of admiration in his voice. "That you are."

Sienna glares daggers into the back of his head, but I just want to hug him.

In fact, Rollins turns out to be right. My first two towers have been on my route forever, but when I appear as a fabulous alpha cat, people sit up and take notice. They smile. They engage with me more. They give me compliments and say things like, *New ears? New boots?*

I play up the queen thing, strutting around and having fun. When they ask me about the change, I say things like, *I've decorated my outfit because I'm the most wonderful delivery cat ever*, or, *I've declared myself queen of the delivery cats.*

My tips go through the friggin' roof.

I'm stunned. The more I work it, the higher the tips.

I'm back out at noon getting the cart for Maximillion Plaza from Rollins.

I'm checking the order on my Meow Pad, which is an iPad that they decided they needed an embarrassing name for, and enter the cart number to check the roster. And there it is. An order for a roast beef and swiss croissant sandwich. Twenty-fifth floor. No office number.

His.

There's always been a strange, sizzling line of knowledge between us like that. Not sizzling hot, but sizzling painful. A sizzle that stings.

It's for sure his.

My heart pounds. It's fear, but something more—a kind of strange exhilaration. I'm going in there. I'm gonna do this.

I make my way to the building, steeling myself. The other deliveries were easy audiences, but Max zeroes in on your weak points. He sees through your bullshit. Queen of the cats is pure bullshit—bullshit that *he* invented.

Will he know?

I keep going back to what Kelsey said, though—her sister never remembers what she wrote even a year ago. Max is running a men's lifestyle empire now; surely the things he put in a book nearly a decade ago have faded into the dust heap of time. Also, his system was for men. He'll never recognize it coming from a woman...right?

Can I actually beat him with his own system? Or at least use it to keep him from humiliating me again?

Anyway, I can't go back now, and my sisters are counting on me. It's this most of all that gives me the rush of courage that propels me through the gleaming steel-and-glass doors of Maximillion Plaza; this that gets me across the high-ceilinged lobby.

It's super lux inside, an assault of white marble and exposed pipes and polished metal beams. There's this ultra-mod lighting scheme, like somebody threw a basket of enchanted glowing orbs toward the ceiling, and they froze midflight in an arrangement that's entirely random, yet utterly perfect.

Naturally.

What you also can't miss are the mammoth photographs of Max on the towering walls. Black-and-white on-brand photos.

I recognize some of the shots from magazine and billboard campaigns for his eveningwear line, his sportswear line, his exclusive wristwatch line.

There's Max leaning in a darkened doorway, all merciless charm in a tux that looks lived-in and maybe even fought in. The tux clings wantonly to his muscular chest and shoulders.

There's thoughtful Max leaning on a railing, looking out over some Mediterranean cliffs wearing a Maximillion brand watch on his very muscular forearm, shot with some type of photographic trickery that makes you really, really want to touch his skin.

Further down, there's a shot of Max surrounded by beautiful women, but not in a cheesy way. Max is never cheesy. He's too smart. Too good.

No, Max is iron-clad. He's a steamship with powerful, iron-clad sides. Your puny little shots ping right off of him as he looks on amused, at ease, a glorious god.

It's no wonder that millions of men emulate Max, strive to be the cool, untouchable man of mystery with the world at his feet, a man whose every move is fawned over by *Entertainment Today*. Max walks into a party on a yacht and everyone on board scrambles for his attention, competes to offer him his favorite cocktail, ready to smile at his quips, but not too hugely, because you don't want to be sycophantic!

The security guard waves me into an elevator area. I wait alongside a bunch of beautiful people with respectable jobs that don't require them to wear ears and make animal sounds.

Sweat trickles down my spine.

I shouldn't have been surprised Max found out I was a delivery cat. Max always finds out everything that is wrong. Everything you want to hide, he finds it and exploits it.

The elevator doors open and I get in with the group. A few of them glance discreetly at me. I hold my head high.

I go over various self-confidence mantras I have.

Many successful actresses were still struggling in their late twenties and thirties.

Another: *You made a choice to reach for the stars, to have a career on Broadway. There's no shame in a delivery job, if that's what it takes. It's called paying dues.*

And when things are at their worst: *You have a right to dream.*

The lines all crumble as I ride up the elevator. Only Max has the ability to pre-crumble me.

Max's floor is the highest floor, but I'm not going to deliver to him first, though in a different building, I would.

The efficiency of delivering up versus delivering down is a raging debate among the Meow Squad delivery cats. I'm a deliver-down girl, especially before three in the afternoon, a decision that has to do with my personal theories of elevator traffic patterns. I'm going against my normal way, partly because I want to make Max wait the longest, and also, I might have to cry afterwards.

So I hit floor five first, in and out of the elevator. Five orders on the sixth floor, mostly sushi; lots of falafels and some wraps to the conference room on seven, nothing else until twelve, and so on.

I deliver in the persona of most wonderful cat ever, but it's fraying at the edges.

I dispatch food to the twenty-first floor and get back in with my cart. Max is next. I remind myself to breathe. I picture Kelsey's and Jada's faces when I check off the first box when they see I'm stepping up for them. And I'll keep checking off the boxes.

Assuming he makes me deliver his lunch more than once. But he will. Max has no mercy. He never did.

The floor buttons blink. My pulse races.

A lot of successful actresses were still struggling in their late twenties and thirties.

The doors squeech open.

The twenty-fifth floor is a crystal palace of breathtaking views featuring the cool angularity of Manhattan beneath a soaring blue sky.

A beautiful woman not in an embarrassing cat squad delivery outfit sits behind the desk.

I suck in a breath. There's still a chance this is all coincidence, or that somebody else in the building requested me. If this is not a setup personally designed by Max, she'll take the delivery for him. One of the main things big money does is to insulate you from commoners.

"Meow Squad delivery," I say.

"Go ahead and bring it down. All the way down." She turns her head to indicate the direction.

With that one command, she shows me that she had instructions to let me through.

Which means Max is expecting me.

She's still looking at me. Again she does the head motion, or more like a graceful torque. It's the kind of move I might memorize and fold into my catalog of character details if I weren't feeling like I was wearing a Lady Gaga-style meat suit on my way to a rabid dog convention.

"Thanks." I head down, cart in tow.

The place really is impressive. The floor is some kind of sparkling white marble and the walls are something white that glows, as though with lights behind; skylights above showcase the blue sky.

All in all, this hallway could be somebody's idea of what the path to heaven is like. But being that every ten feet there's a photo of Max Hilton looking like he's Adonis himself, and I'm dressed up as an animal that eats from a bowl on the floor and poops in a box, it's more like the highway to hell for me.

My neck feels unpleasantly clammy. Sweat is pouring down my back.

I don't have to go in. I could turn around. I could ditch the cart and turn around. It's still a free country. I slow my steps, thinking seriously about going back to waiting tables. Except insurance. Flexibility. My friends.

I reach the door and do an acting exercise where I breathe in the feeling that I wish to convey. I breathe in confidence and success.

I'm cool and confident, never doubting the path I've taken.

Max is nobody special to me. I barely even remember him from high school.

With trembling hands I knock. "Lunch delivery." Because I can't quite bring myself to say *Meow Squad.*

"Come," he says, sounding bored.

I push in my cart.

There across an expanse of white marble tile stands a massive desk. And behind it sits Max.

My mouth goes dry. Butterflies scatter in my belly.

He's typing something onto a laptop, eyes fixed on whatever

he's writing. The light from the screen seems to kiss his cheek-bones, brushing them with an imperious glow.

People talk about resting bitch face, but Max has the opposite. He has resting amused-and-confident-god face, the default expression of a man with incredible beauty and wealth and a magnetic presence that people can feel in their bodies when they get within ten feet. Not to mention an uber-cool mythology about himself where he lounges by pools in sunglasses and likes his women hot and his scotch cold.

I stand there flooded with loathing and something else that I don't have a category for.

He doesn't even see me.

On his wall is a massive photograph of him in a tux, sprawled upon a princely chair; three gorgeous gown-wearing supermodels hang on him. They're all laughing.

I recognize Lana Sheffidy, the most famous Max Hilton girl. She parlayed her association with Max into one of the world's top handbag brands. But she'll still always be a Max Hilton girl first, no matter what she does. Nobody will ever take her seriously, or think she got anywhere on her own.

"Mia?"

I turn.

Our gazes lock.

And for one skin-shivering, heart-thundering moment, I forget how to breathe.

Because it's Max. The familiarity of him buzzes through my veins like a drug. He tilts his head, dark brows a bold slash over blue eyes.

Maybe it's the surprise that makes him look vulnerable for a second, that lets me imagine I see the boy I knew that summer we did *Oklahoma!*, the sweet kid who sang with me and lay on the grass watching the clouds with me. The boy who kissed me and brought me snow cones and helped me with my music theory class.

"Mia. What are you doing?"

I straighten. He's acting surprised? *Seriously?* Who arranges for his high school rival to deliver him a sandwich and then acts surprised?

For a second, I think it's real. That this is some kind of mix-up.

Then the corner of his lip quirks up, all baffled amusement. Like something's funny. Like it's all a joke. Which tells me that this is his *gotcha* moment.

My body heats. More than heats. I'm a nuclear reactor of mortification.

God, when will I learn my lesson? How many times will I think Max Hilton is having a real emotion, only to be slammed in the face with the cynical, cold-hearted truth of him?

I smile my hugest smile. It's not for nothing that I attended Manhattan's most elite performing arts high school. "Max," I say. "Looks like *somebody's* getting a delicious croissant sandwich."

I park my cart and move across the elegant white marble floor of his airy office like he's just another customer. I set the bag and his complimentary mini-bag of potato chips in front of him.

He just watches me. Saying nothing—savoring his victory, I suppose. There's a lot of victory to savor.

But either way, alpha-signaling unlocked!

It's here that I get my flash of brilliance. I put my hand on my hip. "Very nice, Max," I say. "All of this is very impressive."

To most people, that would sound like a compliment.

But Max and I aren't most people.

His lip twitches—that's how I know my little zinger hit home.

I strut back to my cart and push it toward the door, biting back a smile at my cleverness. Still he says nothing. I really, really, really don't want to do the outrageous meow—or really, any meow—but I need to. So I'm thinking about that when he speaks just one more word.

"Wait."

I brace. I turn.

And meet his gaze.

He beams at me, his amused resting face turned to eleven. After a perfect amount of time, he crosses his legs, leisurely king upon his throne.

"What is it?" I ask.

He takes a nice long look at me in my stupid outfit, and finally his gaze rests at the top of my head where my glittering cat ears perch. It's the part of the outfit I hate the most right now, which just goes to show that Max's ability to zero in on my weak spot is still intact.

He lifts the white bag with the Meow Squad logo and website URL and delivery promise spelled out in a fab orange font. "It says right on the bag that I get to choose from an array of chips."

"When no choice is made, you get plain Lay's."

He frowns. "I'd prefer to choose from the array."

I raise my eyebrows. Okay, then. I say, "I have Lay's, cheesy puffs, barbeque, cool ranch, and baked sea salt."

A shadow of a grin plays on his generous lips. "Let's see them." And then, as if that's not enough, he circles his finger.

"Well...I just told you what they are."

"I'm sorry," he says. "But *presented with an array* is a visual concept. I'd like to be presented with my array. I think I'm entitled, don't you?"

My pulse races. So this is how it's going to be. Max going

full asshole. Milking every bit of evil pleasure out of my servitude.

"Oh, I definitely think you're entitled," I say, and I'm definitely using *entitled* as an unflattering adjective. "Very entitled."

His stare is all cold sparkles. "Present me with my array, Mia; I don't have all day."

My belly twists. I'd thought I'd had Greek yogurt for breakfast, but maybe it was daggers that I ate, because they are stabbing around inside of me.

And somehow I can't move. I really should hop into action. The longer I wait, the more obvious it'll be that he's getting to me.

Rule number one: never let Max know he's getting to you.

And of course, there's the little matter of my job. Meow Squad is a customer-is-always-right place, and Max Hilton is more important than most. He could get me fired with the slightest complaint. One disparaging word on Instagram and Meow Squad could go supernova.

I turn to my cart. I grab two bags in one hand and three in the other and walk his floor of glamour—slowly—head held high. If nothing else, I'll waste his time, one of the few ways the powerless get revenge on the powerful.

I smile coolly, an old technique from the Max and Mia wars that raged after that one perfect summer. I recite the names in the manner of a game show hostess, "Lay's, cheesy puffs, barbeque, cool ranch, and baked sea salt."

He makes me stand there while he decides, demoting me from delivery girl to human chip display rack.

"Hmm." He's not looking at the chips, though. He's looking at me.

Max's book is really strong on projecting confidence, so I project with everything I have. I stand proudly, foot out front, a model with attitude. *Eat your heart out, Max Hilton,* that's what my stance says. *You have your empire but you'll never have me. I'm queen of the delivery cats.*

Or at least, that's what I'm hoping it says.

The seconds tick away. My pulse whooshes in my ears.

"Very good," he says with a twinkle in his eye.

Whoosh whoosh whoooooosh.

Literally is an overused word, just as *worst nightmare come true* is an overused phrase. But put them together and you have the perfect description of Max finding himself with the ability to order me around. Literally my worst nightmare come true.

And maybe this awesome power to humiliate me is *his* dream come true. We always were on opposite sides of things like that.

"Well?" I say.

"Hmm." He puts his finger on his chin.

Seriously?!

Time slows. Humiliation is a buzz inside my body, growing more and more intense with every passing moment, until it reaches the level of an agitated hornets' nest, and all of the hornets are trapped and frantic. And maybe they're still a little bit in love with him.

"I'll take the cheesy puffs," he says, voice rough.

I force myself to give him a mocking smile.

"Open them and set them here, please," he adds.

I walk back around the desk, feeling his gaze—not just on my skin, but deeper than that, like he can hear those hornets.

Tears prick at my eyes.

I really want to rip open the bag in a way that either smashes the puffs or sends them flying, but then he'd know I'm upset, so I open it nicely, channeling the dancerly grace of Kelsey. Coolly I set it next to his sandwich.

"Thank you," he says.

I head for the door, feeling warm in my cat suit, and like the ears-headband is a vise on my head. I need to get out of there.

I so don't want to say meow. But what if he decides to make me? I can hear him now: *Did you forget your line, Mia?*

Though that wasn't his criticism of my acting back at the Shiz. It was that my acting was obvious. Without nuance. *Jersey-girl*, he'd call me, mocking my south Jersey accent.

My accent definitely put me at a disadvantage. So did my lack of training—all the other kids at the Shiz had grown up with lessons in everything, but I was lucky to get a bowl of Cheerios for dinner some days.

Still, I'm proud of where I'm from. And I can be proud of who I am. I don't have a plaza, but I have friends who I fight for.

I decide I'll say *meow*, and I'll say it the best ever.

I put my queen-of-the-delivery-cats attitude back on. I whip around, chest lifted, shoulders back, so happy and sure of things. I'm channeling the love I have for my girlfriends and for my sweet cousin, and for Beyoncé and Peanut Butter Kandy Kakes. I'm remembering how it feels when I nail a monologue so hard I feel magic, and that's what I load into it. "Meowwwwww!"

He looks up, features formed into an expression I can't read. What? Did I disturb him? Had he returned to his important business, thinking I'd left, only to be interrupted by my silly antics?

"That'll be all, Mia."

The breath goes out of me. *That'll be all.* As though I'm a ridiculous creature, scrabbling at his feet.

My hands grab on to my cart handle, seemingly of their own will. It's like my hands are saying, *let's get out of here!* And my feet agree. *Go, go, goooo!* They're moving, ferrying me away with whatever shreds of dignity I have left. Somehow I get my servile cart out through the door. I push it down the hallway and all the way down to the elevator. Into the elevator.

I don't remember getting down to the street, but eventually I'm there, grateful for the bracing winter breeze.

One thought and one thought only races through my mind: *never again.*

I can never go back there again. They can fire me, take my apartment, strip me of my insurance. They can send me back to Sadler with its bars and sad little Dollar Store and boarded-up movie theater.

And my mom'll totally understand, because that's the Corelli family curse. Chase your goals and get knocked flat. My folks started so many crazy businesses when my brother and I were coming up, but they're playing it safe now, working at the Foot Locker at the mall. "The higher you shoot, the harder you fall," Dad warned me when I took off for Manhattan.

I walk down the block, trying to keep a spring in my step in case he's watching out his window. And then I go around the corner and cry.

4

Smile like you have a magical secret. The world is your cocktail party.

~THE MAX HILTON PLAYBOOK: TEN
GOLDEN RULES FOR LANDING THE
HOTTEST GIRL IN THE ROOM

Max

I sit there stunned. Pulse racing.

Mia Corelli. My high school obsession. In my office.

Infuriating Mia, with her nonstop talent for singing, dancing, acting, and getting under my skin.

She drove me crazy. So crazy. And I wanted her with the fury of a thousand suns.

I knew she was a sandwich delivery girl, but I never expected her here.

She wasn't at all surprised to see me—I could tell. Almost as if she was ready for it.

Is it possible she engineered this visit? Of course she did. It would be completely outrageous. Which is to say, so Mia.

But how did she get past the front desk? Delivery people can't just come in. Did she convince Meredith to let her through somehow? Mia could always get people to do her bidding. Mia Corelli, everybody's best friend, laughing and flirting, secrets in her eyes, a smile on her lips.

I stab the buzzer for Meredith. Nothing. Where the hell is she? Delivery people are not to be let into my office under any circumstances. Meredith should know that.

The idea that Mia would seek me out, wanting to start it all up again. Thinking she'll just bring it—to *me*. A man who controls a billion-dollar empire, and all of the messaging and mindshare that spreads out from that, and she's a lunch-cart girl, and she decides it's a good time to bring it.

Classic Mia.

I sometimes fly my buddies out to Vegas to see mixed martial arts fights. Front-row seats. Ringside service. If you know the sport, you know that the fighter who is flat on his back can sometimes turn that position to his advantage. There are certain moves that can be downright deadly from the bottom.

Leave it to Mia to think she's going to bring it from the bottom.

A lunch-cart girl. But what does Mia care? The world is her cocktail party.

Back at the Shiz, wherever you heard laughter or gasps and whispers rising up from a group, you could be sure that Mia was at the center of it.

Everybody was in love with her. Including me.

My pulse races. I definitely don't have time for this sort of thing. I buzz for Meredith again and again.

Finally a breathless Jeanetta picks up. "Mr. Hilton? I'm sorry, Meredith's out. This is the week her mother's having that surgery?"

"Right," I grumble.

"Can I help you with something?"

"What's up with the delivery cat?" I bark.

"There was a note left for us to let her through," Jeanetta says. "Was that okay? Would you prefer a hand-off?"

"There were instructions to let her through? Left by Meredith?"

"I'm assuming...I'm sorry...I don't know, it just said to let her through, but if you don't want—"

"No, I don't want. Delivery people aren't ever allowed in. You should know that."

"But—"

"Thank you," I say. I let up off the button.

Impressive.

You had to be a student at the Shiz to fully understand the meaning of "impressive." Impressive meant style over substance. Flash over soul. As if you were striving to impress. It meant you were pandering to the audience as opposed to being a serious artist. Impressive suggested that you cared only about looking good to people.

Suggesting that I built my empire to impress—maybe even impress *her*. Oh, I'm sure that's what she thinks. It's maddening.

She's maddening.

Completely distracting. Completely...there's no word invented for Mia.

In your room full of balloons, Mia is the one holding the needle, dancing around like a dervish, laughing her head off.

Something in my gut tightens, thinking about those pale pink flags on her cheeks when I asked her to display the chips. I remember that so well about her—how the pink would show up when she couldn't conceal her emotions. And how her eyes would shine. Most people didn't see it, but I always did.

And when she was really off balance, the old accent would peek through—just the edges of it. When you took the actual time to observe her, you'd see she wasn't always so polished.

I should bar Meow Squad from the building. It's what I should do. A different man would do that. A different man would have no time for somebody like Mia.

It's what I should do.

God, the way she stood there—just her stance was outrageous. Glowing. Mia never settled for anything less than the maximum effect. And here she is—to what? Wrap me around her little finger again?

Unfortunately for Mia, I'm not that sullen, awkward, insecure kid anymore.

Also...*impressive?*

No. She doesn't get to do this. I ping Jeanetta. "Never mind. She's to be let through."

"The Meow Squad girl?"

"Yes. If she comes again, she's to be let through."

"Okay," she says, mystified. She knows not to ask.

"Thank you." I click off.

Impressive.

I sit back in my chair. *You bring it, Mia,* I think. *Bring it on.*

5

Remember, you're the alpha. You're the pursued. Let your reality be stronger than hers.

~THE MAX HILTON PLAYBOOK: TEN
GOLDEN RULES FOR LANDING THE
HOTTEST GIRL IN THE ROOM

Mia

Kelsey, Antonio, and Jada are waiting for me when I get back home, along with a redhead who rises from the couch with the poise of a dancer. She rushes up and shakes my hand before I can even take off my coat.

"I want you to know that I dated a guy off that capricious-god-escalation move," she says with confidential urgency. "And I found half the things he ever told me in the back of that book. I kept giving him chances because of those stories and it was all Max Hilton material!"

"Oh, no," I say.

"This is Francine," Kelsey calls from the couch. "Francine is in."

Francine says, "I'm putting a hundred toward buying your heels because you are so amazing for doing this, and here's another hundred from my sister, who fell for half the lines in there, too. Kelsey told us to read that book, and we've been freaking out."

"Thank you," I say, "but I don't know...this whole thing..." I give Kelsey a desperate look.

"Are you gonna have him on his grovelly knees soon?" Jada asks excitedly, not picking up on my distress.

Kelsey gets it, though. She's on her feet. "What?"

"It was harder than I thought it would be," I say. "It might be a little ambitious, thinking I'm going to put Max Hilton on his knees. After today, I'd settle for retaining a shred of dignity. It could not have been more demeaning."

"Demeaning the woman who inspires my dreams?" Antonio growls from the couch. "Perhaps my character needs to teach this man a lesson he won't forget."

"Don't," I say, not sure whether I want to laugh or cry. "It's not funny."

Kelsey wraps me in a big long hug. "You got this." She gives me one final squeeze, then lets me go. "You got it."

"Yeah, I don't know," I say.

"What happened?"

I peel off my coat and sink into the couch next to Antonio, who's studying his phone now. "It was just the worst experience of my life is all."

"So, you wore the ears?" Jada asks softly. "Did he notice?"

"Hard to say. Max is a man with a carefully curated surface.

I know in his pictures he looks all natural and warm and friendly with his enchanting smile, but he's a cold, calculating metal robot. He gives you nothing. Though he did try to act like he was surprised that I was there, and then he got off on ordering me around. It was just...uhhh." I tell them about the chips array thing.

"I would die," Francine says unhelpfully.

"I wanted to," I say.

Jada scowls. The silver glitter headband that holds back her thick blonde hair seems almost to sparkle in sympathetic anger. "Why is he such an asshole to you?"

"Because we're natural enemies in the wild. Why is the lion an asshole to the antelope?"

"I think that's a negative way of framing it," Kelsey says. "It positions you as the prey of the lion. You're more like the giraffe."

"A giraffe can't take down a lion," I say.

"Hyena?" Jada offers. "The lion can rarely get the best of a hyena. You're the hyena."

"The hyena. Thank you, Jada. Why not *a plague of locusts*? Or *a noxious cloud*?"

"I didn't mean—"

"Kidding," I say. *Kind of.*

"Anyway, I'm a long way to bringing him to his grovelly knees. It's not just about his heartless power. There's a massive flock of supermodels that will be keeping him from sinking to his grovelly knees for me. With gossamer threads. Lifting him up."

"Max Hilton girls," Kelsey groans.

Antonio looks up from his phone. As a male member of the species, it's his duty to perk up whenever Max Hilton girls are mentioned. "You don't think those girls all actually..."

"Fuck him? No way, it's just publicity," Jada says.

"Socialites and models and designers use him for his name. And he's using them for the Max Hilton illusion."

I study her. She's quite the Max Hilton expert. "Yeah, they'd flee like rats if he went out in sweatpants with socks in sandals."

Kelsey snorts.

"Give them a break. The Max Hilton girls are sweet," Antonio says. "They're very attractive and clever too. On Instagram…"

"Uhhh." Kelsey tosses a cork from our cork bowl at him. And then another and another.

Kelsey tosses more and more corks. I grab a handful and completely nail him.

Antonio's cringing, laughing. "What?!"

"It's PR, Antonio," Kelsey says. "That's not who they are."

I'm feeling better. Slightly. Antonio watches Kelsey out the side of his eyes. Did he say that to get a rise out of her?

"It was only your first day working his own rules on him," Kelsey says. "Do we need to get out the Hilton Playbook and read what it says about perseverance?"

I snort. "No."

"What does it say?" Francine asks.

"To not get discouraged," Kelsey says. "Hold your head up high and keep moving forward. You can do anything."

"As long as you have Max Hilton telling you what to do," Francine grumbles.

"It's a good system," Antonio says, gazing over at Kelsey, who's all smiles back at him.

Antonio and Kelsey—is it possible?

"You have to deliver sandwiches to him either way," Jada points out. "You may as well check off all of the boxes. Worst-case scenario, we buy you those shoes. Best-case scenario, he's on his knees and you are wearing them as you crush him."

"You can do it!" Kelsey grabs a marker off the side table and holds it out to me. "Put an X in that alpha-signaling box! You nailed that rule. One golden move down, nine to go."

I just stare at the marker.

"And you're fighting for us," Francine says. "For all of us who went home with a clever, exciting guy and woke up with a loser. You're showing Max what it's like for somebody to do a system on him. Please don't quit."

"Pleeeeease," Jada says.

Something swells in my chest. They're counting on me.

We used to play this nerdy guessing game in acting class where you had to pantomime things in a really specific way—like you'd pantomime washing the dishes smugly or charmingly or happily or anxiously or whatever, and the others would have to guess the adjective you were going for. It's a fun game—if you're an actor—and great for building nuance.

So I'm looking at my girlfriends, old and new. And yeah, maybe I'm fighting a losing battle, but I'm fighting for them, and that means something.

I grab the marker and march over to the chart *swashbucklingly*. I slash out an X *resolutely*, and spin around. *Boldly* I jam my fists onto my hips. I'm fighting for my friends. I'm fighting for all women. I'm Joan of Arc in kitten ears. "One golden rule down, nine to go, bitches!"

Francine hoots, and Jada claps. Kelsey's hands are clasped. Antonio looks on smolderingly. He has resting smoldering face.

The other nine rules won't be so easy, but I'm acting *as if*, and that's important.

"What rule are you doing tomorrow?" Kelsey asks.

I eye the chart. "Reverse-chasing is next."

"Reverse-chasing?" Francine asks

Kelsey raises her hand. "I know all about reverse-chasing," she says to Francine with a murderous look in her eye. "*Reverse-*

chasing is where you act like the woman you want to pick up is after *you*, even though she totally is not. And you're all like, get away! Even though she's not at all after you, but you act like you think she is, and it intrigues her. That's how my cheating ex kicked things off with me. He reverse-chased me and I fell for it. If only I'd known."

Francine shakes her head disgustedly in solidarity with Kelsey, then she turns to me. "So you're gonna reverse-chase him? What are you gonna say?"

"I don't have it worked out. But I have some ideas. I want it to feel spontaneous."

"Mia can improv like a boss," Kelsey says. "Mia'll reverse-chase his ass so hard, he won't know what hit him."

"Do not forget prize-baiting." Antonio puts away his phone. "Where you position yourself as a prize. A sought-after partner, desired by others." He smiles, all sexy man-mystery. "I've been working on my backstory, *cara*."

"You have?" I try to act like that's good news, and not the worst news ever.

"And when I dress in Hugo Boss?" He kisses his fingers. "With this backstory I'm creating?"

"You in a suit, that's probably all we need, right there," I say.

"But to add this backstory," he says.

"We'll see. I *did* see Max cross the street from afar, going between his two buildings, before the last delivery. Around eleven. So we could set it up so that he sees you talking with me out there, but you wouldn't have to interact with him."

"You saw him before the delivery?" Kelsey asks.

"Just from afar. Max's company owns this rehabbed work-shop space across the street from Maximillion Plaza. If he goes back and forth often at that time, I could get the driver to park at a spot where Antonio would be visibly admiring me."

Antonio rubs his hands. "I will be such a suitor. He will see my passion."

"My plan is that you just smile at me a lot and laugh at whatever I say. It doesn't have to be over the top."

"He would see my desperation for you."

"Just passion is good," I say.

"No, it's desperation." Antonio puts on a dark expression. "I grew up poor in the streets. My father rejected me. My mother was cruel but beautiful. So poor were we that they sold me to a brothel when I was but a boy. I was forced to sell myself in the alleyways of Milano."

"Double Dark Chocolate Milano is my favorite cookie," I say, trying to lighten the mood.

"Milano is not a cookie," Antonio growls. "It's a city."

"Sorry, Antonio..." Jada winces. "In America it kind of *is* a cookie."

"If you knew the underbelly of Milano as I did," Antonio says, "you would not think it."

"The underbelly of Milano," I say. "Is that near the hard-scrabble alley behind the Keebler Elves' Factory?" I ask.

Jada raises a finger. "I believe it's located east of the Pepperidge Farms killing fields."

"Stop it, you guys! Let Antonio tell his backstory." Kelsey turns to Antonio. "Ignore them, Antonio. Please go on."

Antonio fixes her with that dark expression, something I might describe as Scarface meets Blue Steel. "I grew up fighting hoodlums. The fist, the blade. What did I care? What did ever I see of life?"

I suck in a breath. "Too many productions of *West Side Story*, maybe?"

He gives me a dark look.

"Dude, I'm just saying you should save this backstory for a real role where you have lines and things," I say.

Antonio's unperturbed. "So many shameful acts I did until I hit rock bottom, so desperate was I for a kind word from my mother."

"Your mother?" Jada squeaks. "Are you going Jerry Springer on us?"

Kelsey scowls at Jada. "Come on, you guys!"

"Italian men prize the love of their mothers," Antonio says. "It is a pure and good thing." He turns to me. "Then, at my lowest, lying in the gutter, I see your Yummies ad."

"Oh my god, Antonio, no," I laugh. I actually *was* in a Yummies caramel-pops commercial that got made into a print ad. "I don't think they have Yummies in Milano."

"They don't have Yummies there because all the people are eating Milanos," Jada says.

Antonio waves her off and continues with his backstory, which involves him lying injured in a pool of blood—the blood of his rival, he clarifies—and then a pedestrian comes by and casts a magazine down onto his face in disgust, and when he regains consciousness, he sees my ad.

"It is your beauty and talent that inspired me to clean myself up and climb from the gutter and come to America," he continues. "To seek you out. You are the light of my life."

"Umm...that's a crazy backstory, Antonio," I say. "Not that you'll be able to use it. But I guess there's no harm in having that on your mind as you appear to admire me when Max walks by."

The operative phrase there being *on his mind*, as opposed to *leaving his mouth*. No way do I want him saying such things to Max.

"Will we kiss? We could make a signal," he says. "I remember every one of your expert stage-kissing pointers."

I smile. I taught Antonio the art of the stage kiss, where the man puts his fingers behind the woman's ear and his thumb over her lips, and then he leans in and kisses his own thumb. Antonio's a very dramatic kisser of his own thumb, needless to say. But then, I'm a dramatic kisser, too.

I sometimes apply my stage-kissing expertise in real life, pouring on the big drama. Even with dramatic kisses, the few long-term relationships I've been in have felt way more convenient than passionate. I wasn't even sad when they were over.

"We won't need a stage kiss," I tell him. "Your character sounds protective and macho. Maybe he prefers his woman to appear modest. I doubt he'd wanna go all PDA."

"Unless he feels his woman is being ogled," he rumbles. "Then he would want to claim her publicly."

"Yeah, but what if she gets carried away and messes up his hair?"

This is a definite threat; Antonio hates when you touch his hair.

"She must not do that," he growls.

I snort. "Well, it luckily won't come to that. It would just be you looking adoringly at me."

If and when the time comes. Which is less likely with every new twist in his backstory.

6

Never ask a woman what she wants. Tell her what she wants.

~THE MAX HILTON PLAYBOOK: TEN
GOLDEN RULES FOR LANDING THE
HOTTEST GIRL IN THE ROOM

Mia

Sienna is down at the rendezvous point when I arrive. She is sitting today, draped elegantly over a bus bench, arms splayed to either side. You can almost hear the lush electronica playing in the background.

She looks me up and down, from my shiny silver boots sticking out under my wool overcoat to my sequined cat ears. "Again?"

I do a little shimmy-dance right up to her, in time with music blaring out of somebody's car.

She sits up. "Seriously? How much did it raise your tips?"

"Does it matter?" I tease. "Sienna, only one cat can be alpha queen."

"Cats don't have alphas," she says. "They're not pack animals."

I hold up four fingers.

"Four percent better?" she asks.

I smile even more widely, shaking my head.

"Forty?!?"

"Forty percent more over my average."

"Are you messing with me?"

I shake my head. "Not messing with you."

She narrows her eyes. "It could've been the shock of the new outfit."

"Maybe. Maybe they were dazzled."

She studies my getup. "Lemme know if the tips stay good. If this thing holds, I'm doing alpha-queen cat, too."

"I'll let you know," I say.

And I will. Sienna's not the nicest, but we all deserve more money.

I do my route, taking my pair of financial industries buildings first, because those guys are all at work at five in the morning, so lunch for them is around ten. I head to the next building, a mammoth office complex. I check my tips between buildings, and they are definitely staying high. In fact, the more expressively I do my meow, the higher they go. I'll definitely let Sienna in on that.

It's half past twelve by the time I hit Maximillion Plaza. I deliver up, and before I know it, I'm on the twenty-fifth floor. I walk down past the glorious receptionists and continue on down the glorious hall and knock. "Meow Squad," I say.

"Come." Because he can't be bothered to say come in.

I push in with my cart.

My belly turns upside down like it always does when I get into the presence of Max. His beauty crackles through the air like an electric charge. It gets inside you and melts your will to hate him.

He sets down his phone and leans back in his chair, stretching his arms slowly upward, then places them behind his head as a lazy smile overtakes his face. It's as if every fiber of his being is saying, *Ah! A big, delicious dish of humiliation. Can't wait to dig in!*

I grab his bag of cheesy puffs from the cart and head toward his desk—that's a Meow Squad thing; you're not supposed to pull the cart right up to people's desks. It gives the illusion of table service.

In an office with as much square footage as Max's, I have to cross several feet of tundra.

He nods at a space that's been cleared in front of him. "Lay it out here."

I put down the bag that contains his roast beef croissant sandwich, and set the cheesy puffs next to it. Now's my chance to reverse-chase him. I have a few ideas.

"Mia," he says. "Did I not say to lay it out?"

"What?"

"Lay. It. Out." He waits, all sparkling arrogance with a streak of smug pleasure.

I suck in a small breath and hold it. Like maybe if I don't breathe, somehow this won't be happening.

Lay it out.

Lunch layout is definitely something he has a right to request, but our layout service is designed for conference scenarios, in order to minimize distractions during meetings. So that people can keep their attention on the project instead of on crinkling bags and switched orders and extra napkins.

What is it not designed for? A jerky billionaire in an office ordering you around.

Now I have to set his place for him like a servant? But of course, it's what he wants.

I give him a cool stare. "You're asking me to lay it out?"

"Yes," he says.

I regard him with amused consternation, like it's such a ridiculous request I can barely process it. *Acting skillz!*

"Is there a problem?" he asks.

I smile. "If that's what you *need*," I chirp. As in, *If that's what you need to feel good, jerk.*

His eyes glitter. "It is what I need, Mia. Thank you."

It is what I need, Mia. Thank you.

Millennial Dean Martin, thinking he's ending our rivalry once and for all in a blaze of glory that leaves me eating his dust.

Eating the dust of his dust.

With perfectly steady hands, I take the sandwich from the bag and set it aside. I form the bag into a placemat in front of him. Meow Squad is an eco-friendly place where we repurpose the packaging wherever possible—there's a whole training video on it, but I'm taking it further. I'm smoothing it down with an extra fussy flourish, like he's such a ridiculous person to have requested a layout. I'm also taking an obnoxiously long time.

I unwrap his roast beef and swiss croissant sandwich, set it upon the bag, and pull up the four corners of the wax paper by the edges. The video doesn't have you unwrap the sandwich, but how can I resist? I happen to know that Max is the kind of guy who gets annoyed by fussy inefficiency.

I get each of the wax paper corners to curl slightly outward, as if to say, look at how fussy your demands are.

"This is how you lay it out?"

"Shh." I take the three mustard packets from the bag and arrange them to splay out from the upper left, like a small hat—a fascinator, if you will—for the sandwich.

Sir Ian McKellen himself couldn't squeeze more mockery out of a performance if his life depended on it.

Max, of course, shows me nothing, unless you count the slight enlargement of one of his neck muscles, which I definitely do.

I set the chips down, pull my hands away and make a square with my thumbs and pointer fingers, as if to examine the presentation—picture hands is a funny thing my girlfriends and I like to do.

"Are you quite done?"

"No." I reach back down and set the chips at a jaunty diagonal. "There we go."

I look up and find him watching me sternly.

His pillowy lips twist.

My heart does a lightning-bolt zig zag.

"Or perhaps you'd prefer something more symmetrical," I find myself saying. I line the mustards up, three soldiers in a row. It's hilarious, what with his gaze so stern.

I proudly cross my arms, looking over this new arrangement. "Now we're done."

I sneak another look at him.

He frowns. "Did you forget something?"

"What?" There was a time when I imagined I could read him. I thought I knew his heart as well as my own. I thought he had a heart. But it was all a cynical joke. It was Max pretending to have a heart.

"Where's my array?"

"You picked cheesy puffs. There they are."

"That was yesterday," he says. "I might pick something different today."

My pulse pounds. Is he really going to make me do it?

He wouldn't.

But there he is, waiting. Cruel, perfect Max. He does the finger-twirl.

I grab the chips from their jaunty angle next to his sandwich and take them back to my cart and grab the other chips. I hold them up and list them off, knowing he'll choose the cheesy puffs. The understanding rushes between us, strong as an ocean current.

I know, and he knows I know. I guess that's what makes this fun for him.

"Very good. Now let's see." He folds his hands and rocks back. His gaze is heavy on my skin, a cool, smooth weight.

I grit my teeth, heart drumming inside me. But all he sees is my cool smile—I make sure of it.

Finally he speaks. "I'll take the cheesy puffs."

I see right now he's going to make me show him the array every time. And he'll choose the cheesy puffs every time. Even if he doesn't want cheesy puffs, he'll choose cheesy puffs, because that will upset me most.

It's as if we're connected by some horrible thread. Just like always.

I tuck the other chips back in the cart, wondering what he'd do if I smashed them. But I'm here to check off boxes, not to crush his chips.

I remind myself to get with the program. If I'm going to reverse-chase him, now is the time.

Even though it feels pathetic, like spitting at a hurricane.

He smiles as I bring him his cheesy puffs. He's so much more substantial now than he was in high school. Solid in places where he once was slight. Hard where he was soft. A bright and beautiful glacier, shining above the globe. An aggressive winner leading a charmed life.

I focus on my girlfriends. I'm doing this for them.

"You know," I say, placing the chips at a jaunty angle, "if you wanted to ask me on a date, there were easier ways than having me deliver your sandwiches."

He stiffens slightly, looks at me quizzically. Did I manage to surprise the great Max Hilton?

I lower my voice. "I get that you wanted to bring me here in hopes that I'd see all of this...*success* of yours." I say the word success with everything but the quote fingers. "Hoping that it would help your chances with me, but I'm sorry...you should've messaged me—"

"I brought *you* here," he says incredulously. "To ask you out."

"Yes, to ask me out, and I'm flattered, I want you to know that." I act like I'm arranging things in my cart. "And maybe if things were different, my answer would be different..."

He looks baffled. Like the whole idea is ridiculous, and it is —he's always been too good for me. He always made sure I knew that.

I force myself to think about the advice in his book. *Keep pushing the illusion no matter what. You're the alpha. You're the pursued. Your reality is stronger than hers. Go ahead, shoot for the stars.*

"I know you're disappointed, Max. I'm sorry you went to all this trouble to woo me—"

"This is what you're going with, Mia? That I arranged all this?"

"And I do want you to know I'm flattered, Max. It's not that you haven't impressed me."

That muscle in his neck twitches. Was *impressed* too much?

He turns back to his computer. *Tap-tap-tap.* "Yes, I'll cry every night. I'll rest my head into the bosoms of supermodels and just weep."

Something unpleasant twists in my belly. Probably the bosoms of three supermodels at once, like in the picture. Why did I ever think this would work? Max is winning. Max always wins.

I'm back to thinking about his book, finding strength in his book. His book says, *Keep pushing with the illusion. You're the alpha. You're the pursued. Don't give up.*

"All this trouble you went to," I say. "I'm sure you'll find a wonderful real-life girlfriend someday who appreciates you the way you deserve..."

"Compelling as your little lunch-cart-girl monologue is, I have work to do, so..." He circles his finger and returns his attention to his computer.

Little lunch-cart-girl monologue? *Lunch-cart girl?*

"It has my attention," I continue. "Don't get me wrong. I di-int think..."

Right there I freeze.

His gaze snaps back up to mine.

Di-int. We both heard it clear as a bell—the dropped "d" of didn't, so it comes out di'int. A glottal stop, my voice coach called it. That's a central feature of the south Jersey accent I worked so hard to erase. *I di'int think. Di'int think.*

My heart bangs in my chest as he watches me, sizing me up like old times.

And then he goes in for the kill, which is, in this case, a smile.

Or to the world it would look like a smile. Between us, it's him enjoying the Jerseygirl slip, softly and silently plunging me back to those years in high school when I wanted to overcome my accent. To have a shot at the lights of Broadway. To beat the Corelli curse of big dreams and even bigger failures.

Jerseygirl. The name hangs thick in the charged air between us, all the more hurtful for being unsaid.

My face heats. Even my ears lose a little sparkle—I can feel them dimming on top of my head.

With as much grace as I can muster, I put my lunch things back in my cart. I enunciate my words in my best, most aristo-cratic-sounding version of General American English, what my voice coach calls GA, "That's all I'm saying, Max. Sweet of you. I *am* flattered."

Still he says nothing.

I turn and walk. I need to say *meow* now, but I don't have it in me. I just don't have it in me. Except then he'll make me say it. I run the exchange in my head:

Forget your line?

Please, just let me go.

You're the lunch-cart girl.

"Mia," he says softly.

Something about my name on his lips like that, sounding genuine, even full of feeling, it reaches deep into me and squeezes my heart.

But when Max is nice to you, that's the time you can least trust him. He's going to make me say meow now—I know it.

I refuse to give him the satisfaction.

I turn, full of breezy determination, holding up a finger, smiling like I have a wonderful secret. I breathe in all of the magic that I can possibly breathe in. I am the queen of the cats, pursued and loved.

I straighten my spine against Max, against everybody who ever doubted me. I press my hands on my hips and let loose. "Meeeeow."

He tilts his head. "Oh, I was just going to say, I'll only need two mustards going forward."

My pulse races. My cheeks heat.

But I don't lose my aplomb. "We'll see," I say. Like I may or may not comply. With that, I leave.

This is what I've been reduced to, I think, heading down his faux-heaven hall. Max has everything, and my only recourse is maybe giving him the wrong number of mustards. And then he'll just make me correct the mistake in the most demeaning way possible, so what is the point?

I'm dimly aware that I ride the elevator with other people. Some people get in. Some people get out. I barely see them. I'm too focused on myself. Or more, the naive girl I once was, trying so hard to be sophisticated. The world's greatest fraud.

I di-int think.

I spent so many hours with that voice coach, trying to polish myself up in order to be worthy of the glittering, glamorous Broadway scene.

I thought maybe I was, finally. But then Max had to come back into my life to remind me of my station. Because it's not enough to be king of the world—not for Max.

I burst outside onto the busy sidewalk, into the chaos of honking cars and hurried pedestrians. I pull my jacket from the cart pocket and wrap myself against the cold, wet wind and set out to the meeting point.

Didn't didn't didn't didn't.

A lot of really prominent teachers cycled through the Shiz. Famed director Strom Windmeyer. Choreographer Fanny Forlio. Actors like Jean Stern and Marcel Rhodes.

Many of them had encouraging words for me. Some of them even singled me out for praise.

But it's Max's biting words I remember. *Obvious. Without nuance. Not there. Not her best.* He never said them directly to me—we didn't speak except for that one summer. But other students took glee in passing our insults along to each other.

I'd always laugh dismissively at them. I'd say that Max was just some sullen rich boy who hated me. What did I care what he had to say?

But I remembered each and every word he spoke with the clarity of a near-death experience. Sometimes I'd lie in bed staring up at my autographed *Mamma Mia!* poster and dissect his words, turning them over and over, painful artifacts.

I pull out my phone. Rollins is five minutes away. I punch in my location, hit send, then sit in the shadowy doorway, feeling small and cold. I need to compose myself.

Didn't didn't didn't didn't didn't. I enunciate the word with the tip of my tongue at the just-right spot behind my teeth, just the way my voice teacher taught.

How can I let him do that to me still? Why did I ever think this would work?

I yank the blinged-out cat-ears headband from my head and scrape off the sequins, ripping them off with my fingernails. This whole thing was a mistake! The threads break and sequins go all over the sidewalk.

Didn't didn't didn't, I say. But it's not enough. It'll never be enough.

I'll never be enough. Never good enough for Max.

I hate how tuned into him I still am. I always was. Though really, everybody back at *the Shiz* was tuned into Max. Fascinated by Max—the awkward, sullen rich boy with the famous parents.

But it was more than that—he had this quiet, brooding thing, even then. And then there was his legendary talent. He knew music theory inside out, and he could sight-read wildly difficult piano scores. He'd had lessons practically from birth, but still, his virtuosity was stunning.

Max and I were polar opposites in every way—he was in the classical music track and the more affluent student group; I was dirt poor and in musical theater, and on a full housing scholarship.

I'd never ridden on a plane or slept overnight in a hotel, and by the time high school rolled around, he'd lived in every glamorous international capital you could name with his fabulous parents.

And beyond that, the musician kids didn't like the theater kids and vice versa.

Unfortunately for the musician kids, they were *musician kids,* a socially awkward if not downright nerdy bunch, and we were theater kids, all outgoing and fabulous and way better prepared to make fun of the musicians. We had nicknames for a lot of them—I named Max Mr. Roboto—and we did impressions of the way they walked and talked. I actually did a great Max-Mr. Roboto impression where I mimicked his way of playing piano. We put it up on YouTube, and it got a ton of views.

Sophomore year, he composed a song making fun of my laugh—the one from before I changed it. The song had a dance move that went with it—the Donkey Honk. Even the name was catchy, and it spread through the Shiz like wildfire—he had the entire school mimicking my laugh as part of the song. Performing arts kids are hungry for that kind of thing.

I acted like I didn't care, and I even sometimes laughed and danced along, but truly, it devastated me. All the more because of the truth in it. I was a poor girl trying to pretend I was above my station, and the most talented boy in school utterly had my number.

Yes, my laugh did honk at one time. I'd worked hard to make it sound prettier and more bell-like, but Max's song made it so nobody could forget what it sounded like when I first came to the city, a naive girl hell-bent on clawing her way up to the bright lights of the Broadway stage.

If you would've told me then that years later I'd be delivering sandwiches to Max as he sat behind a desk in a grand office tower that he personally owned, I would've asked you to put a bullet through my head.

All that heartbreak. That mockery, secretly stinging.

The mockery mostly hurt because I had this idea that the production of *Oklahoma!* was the real him. I thought I was the only person who knew his sweet side. I thought that I was the only one he showed his true face to.

I had it backwards.

The few friends that I told about our strange, *Oklahoma!*-based summer romance warned me not to trust him—they said he was just using me, that he'd toss me aside like garbage come fall.

I felt sure it wasn't true. I felt like I knew his heart. We'd bonded fiercely and even magically, and we hadn't even had sex yet—if he was using me, wouldn't he be trying to get in my pants? I showed a few friends our texts—we were texting constantly, full of inside jokes and a use of emojis that nobody else would understand. Like he could send a musical note and wry smile cat face and it would have a specific sense of humor and specific meaning between us that nobody else could get— that's how much we were on the same wavelength.

I even went shopping with my friends for homecoming dresses after the production ended and before school came back in. They weren't sold on me and Max, but I knew us together.

Max hadn't asked me yet, but I felt so sure of him, I spent more money than I should've on a gorgeous secondhand gown, like an Oscars gown. Blue, his favorite color. So pretty. I wanted him to be proud of me in front of the school.

I even bought condoms.

His parents had whisked him off to Europe, and our texts were getting sparse, but I still believed in us.

I couldn't wait for my friends to see us together, to see how amazingly we clicked. They didn't believe when I tried to explain his transformation. I even sang some Curly McLain songs, demonstrating his goofy attitude. I wished I had footage.

Then I got a *kinda busy* text in response to a long, unanswered string from my side.

Then I stopped hearing from him at all.

I told myself it was something with being overseas, like maybe their data plan was screwed up. Or maybe he got some opportunity that had him exhausted from practicing.

Kinda busy.

Maybe I knew, because I felt sick the day school started back up. And he was there in the lunchroom with his friends. And he looked at me so coldly. Like he didn't even see me. Even so, I went over to say hello to him like a fool. And I tripped and fell.

It was a dramatic fall. Spaghetti everywhere.

The whole lunchroom was laughing. And Max just sat there blinking. Staring.

My heart fell through my shoes.

Too good for me.

He went back to eating his lunch. Like he didn't know me. Like he didn't even care.

I was devastated.

I couldn't believe our whole summer was a lie! That us singing and laughing and drinking bubble teas at Vo's and our secretly mind-blowing stage kisses was fake.

I went to the homecoming dance anyway—my friends circled their wagons and brought me in my blue dress. I acted like I was having fun without him. I got drunk on Strawberry wine and cried.

I'd thought *Oklahoma!* was real, but he was just playing a part. Having fun at my expense. This was the real Max, as it turned out.

Even his playing sounded different after that summer in Europe—way more robotic. Or maybe I just saw him for what he was.

I made sure everybody knew how sappy he'd sung. People didn't believe me, but he knew. He was the only one who mattered.

A rumor soon went around that he'd made a fool of me that summer. My friends started a counter-rumor that I'd made a fool of Max, and it took forever for him to catch on.

I tried like hell to get my hands on footage, but there were only really bad clips with bad sound, mostly taken from the back of the theater where you couldn't see faces—nobody in that production wanted to be in that production, so nobody took care with shooting it.

We went on to develop factions. We ruined each other's dates, critiqued each other's work in harsh ways. He'd call me Jerseygirl. I'd pretend I thought he was in love with me, like every mean thing he did was because he was in love with me, which drove him crazy. There was recital sabotage. Our war was one of the central dramas of our class. Storied. Epic.

I wait for Rollins, keeping the breath going through the words. *Didn't. Wouldn't. Shouldn't. Couldn't. Mightn't.*

Why do I still care?

Then I remember my friends. That's why I care.

I picture Kelsey's face when she realized the part Max's book played. That's why I care.

I get on my hands and knees to pick up the sequins now. It would be easier to sew on new ones, but I'm imagining pigeons trying to eat them and getting sick, and I would feel so bad if that happened.

Whatever. I may be the world's most loserish Broadway hopeful, but that's not a reason to be hurting birds.

The most painful critique of his came down after my senior project, a solo monologue and song-and-dance number from a musical adaptation of *Age of Innocence*, all upscale NY society women. The perfect part for a well-mannered girl. I felt like I'd internalized the character of May, and I had that polished accent so deep in me, I felt like I was even dreaming in it.

And then word came back that he'd seen a clip of it and passed his judgment. Two words. *All wrong.*

It was as if he alone knew. As if he alone saw the poor girl burning through.

Didn't didn't didn't didn't didn't, I emote silently to all of Manhattan. *I didn't think.*

Maybe they can all hear it.

7

Never fixate on any one woman; you're playing a numbers game.

~THE MAX HILTON PLAYBOOK: TEN
GOLDEN RULES FOR LANDING THE
HOTTEST GIRL IN THE ROOM

Max

I stare down at her arrangement of mustards in disbelief.

She doesn't get to do this—not again. No way. I won't have it. I won't allow it.

Leave it to Mia to turn the activity of laying out a sandwich into a master class in driving me crazy. I could own the planet and she'd find a way to get to me. She's a force of nature—she always was.

Suggesting I brought her here as my sandwich girl—is it possible she actually *didn't* arrange all of this?

No way. She's having too much fun, just like always. Too much fun for this to be an accident or coincidence. And she wasn't surprised to see me—I can't forget that.

After all these years. What the hell?

I push away the sandwich.

She doesn't really think I'm trying to hit on her—there's no way she actually thinks it. She just wants to get to me. Some things never change. I go back over our exchange. There's no way.

Mia's talent for being a thorn in my sock is mind-blowing.

Thorn is surprisingly accurate, actually. You could be in the most beautiful place at the top of the world, and let's be honest, I have reached that place, but something as small as a thorn in your sock is enough of a distraction to destroy any sense of satisfaction. Small, powerless, but utterly aggravating.

Fucking Mia Corelli.

Though, it *was* fun to watch her bristle when I told her I wanted to see the array of chips again. More fun than I've had in such a long time. The pink on her cheeks. Fuck.

I have a one o'clock to prepare for, but I can't stop picturing her standing there. Just the way she stands does something to me.

I need to get laid, that's all. It's been a while. Too long. I have my pick of women now. I love women. I love the way they feel, the way they laugh, the way they sound when they come apart underneath me.

The women in that photo are more like friends and colleagues than anything. We help each other's businesses. It looks like they're hanging all over me, in public and in pictures, but it's more about joking around. A lot of those poses are inside jokes, mugging for the camera. The whole Max Hilton girl thing is part of the Max Hilton brand that Parker and I have carefully and seamlessly created. It took on a life of its own. Now any woman I date tends to get branded as a Max Hilton girl. Most women are fine with it.

There was this heiress I was dating for a while who I had a lot of fun with, and she was down with the Max Hilton girl thing, but then she left for France. It occurs to me that she should be back...I scan through my texts, trying to remember her name. Vella...Nella. I find her—Wella. A year ago. That long? I need to think of something to invite her to. I pause over her last message, thinking about Mia. The way her lavender scent filled me as she was laying out that bag. How it swooped me back to that summer we did *Oklahoma!*

I don't know how she's making me so crazy.

Just like Mia to still wear that same lavender scent from high school. She was always the most stubborn person—tenacious, once she fixated on something. I respected that about her, I suppose.

Lavender is such a commonplace scent. Not that it's a bad one. We actually use it in Maximillion brand colognes and some of our men's grooming products. Personally, I find that adding lavender to a blend introduces a wistful note of longing, a nostalgic edge, an ache for what once was, what never could've been. In the end, that's what nostalgia is; the past seen through rose-colored glasses.

Like *Oklahoma!*

Maybe she can't afford a better scent. Most of our graduating class have actual jobs, if not in the arts, then in teaching the arts, or in marketing or TV production, but Mia was always an all-or-nothing kind of girl. She shot for the stars.

Mia Corelli, everybody's favorite sassy thespian, with her brave stance and witchy gaze and compact, curvy little body, finely honed instrument of her craft, singing and dancing her heart out, finding fun in unexpected places. And her carefully polished accent designed to conceal her hardscrabble background, one genuine, pitch-perfect note concealed in layers of noise.

Going around imagining my entire empire is all about her. Of course.

The intercom blares. "Tarquin Milbauer's here for your one o'clock."

"Let him in," I sigh.

The door opens and there he is.

"Rattling Meow Squad girls?" he says, strolling in, smiling.

I frown, wondering what he means. *Rattling?* Was Mia rattled? Is she okay?

He watches my face a little too intently. Does he sense a story? The last place I want Tarquin digging is that summer with Mia, or that fucking production of *Oklahoma!*

But you never want to underestimate Tarquin Millbauer, intrepid reporter. You never want to give him anything.

"Rattling, you say." Ever so casually, I go over to my coffee bar, pour him a coffee. Like it's not that important, but it is. "Cream?"

"Black, thanks," he says.

I stir mine.

"Tell me, how was I rattling Meow Squad cats?" I turn to him with a smile.

"She looked like she was about to cry."

Something twists inside me. I need more. Did I upset her? For a wild minute, I think about ejecting him from my office and going after her.

Or is Tarquin exaggerating? I replay the end of our encounter. Mia, acting like my goal in life is to impress her, because of course, what else? And her accent had even slipped a bit, and it was her old natural voice from when she was first at school. And then that sassy meow, and I sat there marveling at her fucking nerve. And I asked for the mustards.

No way was she rattled. Mia doesn't get rattled.

I shrug. "Seeing me is always a religious experience for women," I say.

"Come on," he says. "Level with me. You're having a delivery girl all the way in? And she runs out crying? Do tell."

I tighten my jaw, not liking this angle he's sniffing out.

Tarquin's doing a celebrity profile on me. The goal of a celebrity profiler is always to get something more than you want to give. Exposing the man behind the myth, as it were. And a tawdry delivery girl sex drama would be perfect for his purposes.

I can see the headline now—*The Max Hilton Girl Casting Couch* or some such shit. I could deflect and absorb it, but Mia couldn't. It would affect her career.

Sure, it's ridiculous—maddening, even—that she thinks she can blow back in and get under my skin. But I wouldn't let her career get ruined over it. I'm not that much of an asshole.

Luckily for Mia, I'm a master at what I do. I can wrap the media around my little finger ten times over. And I happen to know the best way to handle Tarquin is to be his buddy—that's his weak spot.

"You want the real Max Hilton?" I put my arm around his shoulders and my lips to his ear. "Would you like the Max Hilton with an addiction to peppermint schnapps and tormenting delivery girls in stupid outfits? Or maybe an underground fight club Max Hilton, full of rage and trauma and strange neck tattoos? Or we go with a Max Hilton who sings weepy show tunes and who still can't get over his first love who rejected him?"

"Don't give me a bunch of bullshit, I want something real. Some interiority, Max."

"Tarquin, the side boob has come back in style, and the Verona Club has Delmonico steak back on the menu. Let's grab a window table and get day drunk."

"You're not doing that to me again," he says. "Work with me, man."

"Interiority is so overdone. You can quote me on that."

"Fuck you," he says, but he's laughing. He can scratch the surface for years. He'll never get in.

8

A cool smile is never out of style.

~THE MAX HILTON PLAYBOOK: TEN
GOLDEN RULES FOR LANDING THE
HOTTEST GIRL IN THE ROOM

Mia

Kelsey's been working on the chart—she mounted the picture of the Louboutins on a pink background and pasted glitter stars around them.

She's so funny to make a fuss about the shoes. These are my friends who know my heart and my quirks. They know where I come from and how hard I work. They don't ever hear my real accent, but it's not because I'm fooling them, it's just that I've grown up from that girl.

Leave it to Max to zero in on that one thing from my past.

Kelsey has her dance stuff on when I get home. "Petra canceled her jazz dance class—we have the studio for two hours. The one with the piano. Come! Hurry!"

"Oh my god, I'm there." I hand her a bag—a double-order mistake. "Korean fried chicken with spicy dressing. You're gonna die."

"Smells...mmm. I'm eating half now. But only half." She digs into the bag while I rush into my room to get ready. Kelsey teaches at the dance studio just up 45th Street.

I scrounge up my dance workout clothes. Kelsey's helping me with my dance moves for the audition, and I'm helping her nail her song. Usually we practice with recorded piano, but it'll be good for her to do it live.

"Now I want to eat it allllllll!" she calls to me.

"Don't." I go out and whip the bag out of her hand. "You'll get a side stitch."

"Eating doesn't cause those." She takes it back. "I'm eating it all. So how'd it go today? Did you reverse-chase him?"

I grab my coat and my phone and then the marker. I put an X in the reverse-chase box. I also alpha-signaled, what with my awesome outfit, but there's already an X in that box. Then, just because I had a bad day, I make another X over the first X.

Max says the techniques are to be layered onto each other. I layered like a boss!

"You so rock."

"Uh, I don't know." We get out of there and head down the stairwell.

"Did he respond?"

"It's gonna take a little more oomph to crack that nut."

"What happened."

We burst out onto the street and hoof it down the block. "I acted like I thought he brought me in as a delivery girl as a way of hitting on me, and I was all about letting him down easy. I go, I'm sorry you went to all this trouble to woo me."

"To *woo* you," she snorts. "Love it."

"I was really going for it. Just putting up this wall of belief, as though my reality is so much stronger than his. Like he says in the book."

"Which is something you're actually very good at," she says. "You know you have a talent for that."

"Well, he wasn't all that moved. He opened with disbelief— he was all, 'that's what you're going with? Really?' and eventually he moved on to informing me that he'd be weeping into the bosoms of supermodels."

"What a jerk," Kelsey says. "But maybe you were getting to him. Maybe a little?"

We hold up at a corner. "Doubtful. From what I could see."

"Well, don't forget—the target will act like they wouldn't ever even give you the time of day. But they'll keep on engaging you, and that's how you'll know."

"I won't give up, don't worry." We grab hands and run across the street, hopping a puddle to get safely to the other side. "He's messed with the wrong Jerseygirl."

"Yeah, motherfucker!" Kelsey says. "Don't you flip my girl's bitch switch."

I snort. "Though he has been giving me good tips. Or at least, his receptionist or whoever handles that."

"He's a billionaire," she says. "Billionaires and celebs have to tip extravagantly or people think they're cheap."

"True." We sidestep bits of soggy garbage and head in under the bright red dance studio awning.

"I still can't picture him as the goofy cowboy in *Oklahoma!*," she says as we climb some more stairs.

"He was great as a goofy cowboy."

"How did you guys even co-exist in a summer production?

And what was he doing there anyway? If he was mister classical?"

"It was part of the cross-genre requirement we all had. Where a teacher puts you in a production out of your comfort zone and the other kids have to help you. He was Curly and I was Laurey."

"Wait, you were romantic leads?" She stops at the landing and turns to me. "You didn't tell me that part."

"Yup. I had to play a poor rube girl in love with Max. And he played the cowboy in love with me. It was...whatever."

We head on into an unfinished hall. "It doesn't sound *whatever*," she says, slightly accusatorily.

"It was," I say. "Very whatever." A lie. The setup was very close to the truth. I did fall for him. Hard.

She unlocks the door and we go in. It's a massive room with mirrors all around the perimeter, and an upright Yamaha piano in the corner. We put down our stuff.

Kelsey goes over and hooks her iPhone to a speaker and starts up the music. She claps twice. "This music is mellow— Mia, tell me, what do we need?"

"Back grooves!" I say.

She starts in, rocking her hips, and I mirror her. "You were romantic leads?" she asks again.

"Yup," I say. "And it was a summer show, and summer shows are always weird, like summer school where you don't want to be. Like this one was full of younger kids, mostly from other schools."

She turns to the side and I copy her.

"It felt like we were stranded on a deserted island," I continue. "Away from our friends. It was the one time we got along. Or I thought we were getting along. He was playing games with me."

"Define *getting along*." She demonstrates a move to spice it up. We dance side by side in the mirror.

"Okay, I'm going to confess something to you here—we had kind of a fling. Or, to me it was a fling."

Kelsey stops and turns to me, eyes wide. "Excuse me?"

I keep dancing. "Not a full-blown fling," I say. "More like, the stage kisses were getting hot."

"Hold up. Stage kisses getting hot. With Max," she says.

"Come on!" I say.

She starts up again. "Switch!" she calls out.

We hop around to face the east wall.

"And?" she presses.

"Let's just say we rehearsed the kiss a lot," I tell her. "It was a joke with us—even knocking around backstage, one of us would say, we need to practice that kiss. And we'd make out. And we'd get bubble tea afterwards and do homework together and stuff."

"Mia," she says. "You had a fling with him. That counts as a fling."

"It wasn't a fling to him. To him it was more like, he was trapped in an uncool musical with an uncool girl. It was a game to him. I was his amusement."

"Ugh. I didn't know. I'm sorry," she says. "Switch!"

I hop in unison with her. The beat is picking up, and I'm thinking back to those long afternoon rehearsals. I played the prairie girl with a rope for a belt, so smitten. And Max would shove his thumbs into his pockets and play the goofy cowpoke. He couldn't sing, but he really seemed to enjoy being in the show. It was fun, like we had this entire secret life together of being all in with stupid *Oklahoma!*

I fell for him hard. Hard as in daydreaming, name-doodling, social-media-orbiting hard. "I was such a fool. My heart would just hammer to think about him," I say. "The force of my crush on him could've powered a small nuclear sub."

She starts us on a dance move called *oppositions*, getting more core involved.

"I had this stupid idea that the production of *Oklahoma!* was the real him," I continue, keeping up with her, heart pumping. "I thought that I was the only person who knew the real him."

"But he was just playing you," she supplies.

"Yup. And then school was back in session, and it was the worst. Our texting had been sparse during August. That should've been an alarm bell." I tell her about the lunchroom fall. How cold Max was after we'd been apart for a month.

Like he'd gone from sweetness to pure ice.

"You're sure he was playing you?" she asks. "What if something happened?"

"He could've told me," I say. "Though, he did come later and apologize."

"What did he say?"

"I don't remember. I was upset. I was all, fuck off! Don't pretend like you care. And by then, we had warring factions going."

"You never found out why he went cold?"

"He was playing me like his piano," I snap. It hurts to admit even now.

"Hmm," she says.

"What, hmm? Are you being skeptical here?" I say. "The whole school laughed at me and he ignored me. He went on to ridicule me. To write a mean song about me."

"Okay, okay," she says.

After our warm-up, we move on to my dance for my audition, a combination of contemporary and classical ballet moves we worked out, with music that Kelsey picked. There are a few combinations I haven't been nailing, so we concentrate on those.

I'm dead on my feet an hour later. Luckily, it's switch-off time. I seat myself at the piano and take Kelsey through her vocal warm-up. We've chosen *Midnight Blue* as her audition song, but we think if it goes well, the casting director might ask her to sing *Blow, Gabriel, Blow*, so we're preparing that one, too.

Getting this show would be so major. As in breakout major.

People are saying it's going to be the next *Waitress*. Maybe even the next *Hamilton*. The group behind it has had massive hits before, so who knows? Needless to say, the best actors are vying to get a part in this production.

Sometimes I'm afraid to hope for landing the part of confident, sassy Reno, like am I dreaming too big? But when people who know the show hear I'm going out for it, their eyes light up. It's a very *me* part.

At home I eat rice and cheese and watch YouTube videos. I go to bed early to read, but eventually the evil phone is calling out to me, and I'm on Max's Instagram feed.

Why I bother, I do not know. I guess I have this desire to find out something vulnerable and sensitive about him. A post where he isn't perfect. Where he shows his belly.

Some of the posts are familiar to me from late-night Instagram scrolls, or let's just call them what they are: drunk scrolls.

There's Max with the captain of his yacht. They're standing in front of a giant steering wheel and Max's hair is all windblown, his cheeks are kissed by the sun and he's in a perfectly worn-out T-shirt with rugged tan shorts, making the captain look like a sad vision of manhood indeed.

Caption: *Rough weather ahead. Prepare the martini shakers.*

There's a series of pictures of him with his arm slung around a woman with dark, curly hair. Caption: *Happy Saturday.*

There's a shot of Max sitting in the front row of some basketball game next to the coolest movie stars ever.

Caption: *Down five points!* Though you'd think he was a child trapped in a mine shaft hundreds of feet down rather than a man watching his favorite team lose, judging by the outpouring of sympathy in the comments.

There's a shot of Max the fierce entrepreneur, hands planted on a drafting table, necktie loosened just enough that you can get a hint of his corded neck. From that corded neck, one might infer an entire body of muscular perfection. He's surrounded by fiercely photogenic twenty- and thirty-some-things in an array of genders, set against the grunge-chic background of his "studio complex."

Caption: *Never feels like working when you're doing what you love.*

There's an arty shot of a woman in an elevator, head tipped back against the panel, as if in pleasure—you can't see her face because of the light from the elevator chandelier reflected just above her, but a man's hand is planted on the panel next to her.

Caption: *This elevator has everything it needs except a well-stocked liquor cart.*

There's Max at work, surrounded by models, and they're all laughing their heads off—one guy is doubled over.

Caption: *Shoot crew made my day.*

I definitely feel like that caption lies; if you study the picture long enough, you can see that their energy is directed at him, like he said something funny. He made the shoot crew's day, not the other way around, but Max is clever like that.

It made him a dangerous enemy.

There's Max holding a lady's hand over a candlelit table. The hand is the only part of her that we see because it's Max we care about. But presumably it's a Max Hilton girl, possibly it's Lana, his most famous Max Hilton girl.

Whoever it is, she has pretty blue fingernails and wears several vintage cocktail rings. And Max gazes intensely across the table at her with an expression that is so full of desire, it makes my heart hurt.

Caption: *No words.*

I tell myself it's not the girl he's looking at, but that's a lie, because it's obvious that he's staring right where her face would be if the picture hadn't been cut off.

Then again, who can say what she's doing with the other hand?

I decide she's holding a pork chop in front of her face with her other hand, and she's about to bite into it. And it's the pork chop—and not her—that Max is staring at, lusting over.

New Caption: *Why the hell didn't I order the pork chops? I wonder if she'll trade with me. I am Max Hilton, after all.*

I shut off Instagram. Max Hilton's Instagram feed is not helping my mood. But then there's that slice of his tower, right out my window.

"Yeah, I'm not done with you," I say. I give his tower the finger and go get my uniform. I empty the sequins out of my pocket from when I ripped them off my ears in fury—oh, how Max would've loved to see that!

Carefully, I sew them back onto the cat ears. Because I'm doing this thing. I'm fighting him on behalf of all the women who ended up going home with losers because of his stupid book.

I sit in bed, pulling the needle through one tiny sequin hole after another. I don't care what it takes, I'll stuff my painful lust for him deep down and I'll keep alpha-signaling and reverse-chasing and all of the rest until Max sees what he's done.

9

Women are like dogs. They enjoy knowing you're in charge.

~THE MAX HILTON PLAYBOOK: TEN
GOLDEN RULES FOR LANDING THE
HOTTEST GIRL IN THE ROOM

Mia

Sienna slips from her pose of leisure into a pose of attentiveness when I arrive at today's meet place. "So?" She looks my blingy self up and down. "You're wearing it again. Does that mean the tips stayed good?"

"Oh, they stayed good, my friend," I say.

"Really? Forty percent good?"

I smile. Raise my brows. *Yes.*

"And you didn't do more deliveries? It's per delivery?"

"Per delivery, an average of forty percent better."

"That settles it," Sienna says. "I'm doing it."

"You should."

"You don't mind?"

"Of course not," I say. We may be in bitter competition for musical theater roles, but we're a family at Meow Squad; one of us getting better tips doesn't take away from the others.

"So is this the sort of shit you'll be wearing for the *Anything Goes* tryouts?"

"Not sure yet," I say. "Did you pick your outfit?"

"Not sure yet," she says, resuming her picture-perfect pose of leisure.

Neither of us want to reveal what we're wearing. The audition outfit is a delicate balance—you want to *feel* like that character to the casting director, but it's a rookie move to go full-on dressing the part.

Sienna could be real competition. She has a bell-like voice and perfect diction. She has a big ballet pedigree, too. She's a better dancer, but I'm the better overall singer, and a way better soprano.

A few hours later, I'm heading into the lobby of Maximillion Plaza with my trusty cart. I'll be doing the *Show You're in Charge* rule, which is exactly what you'd think it is.

It's not easy to take charge when you feel like a tiny little plastic figurine living in a snow globe on Max's desk. And Max gets to shake up your world and make it snow whenever he pleases.

But that doesn't stop me. I have a little something in store for him. I may not be in charge of much, but there is one thing that I am in charge of—Max's lunch.

I practice bossing the customers on the lower floors. I give people unasked-for mustards when they've ordered sandwiches that should have mustard, and when they push back, I look them in the eye and I say, *you need mustard with that. You're going to open up that packet and you're going to spread it on there, okay?*

At first people are surprised, but most seem to enjoy it. I override some customers' chip selection. *You've ordered Lay's every day this week. It's time for cool ranch.*

I'm stunned when people go along. Max's book is actually kind of brilliant, aside from being the pickup guide that helped to ruin women's lives.

There's a sweet guy on the twentieth floor who has lots of *Blade Runner* stuff in his office. The first day he was all, *the cat thing is working for you!* and we had a charming exchange. When I notice him opening his chips first thing, I tell him he has to eat his chips after he eats his sandwich, because otherwise it spoils the taste, and I'm very firm about it.

He seems surprised, but he puts them aside, and then we bond over *Blade Runner*, and I tell him I'll be calling him Blade from now on.

Blade is the kind of guy I'd normally fall for if Max wasn't looming up there, poised for another round of his favorite new game, jerky billionaire vs. delivery cat.

PLAYBOY BILLIONAIRE EXECUTIVE and supposed woman expert Max Hilton is on the phone when I arrive.

It's a problem that he's on the phone; if I'm gonna show him I'm in charge, I need him to be paying attention. I've taken the liberty of changing his order entirely to a selection of my choosing.

He motions to the corner of his desk, not even looking at me. Like I'm a dog who needs a hand signal to understand that the master needs his food laid out.

Ugh! So arrogant. I'm flooded with memories of passing him

in the hall. He would sort of tip up his head when I was around, as if he didn't even want to breathe the air at my lowly and pathetic level.

I look away, because maybe I can't be bothered to glance at him or breathe his air.

Looking away turns out to be worse, because there's that giant photo of models hanging all over him. I avert my eyes after a quick, hate-drenched glance.

I go around and extract the sandwich. I work really hard on flattening the bag out to form his little placemat. He's talking scheduling, something about Tuesday night being out.

"No, it's out, always out. The entire evening. A foundation commitment."

Slowly I unwrap his sandwich. I'm detecting a definite emotional charge around this Tuesday-after-work thing.

And I have this intuition that he's lying.

I should know.

The relationship of prey and predator is a fierce form of intimacy, especially in high school.

I watched him closely. Listened to his conversations from across halls and classrooms, listened with rapt attention, tuning out all else. And it wasn't just real-time stuff; I kept his every utterance alive in my mind for later dissection and analysis. Understanding your enemy is an important survival skill.

So I really think he's lying to whoever is on the other line. *Foundation commitment* is the sort of vague term a man like Max would use as a lie. Maybe he's really going to be out having a foursome with his three best friends' wives. Or visiting a children's hospital dressed as an evil clown.

I set the sandwich he didn't order on the perfectly flattened bag-bed, showing meticulous care, adjusting it just so. I'm close enough to feel the heat of him, the electricity of him, and something else—annoyance, maybe. Anger. Some high emotion.

And I'm pretty sure he's watching me, too. Discreetly watching me.

It feels amazing. I don't know why, it just does.

I decide to push things even further by making presentation hands, like a game-show hostess presenting a special prize.

I peek up. A muscle in Max's jaw fires.

I bite back a smile, imagining how Sienna's jaw would drop if she saw me doing presentation hands like this. Especially if she knew that this wasn't even the sandwich Max ordered.

I spin around and go back to my cart. I can literally feel his eyes on me, like an angry caress, waking up my skin.

The only good thing about my outfit is the short multipocket apron that covers most of my middle and is designed to hold utensils and stirrers and salt packets and things, and in my case, it doubles as a really effective tummy hider.

I fuss in my cart, like I can't find something, trying not to smile or laugh.

I sneak a glance. Quickly he looks away. My pulse races.

He totally hasn't noticed that I gave him the wrong sandwich yet. I can't wait. This shouldn't be exciting, but it is!

"Yes, that works. The nineteenth. It's a go." I hear the click of the latest model of iPhone being set on a cold glass surface.

Call ended.

Most people say goodbye when they hang up, but Max dwells in a special world where people don't say goodbye when they get off the phone. They just hang up. Like in movies.

I finger the smooth packets of mustard, feeling his gaze on my back. The sensation is physical, as if the Lycra cat suit has taken on an electric charge.

"You like it?" he asks.

I turn. "What?"

He tips his head at the wall. "The photo. You look at it

enough. I could get you a copy for your bedroom wall. For... personal purposes."

I snort. "As if."

"And to save you the extra labor, I could have my assistants angrily pre-snip the women out of the picture. Or would you prefer I have them scratch their eyes out? Or maybe both? A two-step process?"

"Do those poor women know you're a robot with no feelings?" I ask.

He leans back, so cool. "I like to keep that a surprise to whip out on the second date."

Heat steals over my face. Is he dating one of them? All of them? I can't think of what to say back. Never mind; he's looking down. He's noticed the sandwich.

I bite back a smile as he lifts the bun.

"What is this?" he asks.

"Grilled whitefish with a spicy curry sauce. It's only available in December."

"I ordered the roast beef and swiss cheese croissant sandwich."

I fix him with a steady gaze. Max's book stresses the importance of believing in yourself, or at least looking like you do. *Fake it until you make it* is a recurring theme, though he never puts it like that.

"I know what you ordered," I say sweetly, "but *this* is the sandwich that you *want*. You'll like it much better."

"I'd like a roast beef and swiss croissant sandwich much better."

"Wrong," I say.

He frowns. "You can't just change my order."

I blink, all sunshine and innocence. "This special-edition grilled whitefish sandwich comes from a food truck on Seventh that was recently purchased by a five-time Michelin-rated chef. Way better than your stupid croissant sandwich."

He looks between me and the sandwich, baffled. "You can't just..."

I cock my head, feeling happy and excited. Max needs to do a revised edition of his book, because nowhere does it say how crazy fun the process is. "It's the superior lunch," I say, with the attitude of being in charge, as his book instructs.

The secret truth is, he *will* like it best. Not only is it objectively the superior meal, but it matches his taste. I might not be able to tell you what my best friend in junior year preferred for lunch, but I can tell you what kinds of food Max always went for, yet another unfortunate side effect of the kind of concentration it took to be enemies with him.

I'm excited for him to take a bite. Not that my life's goal is for him to have a delicious sandwich, but I like the idea that he'll see I'm right. I'm showing him that I'm in charge. I'm X-ing that box off like a boss!

He stands. Gives me a hard look.

Max was always much taller than me, maybe that's why he stands. To intimidate me from across the room.

Shivers go over me. Does he think he can intimidate me? Or is it more than that?

He comes around his desk.

I swallow. "Try it, you'll like it."

He keeps coming at me, eyes on mine.

What is he doing? Naturally I can't tell. He never shows you anything.

My skin tightens as he nears. "I'm telling you that this is the one you'll like best. I've chosen it for you," I say, with a hopefully smooth tone.

He keeps coming until he's right in front of me. I gaze up

into his eyes, awash in a feeling of hilarity and something else—a strange alertness. My nipples strain at the fabric of the cat suit. What's up with the AC in this place?

"Do you want to get fired? Is that it?" he grumbles.

Why does that sound like a sexy threat? My heart is basically banging out of my chest at this point. I swallow with difficulty. "No, I don't want to get fired. I'm telling you what sandwich you want."

Emotion flares in his eyes.

It's been forever since I've been this close to Max. Forever since I studied his intensely blue irises, pale at the center, like a ring of ice formed in there. Even when he's being an asshole, he's irresistible.

"You're telling me what sandwich I want," he gusts out, words like feathers on my forehead.

"Yes, Max, that's right," I say, dizzy from the sensation of him. "It's the sandwich," I enunciate sassily, "that you *want*."

"If I'd wanted that sandwich," he rasps, "don't you think I would've ordered that sandwich?"

"Not necessarily," I say, "being that you have no idea of how amazing it is. All that you've missed out on. So sad..."

Something in the way he looks at me changes. His jaw tightens.

Energy shivers up my spine.

For a crazy second, I think he's going to kiss me.

For a crazy second, I want him to.

I'm the amazing one, I think. *I'm the one you missed out on.*

The moment stretches on. My own breath is the only sound I hear. His heat is all that I feel.

I don't know where we've gone, but the sandwich is nowhere to be seen.

Suddenly he blinks. He straightens. He turns and walks the few feet back to his desk, him and his perfect suit.

I stand there, breathless, watching him. His suit pulls tight through the shoulders as he moves, this way and that, giving the optical illusion of a perfect body, strong and lithe and predatorial like a lion, accentuated by the finest fabric. Only the best will do when it comes to kissing and cupping Max Hilton's muscular torso as he prowls his office.

He grabs the sandwich and turns, leans back, butt against the desk, eyes boring into mine. Then he takes a bite, eyes never leaving mine.

My stomach tightens as he chews.

I have a lot of customers to attend to, a lot more tips to get for myself. I have the Edgar building next. If I take too long, people will be mad.

But none of that matters.

I'm furious with excitement and something that feels strangely like happiness.

He chews, looking deliberative.

And then his gaze drops to the sandwich.

He thinks it's delicious—I can tell. I feel like my smile might crack my face. "Right?"

He looks back up. Narrows his eyes.

"Oh, snap," I say. "Who's your daddy?"

He snorts, and for a second, he's not my enemy. For a second, it feels amazing to have introduced him to this sandwich, one of my personal favorites. He dabs the sides of his mouth with a napkin.

"Like I said, it's the *sandwich* that you *want*," I say.

He watches me. Battling with himself, no doubt. Trying to find some loophole where it's not true.

"Right?" I add. "Admit it."

"Why is it so important to you?"

Before I know what I'm doing, I go to him. I can feel his

power as I near. Like he has a force field of smooth, suave perfection, and I need to break through it.

I get in his face. "Because people should admit things."

"Yeah?" he says. One word. Voice calm like steel.

"So delicious. Oh, the deliciousness that you've been missing. Poor, poor Maxfield Miller," I joke.

I may be joking around, but his stern gaze is locked on mine in a way that's anything but jokey.

The floor seems to dip beneath my feet.

Slowly, without warning, he reaches up and touches the side of my face—one lone fingertip. A featherlight touch that sizzles.

He holds my gaze with those eyes, the bluest of blue with that pale ring of ice. One cool fingertip traces along the edge of my jaw, heading slowly for my chin.

I feel like he's looking into my soul with those eyes.

The air thickens between us. My sex turns molten with excitement.

I should laugh at him and push his hand away, but it's the last thing I want. *Don't stop* is more my thinking.

I'm nearly panting by the time he reaches my chin, but his wicked finger isn't finished—oh, no, not by a long shot! His wicked finger has turned into a knuckle now, and it's reversing course, slowly trailing backwards across my sensitive cheek.

I'm dizzy with the feel of it, dizzy with the look of him, so close up and serious. His touch is gentle, like he's petting a tiny wild bird.

Neither of us says a word, as though that might break the spell.

My breath is quick and shallow—okay, I'm panting—but hopefully not hard enough that he notices.

Not easy.

Every molecule in my entire being is focused on the

progress of his knuckle. Yearning for more. Silently keening for more. All I want is to turn into his hand and kiss his palm.

It takes effort to keep my face neutral.

He's trailing my cheek with the soft pad of his finger now. He reaches the tender skin below my ear; then and only then does he stop. He gazes at me even more deeply, as if that's possible. Something in my belly melts.

I have no breath.

He leans in and presses his lips to my cheek.

One tiny brush of a kiss. A seismic event in my belly.

Somewhere on the other side of the globe in some tiny island nation, Richter scales are going crazy. Animals are racing into the hills. Nobody understands what has happened. But it's me, standing in this Manhattan office tower, cracking apart in shards of secret lust.

He pulls back, watching me.

"S-soooo, you really *did* like the sandwich," I say.

His lips quirk in a half smile. It's a smile that I haven't seen for years, and it lights something deep in me. "Thank you."

It comes to me that he's thanking me for the sandwich.

It seems like madness, but yes, what else could he be thanking me for? I put on a sarcastic expression. Like he's such a freak. "Oh-*kay*, then."

His lip twitches. "Chips would go great with this," he says. "What do you have?"

I give him a look. *Don't you dare*—that's what my look says. *You can't make me show you the chips array. You can't be an asshole after that kiss!*

He circles his finger.

Heat fills my face.

I go back to my cart, grab a bag of cheesy puffs, and toss them at him.

He catches them, eyes never leaving mine. "You're not going to open the chips for me? What would Meow Squad say?"

"Call 'em and find out."

He stares at me a bit. "Are you going to get my order right next time?"

"Unlikely." I grab my cart and turn, pulse racing.

10

Show her you're the one in charge by creating a system of rewards for good behavior and demerits for behavior you don't prefer.

~THE MAX HILTON PLAYBOOK: TEN
GOLDEN RULES FOR LANDING THE
HOTTEST GIRL IN THE ROOM

Mia

I attend an acting seminar over the weekend and take off Monday to do some work as a film extra, which goes late into the evening. I don't get home until after three in the morning, which I'm a little unhappy about. I wanted to be well rested for Tuesday. But even on five hours of sleep, I'm feeling strangely chipper, and looking forward to doing some more of Max's system on him.

I don't know how to feel about the way he touched me on Friday. All weekend I've been processing it, which is a euphemism for replaying it over and over in my mind.

Today I'll be doing rewards and demerits.

In his book, Max suggests giving the woman a Hershey's Kiss whenever she does something you like. To get her to associate pleasure with being agreeable.

"What the hell!" Kelsey had exclaimed when I read that part aloud. "Like we're Pavlov's dogs?"

Tell her playfully that she has to earn her chocolate candy. She won't like it and will probably find ways to resist, but hold your ground. Do what you need to do to stay in the alpha position —you are the judge of her, the one who gives rewards for good behavior. If you feel your control slipping, simply give another reward for something. Or a demerit.

"Oh, you have to go after him with everything," Kelsey had said.

I just snorted. "Don't you worry, sister." *And I won't think about kissing his palm this time, either!* But I didn't say that part out loud.

We decided that following his system exactly would be too obvious. Like if I start giving him Hershey's Kisses, it might jog his memory.

In order to position myself as approval giver, I've decided to go with a gold-star grading system like they have on Amazon.

He'll hate it. I smile whenever I imagine how much he'll hate it.

Max is behind the desk when I get there, the king in his castle. His white shirt fits him just so, his tie slightly loosened, brown hair perfectly tousled.

He gives me a smile, but it's not his real one. It's his Max Hilton smile, the smile of Maximillion magazine ads and billboards above Times Square. Enchanting Max who knows all the fun secrets. Max who wears a tuxedo to the many glamorous events you will never be invited to. Max having fun elsewhere without you.

It's a beautiful smile that feels like a wall.

"Is it too much to ask that you've brought the sandwich I ordered?" he asks.

"I've brought the sandwich you *want*," I say.

Blue eyes simmer behind lush lashes. "We'll see."

Fun electricity trills through me, much as I try to clamp it down. I proceed, conscious of him watching my every movement. The taking of his sandwich bag from my cart. The bringing of the sandwich to his desk. The extraction of the sandwich, the smoothing out of the bag.

I've done lunch layout for hundreds of conferences, but until Max, I've never been so aware of how much I'm invading somebody's space when I do it. I've never felt so acutely the hum of another person's nearness. The electric charge of another body up close.

He's not even pretending to work this time. He just sits there enjoying my servitude. Maybe thinking about the way he touched my cheek.

God knows I'm thinking about it.

I blot all sexy thoughts from my mind. I'm on a mission. I position the knife and fork perfectly. I clear my throat. "You know, I can see your tower from my bedroom window."

"Can you," Max rumbles, velvety cool.

"It's a beautiful building, it really is, but..." I trail off.

"But what?"

"I'm afraid I can't give it more than three stars."

His expression is just a little bit stony; no sign of emotion whatsoever unless you count that muscle twitching at the side of his jaw.

"I know you would've wanted at least a four-star rating from me, if not a five. I hope you're not disappointed."

"I can't say I'm disappointed," he says dryly. "Disappointed is not the word I'd use."

"I'm glad," I say. "You're a good sport."

His jaw twitches. "And what piece of Manhattan real estate would the *lunch-cart girl* have me purchase?" he asks.

Again with the *lunch-cart girl*. Deep inside my chest, small demons stoke a fire of outrage. Somebody needs a demerit.

"That's not something I can solve for you, unfortunately." I arrange the mustards, feeling his gaze fixed on me, which makes it difficult to think. I keep thinking about the way he touched me. Feeling the sizzling path of his finger. Imagining primal moves.

I nod at the picture on the wall. "Three stars," I say.

"What's that?"

"The Max Hilton girls. Please. They're not as pretty as I am, and probably not as fascinating as I am, either." This sort of thing comes directly out of his book. *Talk yourself up*, he's always saying.

Everything in him seems to go still, except his eyes, which are busy boring holes in the side of my face. Maybe stunned at how deluded I am.

Because let's face it, the Max Hilton girls in the photo are all objectively prettier than me.

I mean it—they are prettier by every pretty parameter, killing it in the categories of nose-straightness, hair silkiness, and symmetry of features. They especially dominate in the willowi-ness-of-limbs area, whereas I'm short and sturdy. My boob size disqualifies me from being able to pull off the drapey dresses they're wearing. They might be more fascinating, too.

But I'm going with it, even though, standing there under his stern scrutiny, I feel less and less confident.

Never let them smell blood in the water, that's another one of the concepts in his book that comes to me now. Like women are sharks, always ready to attack.

The only shark here is Max, of course. With his harsh good looks and his merciless precision and his billion-dollar empire that eats other billion-dollar empires for lunch.

I lower my voice to a confident whisper. "Probably not as fascinating *or* as fun. I think you know it's true. I might even give them a two. As compared to me. Especially..." I adjust my sequined ears. "Oh, what the hell, two-point-five. I'm feeling generous."

He clears his throat. "Are all of your visits going to be this disruptive?"

I sigh like I have a wonderful secret. *The world is your cocktail party*—that's an attitude Max suggests in his book. I actually liked that one—it really resonated with me. "We'll see."

I grab the five bags of chips before he can demand his array. He watches, expression intense.

Of course, in the cocktail party I'm imagining, I'm not acting as a human sandwich dispenser. I'm having fun and laughing, and Max is watching me, besotted.

And it's not because I have a pork chop lifted to my face, either.

"Are we going with cheesy puffs today?" I ask when he doesn't say anything.

"Cheesy puffs," he says hoarsely.

"Good job," I say. "You made an excellent choice. And just for that, you get an extra bag!"

He tightens his jaw as I snatch up an extra bag.

A reward. I feel like I'm really nailing his system today. I head right for him, all the way around his desk, holding his gaze, because that's what you do to show a dog that you're in charge.

It hits me here that holding a man's gaze and walking steadily toward him, never looking away, is also an incredibly sexy thing to do. Every inch of my skin feels alive with excitement.

He swivels away from his desk as I near, facing me with that strangely serious expression. His shirt cuffs are rolled partway up his muscular forearms. His hands rest on his hard thighs, fingers relaxed. Nails trimmed short. Pianist-short. Some habits die hard.

And those thick thumbs. They're the same thumbs he stuck in his belt loops while he sang with all of that sweet goofiness during that lost summer. Though science tells us that the cells of the body replace themselves over time—nine years for an entirely new body. So he really is a different person in every way.

I stop in front of him, heart jackhammering in my chest, remembering the way he'd sing to me.

Even when there was a full auditorium, it was as if he was singing to me and me alone, gaze dancing under that floppy hat, red bandana around his neck. And he'd make these jerky motions, thumbs pointing this way and that, singing about how the farm animals will scurry when he gets a surrey with a fringe on top to drive me around in.

The song was about young, hopeful love. It's how I felt that summer.

It meant nothing to him. A dalliance of proximity. The second we were back at school, he went back to his cold and cynical mode. Too good for me.

Quizzically, he tilts his head. "Mia?"

Have I been standing there weirdly long?

If you feel your control slipping, simply give them another reward for something.

"And as a reward for *extra* predictable behavior..." I toss one bag onto his desk and pull open the other one with a loud crinkle-snap that splits the air.

His eyes flare.

I remove one puff from the bag and hold it out to him. "Open," I whisper, pulse racing. "Open for your prize."

He watches me sternly. He will do no such thing. Nobody pushes Max Hilton around.

The book doesn't have instructions for outright rebellion. The book doesn't say how sexy that might be. How a person's beauty can squeeze deep into your belly. How you might really want to kiss him. To straddle him. To sink into him and make him remember. Make him come back.

I swallow. "That's not open." I nudge his lower lip with the cheesy puff. "Do better," I say.

He grabs my wrist, encircling it snugly and completely with his big, warm hand.

My breath quickens.

His challenging gaze deepens, like he can see right into me.

The bright orange cheesy puff falls from my fingers.

Slowly, he pulls my hand toward him, pinning me with his eyes.

I swallow, mouth dry. "Are you going to eat my fingers instead?" I whisper.

He brushes his lips over my knuckle. His lips feel soft and warm and smooth as velvet.

More shivers. I'm a fireworks show of shivers.

"Somebody thinks he's quite the operator," I gasp out. "Somebody thinks his robot moves are all that."

A chunk of brown hair has fallen over his eyes, and it's unbearably sexy. He kisses my next knuckle, still watching me.

I stifle a gasp.

Is Max Hilton seducing me? Yes.

Warm lips brush another knuckle, sending skitters across my skin.

My knees tremble.

I steel my resolve. Max doesn't get to think he's actually seducing me. No way. Not him.

But his lips are hovering over my pinky knuckle, and everything between us is electric.

God, I need to get control back, but I'm in a canoe heading over a sparkles waterfall, and control is soaring over the treetops. Control doesn't remember me. It will not come when I call.

Max's eyes are bluer than blue, and his breath is a wisp of silk on my skin. And suddenly I'm imagining his mouth over other parts of me.

Behind those blue eyes I think he's thinking it too. I ball the hand that he doesn't have hold of, tightening it against the overwhelming urge to shove it into his hair, to pull his face to my chest. Or maybe just straddle him.

He looks down at our joined hands. He tightens his grip. We're holding hands. I nearly collapse from the unexpectedness of it. The jaw-dropping sexiness.

He looks up and it's a bolt through my belly.

Holding my gaze, he kisses my pinky knuckle, a brush of a kiss that sends shudders through me.

How is this happening? He's taking me over and he hasn't even gotten past my wrist!

He turns my hand so that his lips are over my thumb knuckle. How could I have forgotten about that one? He's now going to kiss my thumb knuckle.

I wait, barely breathing. My entire world has collapsed to that thumb knuckle. It cries out for his lips.

And omigod, what will he kiss after that? Images of me stretched naked across his desk crowd through my mind. Flashes of his wicked lips hovering over my belly. Pressing to the space between my legs.

My mouth begins to form his name—*Max*. I'm not above begging if that gets us moving along.

It's here I come to my senses. Begging? Moving along? What is happening to me? It comes to me that *this* is probably what he wanted when he set up these deliveries.

Maybe he even wagered on it with Parker—*how long will it take? How many Meow Squad visits until I'm the main course?*

I yank my hand away. "In your dreams, buddy. In your dreams."

I spin around and get back over to my cart, awash in a sense of loss, but you can't trust a man with no heart.

He turns back to his computer. "Are you going to bring my correct sandwich next time?"

"Doubtful." I fling open the door and almost bump into Parker.

I step back.

Parker Westbrook, his brainiac business partner, a budding sax player back at the Shiz.

Parker still has his same chubby cheeks and nerdy glasses and generally disheveled bearing—the pile of folders and magazines he's carrying looks like it's about to explode.

"Parker!" I say, then I remember he was another rich kid who was unkind to me. "Hi," I add, in a more morose tone.

"Mia..." He looks me up and down. "Nice threads."

I do a little shimmy, hips wiggling, while I circle my finger, then point it right at him. "You can't touch this." Just a little alpha-signaling-chase-reversing combo courtesy of Max's book.

"Good to see some people haven't changed," he says, walking in.

"Back atcha," I say.

"Vicious campaign mockups," he says to Max. "Fucking golden."

Vicious campaign. I snort and look back at Max. He just smiles his cool superior smile.

I get out of there and ride the elevator down.

11

The woman will scoff at your rewards and demerits but keep going. Doling out rewards and demerits positions you as the approval giver and her as the approval seeker.

~THE MAX HILTON PLAYBOOK: TEN GOLDEN RULES FOR LANDING THE HOTTEST GIRL IN THE ROOM

Max

"So...not to point out the obvious," Parker says, "but that was Mia Corelli. In your office. In a cat suit."

"I know. She's been delivering sandwiches."

"And?"

"There's no *and*. She engineered getting in here somehow. God knows how or why. Apparently Meredith left instructions for the front desk to let her through before she flitted off to wherever." I shrug. "I'm handling it."

Parker has this odd look on his face. "Mia engineered it?"

"Yes, and I'm sure you'll be happy to know that she finds all of this *impressive*."

Parker snorts. "That's what she said?" He remembers what that means.

"Yeah. Impressive."

"So, what's she up to?" he asks.

"I don't know. It's not as if I follow her on Facebook."

"So you guys aren't catching up with each other?" he asks.

"On the sandwich trends of Manhattan, maybe. She's delivering lunch."

"Right to you in your office," he says strangely.

I shrug. "Let's have it. Where are we on the campaign?"

Parker spins through the media plan.

I'm thinking about the way she added all of that bling to her uniform. Just like her to do something like that.

It reminds me of the way she dressed when she first got to the Shiz, all loud colors and big earrings, as if to proclaim herself center of the room. Later, she made herself over, or maybe her friends did. A new casually elegant style to go with her new casually elegant accent.

Parker shows me another board. "The slate gray is pitch-perfect," he says. "And the look on your face. This is gonna kill. They will eat it up. Don't you think?"

"Agreed," I say. "Perfect."

"Here's our location for your shoot." He flips to a backdrop. "Check out this gritty drama. Set you up here with Lana and a couple of the other girls."

"Yeah, that works." I look up at the image of the Maximillion fifth anniversary photo shoot that Mia keeps staring at. It's a shot of me sitting with my old friend Lana, bag designer extraordinaire. Lana's sister and one of the Max Hilton girls from that year, a jewelry designer, are gathered around us, laughing at something.

It was a good night at the top of Maximillion Plaza, all champagne fountains and A-list celebs and athletes. A whirlwind event where we raised tens of thousands of dollars for charity.

And not once did I look out over the rooftops and wonder what she was doing.

Not once did I sling my arm around a woman's shoulders and think, *you're not her.*

Two-point-five stars. It would be amusing if it wasn't so fucking annoying that she thinks she can launch back into my world like this.

I remind myself that I don't have to care. I'm not that horny kid anymore. And she's not in charge—not in any way, shape, or form. She doesn't get to call the shots. She doesn't get to jerk me around. And if she pushes this thing any further, she's going to find that out.

12

Nice guys wind up in the friend zone.

~THE MAX HILTON PLAYBOOK: TEN
GOLDEN RULES FOR LANDING THE
HOTTEST GIRL IN THE ROOM

Mia

Kelsey's there when I get home from work. I peel off my winter clothes, feeling like a fugitive. Am I running from Max? Or myself?

"So? How'd it go?"

Unbearably sexy comes to mind. *Wild. Confusing. Knuckle kisses of wonder.*

"I'm definitely getting his attention." I grab the marker and put an X in the *mete out rewards and demerits* box. "He got three gold stars for his tower."

Kelsey smiles. It's nice to see her happy and excited like this. "All this time he thought it was such an impressive tower."

"Such high hopes for his tower. And then I gave some supermodels in a photo with him two-point-five stars, and he got an extra bag of cheesy puffs when he behaved well."

"Wow. You are going master-level on his system."

This is the part where I should tell her about the knuckle kiss, but I don't. I can't. I feel so confused. What am I going to do?

It's a beautiful evening, not too cold at all. I put on my hat and jacket and set out with my script teed up on my phone, off to wander the streets and memorize lines. I need to work on my monologue.

And I'm a little bit avoiding further Max discussions with Kelsey.

On the first call with acting and singing auditions, you always go in with your own material, and for my monologue I'm doing something from *Wicked*.

In order to not look crazy, I wear an iPhone headset, like I'm talking on the phone. Though if people listen, they'll definitely wonder about my sanity.

One of the best things about winter is that it gets dark earlier, and you can see in windows, so many windows like bright fishbowls.

I walk and I talk, watching the world around me. The way people move, the way they get into cabs or even wait for a light, all of that goes into my tool bag.

I people-watched a lot when I first arrived in the city as a freshman attending the Shiz.

I'd especially watch the elegant women. I remember how horrified I was when I realized how little grace I had compared to them. I flopped down on chairs instead of sitting. I slammed my beverages instead of sipping. And I didn't talk, I spouted off. Worst of all, that brassy laugh.

I'm heading up Ninth Street, running through my piece enough that it's in my bones. I try incorporating that tip-of-the-head movement that Max's receptionist did, a slight twist of the spine and a tip. It's not right in the piece, but it feels very chic. I like it.

I go along the edge of the park, just over a mile from our place. I re-tie my scarf against the wind coming across it and head back down 8th, which is a reasonable enough street to take back to our neighborhood, but it's also where Maximillion Plaza is.

I haven't forgotten the seeming lie I overheard on the phone. I've thought about it on and off since then. A foundation thing after work on Tuesdays.

What does he really have on Tuesday nights? What is he hiding? I can't quite shake the feeling he's hiding something.

It's 6:30 PM and Max's office lights are still on. Most people would have gone home, but Max is there. He always was a hard worker—I saw that up close during the musical. He seemed to have come in with the songs pre-memorized, and he was so serious about getting the blocking right.

I huddle in a doorway across the street.

Is he working this late? Or maybe there's a supermodel up there, and he's saying Max Hilton things to her. *You're wearing far too many clothes, baby. Come on over here and let's get nasty.*

Or maybe he's kissing her knuckles and melting her mind. And she hates how bad she wants him.

Standing out there, I'm thinking that I could just see where he goes that's so secret and mysterious. What if he's learning to juggle? Attending a jazz-hands-to-the-oldies class? These are things I would need to know. Chances are good that he'll have a driver pick him up and whisk him off somewhere, and it's not like I'm going to jump into a cab and be all, *follow that limo!*

Probably.

In his book, Max talks about the practice of observation.

Guys are stupid and oblivious as a rule. You don't have to do much to rise above the competition. You want a book about how to seduce the woman you want? It's written on her face, in her clothes. She tells you with every word she speaks, with every smile. What does she like? What does she care about? Open your eyes. Start seeing what's in front of your face. Use everything.

I wander up and down the long block, keeping an eye on his window, thinking I'll just linger for a while.

I tell myself it's not weird. I tell myself it's all in that service of my girlfriends—the more ammunition the better, right?

But really, I just want to know.

His light goes off. I step back into the shadows. A few minutes later, he steps out of the building. No car tonight. He's wearing an overcoat and winter hat with ear flaps, pulled low over his forehead. A long scarf slung around his chin.

In other words, a disguise. But I'd recognize that posture anywhere. The angle of his head as he looks around.

He turns right and heads along 8th.

Will he take the subway? Does somebody as rich as Max even take a subway?

If it's an easy ride, I suppose he might, though following him all the way down and onto the train seems like a pretty big commitment. Hard not to be noticed if it's not crowded. And if I'm not in the car he rides, I won't know what stop he gets off at.

I channel every action and adventure movie I ever saw as I follow him at a discreet distance, telling myself I'll decide when I decide.

After high school I'd keep my ears peeled at parties, curious where he was auditioning. I knew he wouldn't go for traditional, more established orchestras or ensembles; that wasn't Max. He'd go for something up-and-coming. The sleek and exciting dark horse trio. Something with the edge and cachet to make you go *ooooh.*

My friends and I were surprised when pianists other than Max turned up in those *ooooh* sorts of positions, whereas Max's name was nowhere, not even sitting in for concerts.

He was so talented and connected. What was he up to?

Then *The Max Hilton Playbook: Ten Golden Rules for Landing the Hottest Girl in the Room* came out. And there was nothing in his bio about playing piano. Like he'd erased that whole part of himself.

We were all stunned, even more when his guide sold millions of copies, earning him more money in a month than most musicians make in a lifetime. A lot of us thought he'd come back to music after that, but instead, he took his mad money and built a global men's style empire.

Max had more talent in his little finger than most serious musicians and he'd cast it all aside.

Now he has his own jet.

And a secret about Tuesday nights.

Much to my delight, he passes the 50th Street station and keeps going. I pull out my phone and text Kelsey. I told her about my suspicions, and she's as interested as I was.

Me: Remember Max's secret Tuesday night liaison? Hot on the trail!

Kelsey: Wut? Girl!

Me: I was monologue walking and...*shrug emoji*

He takes a few turns, walks maybe a total of six blocks until he arrives at a not-very-special building with a Korean noodles place and a Starbucks on the bottom, and five unmemorable stories up top.

Me: Subject has arrived at destination.

I text her a map link.

Kelsey: Don't recall a stalking component in Max's book.

Me: It's there. Know your quarry.

I slink back into a doorway, all the better to watch him. He's in the doorway on his phone, texting, presumably. I snap a picture and text it to Kelsey.

Kelsey: That is no foundation meeting!

He looks up, then turns and leans back against the wall. Waiting? Is he picking somebody up? Going in? The lights in the building are all off except the fifth floor.

The door opens suddenly. A statuesque woman with bright blonde hair comes out. Max kisses her cheek. My stomach jack-knifes as they disappear inside.

I fold my arms, laser gaze set on reduce-to-rubble.

Me: Some woman came out and let him in.

Kelsey: *frown emoji*

I wait, watching for movement or lights to show me where they went. Finally I get what I want—or don't want—up on the top floor, a corner window lights up, but three nearby windows go dark.

And then I see her back to a window sill. Her hands are out on either side of herself, like she's leaning back and talking to somebody in there.

I punch the address into Google and get a series of hits. Eye doctors on the second floor; accountants, fabric wholesaler on the fourth and then a hit on Suite 500, the fifth floor. It's a yoga studio. Namaste Way. Sure enough, there's a neon lotus on the farthest window. The whole half of this side of the top floor is a yoga studio.

Me: They went into a yoga studio and turned most of the lights off.

Kelsey: *frown emoji*

Me: Private yoga lessons? In secret?

Kelsey: But why??????

The woman moves away from the window. I wait a few minutes. Then the neon lotus goes out. Moments pass.

Me: No more movement. What are they doing?

Kelsey: Why does a man ever meet a woman in secret?

Me: Then why not a hotel?

Kelsey: Perhaps he is an exceptionally acrobatic lover?

Something clenches around my heart.

Kelsey: Naked yoga? Troll doll full-costume sex fetish films?

Me: Shit! I was watching the window and somebody else went in!

Kelsey: Did you see who?

Me: IDK could've been more than one person.

Kelsey: Erp.

A few minutes later, somebody else emerges from the front door, all bundled up. The blonde. She turns and walks down the street.

Max doesn't come out. And the corner window up there is still lit. I report back to Kelsey. Did those new people join him? I check the back of the building, but the yoga studio is the only lit-up area.

What does Max do in a yoga studio by himself that he has to lie about? He has a palatial apartment on Central Park; I've seen the photos. If he wanted a yoga studio, he'd have a yoga studio there.

I wait for a bit more, then I give up, cold and hungry. On the way home, I Google Namaste Way. The blonde is the owner, a former gymnast turned yoga teacher, which isn't a big surprise in terms of career progression.

Kelsey and I eat cereal and discuss the new mystery. She's wrangled another donation from another Max Hilton book victim. The woman wants me to know that I'm doing God's work.

"Yeah, I don't know about that."

"You're standing up to him, that's what counts. He's seeing what it feels like to have somebody work a system on him like he's a piece of meat," Kelsey says.

"I'm not going to overpromise," I say. "Max is a man who is surrounded by gorgeous women. He probably has mysterious assignations all over the city, like a bee going from flower to flower."

"And you'll squish him," Kelsey says.

"Well, bees are endangered, so..."

"Squish his overblown ego," she amends.

I try to imagine that, but I can't quite get past the feel of his fingers around my wrist. His lips pressed to my knuckles.

And then it turns to him throwing the yoga teacher up against the wall in the dark stairwell and kissing her. Which is basically like a furious scribble in my mind. Ugh!

In unrelated news, I suggest that maybe it's time for Antonio, and Kelsey's texting him before I can even finish my admittedly weak rationale for my change of heart.

Fifteen minutes after I arrive back at home, Antonio's in our living room modeling a three-piece suit he plans to wear for his star turn, his hair-that-shall-not-be-touched perfectly tousled.

It's as if he lounges around his apartment looking like he stepped right off the pages of a men's magazine.

Kelsey bites her lip, beaming at him.

"Antonio Corelli. Bringing it," I say.

Antonio smiles. "Hugo Boss fall collection. I did a runway show last month and they gave me this one. A ten-thousand-dollar suit if not for a fray by the button."

"It's a wonderful suit," Kelsey says. "Just stunning."

"The bracelet gives it a slight organized-crime twist," I observe. "Very nice. Not that Max will be close enough to see that, so I guess it doesn't matter." This is my gentle way of reminding him that he won't be trotting out that backstory.

He fingers his bracelet. "If you are asking if I am a *friend*—a *soldier*..." He gives his Euro shrug. "This is not something you should ask. I will tell you that my time in the streets made me hard. A very hard businessman. My practices..." Thoughtfully, he adjusts his suit sleeve. "They are not what you call ethical, I'm afraid. Effective, yes. Ethical, not so much, *cara*. Everything I have, I've had to fight for. And now I fight for you. I will follow you up the high-rise. I am not above helping the object of my affection in her menial chores. And if another man even looks at her sideways." He gives Kelsey a dark look and lowers his voice. "I will slit his throat. Without a moment's hesitation, I will do this. I will leave him to die on the street like the dog that he is."

"Dude, too much," I say.

"How will this pickup artist know that I adore you?"

"Remote visual observation," I say.

He frowns.

"And you're not following me. You'll just be out hanging around at the rendezvous truck where I switch out carts between buildings, and he'll see you looking at me adoringly when he walks by. It's usually before lunch, or else right after. Okay? He's not going to come talk to us."

"But if he does..."

"You're a guy on your lunch break who wants a date with me. And you say nothing."

Antonio shakes his head vociferously. "I would not stay silent," he growls. "One sideways look from him—"

"It won't come to that."

"You never know," Kelsey says. "It's good for Antonio to be ready."

I widen my eyes at Kelsey.

Antonio gazes at the ceiling, sucks in a breath. "Even the

smallest interaction with you, when you're loading your lunch cart out on the street, is solace to my darkened soul. Does he think to take you from me? He'll see that the blade is just another tool to me. I am not afraid to tell him that."

"Yeah, you don't want to scare him off," Kelsey says, chastened. "Just watch her with that deep look, maybe a smile. You'll be amazing."

"A smile with no subtext is but a shape of the lips." Antonio turns his deep look to me. "How many men have I killed in this short life? One does not lurk around after a street fight in the alleyways of Milano."

"...cookies," I whisper.

"Roma, then," he growls.

Do something outrageous. You don't give a shit what she thinks.

~THE MAX HILTON PLAYBOOK: TEN
GOLDEN RULES FOR LANDING THE
HOTTEST GIRL IN THE ROOM

Mia

I call Rollins to try and persuade him to use the Maximillion Plaza block as the relay point—I suggest a spot that will be in perfect view of Max walking across the street for his pre-lunch visit. It's just a block over from where we usually are.

Rollins is not so sure—in addition to the innocent-country-boy-in-the-city thing he has going on, he's a dedicated rule follower. Rollins never met a rule he doesn't want to marry in a little white chapel on a windswept prairie.

I promise him I'll tell the other delivery cats and take all the heat, and he finally agrees.

I arrange my delivery schedule so that I can meet Antonio out there just before eleven.

It's a brilliantly sunny afternoon, warm for December, and the timing works like clockwork, which I guess is the point of using a clock. Rollins brings me a new cart and switches out the old like the Indy 500 pit crew of sandwich delivery that he is. I'm refilling the chips and utensils just as Antonio strolls up in his beautiful suit.

"Can I help you?" Rollins asks, because Antonio looks more like somebody we'd deliver to than somebody we'd know.

"I'm past help," Antonio says darkly. "So far past help."

"It's cool, he's my cousin," I explain.

Antonio slides his hand up the side of the truck, gazing down at me. It's a smoldering, sensual, uniquely male stance. "Do not minimize it, *cara*," he says. "Do not minimize what we are to each other. We are more than mere cousins."

Rollins straightens, nervously restocking chips.

I widen my eyes at Antonio.

Antonio turns to Rollins. "I came to look at her beauty, hoping that it would ease the despair and darkness in my heart."

"Oh," Rollins says.

"Antonio, stop being funny."

"*Pah!* You wish me to hide my love. I will not. I had no beauty coming up on the streets of Roma, you know." He turns to a wide-eyed Rollins. "I sold myself, I hurt people. The blade was my friend. I am not proud. But everything I went through is worth it..."

"Okay..." I say. "But do you remember our discussion?"

Rollins is busying himself with the condiments box.

Antonio glances significantly over my shoulder, then back at me, and he turns a thousand-watt smile on me.

"I ask you," he says, tilting his head, which adds hot-guy dimension to the smile. "Who is that dog over there who thinks he can look at you? I will cut out his heart as easily as I'd plunge a knife into a ripe tomato. Your body is not for men to feast their eyes on."

He's spotted Max. I pull out my phone and put it on selfie-mode. My breath catches as I see that familiar pair of shoulders some distance away, crossing the street.

I gaze up at Antonio, who looks down at me besotted. Beatific, even, like a monk, having endured years of darkness for this one chance to gaze upon the divine. "All my problems disappear when I set my eyes upon you," he whispers. "All of them!"

I smile back at him. Now I'm turning on the drama. "You really are amazing," I say.

"I know I am," he says.

"I appreciate it, I do." I'm also relieved that there was no weird confrontation.

"Well, all the lessons you have given me. You have taught me so much." Acting, he means.

"You've been putting in the work."

Antonio sighs and shoves his hands into his pockets.

"Gone?" I ask.

"Gone, *cara*."

I lower my voice. "You think he even saw?"

"I don't know. He seemed...absorbed in thought."

"Do I get to check off the box if he didn't see?" I ask.

Antonio looks at me sadly.

Rollins stands behind him, fussing with a cart, a look of alarm etched upon his features.

I EXECUTE my deliveries for Maximillion Plaza at peak efficiency, getting peak tips. I never looked forward to my route this much before.

Blade, the guy on the twentieth floor who really loves *Blade Runner*, is excited about the whitefish I recommended. He's been talking me up on the floor and it's suddenly my most lucrative floor. He asks me whether I'm appearing in any shows coming up and I tell him about my upcoming audition for *Anything Goes*. He's sure I'll get it.

By the elevators on Blade's floor, there's a pair of enlarged photos of Max.

In one of them, he's looking bored in a fabulous suit, sprawled on a kingly piece of furniture. A woman stands behind him with her hand in his hair.

My belly grinds at the sight. Which just goes to show the devastating power of prize-positioning, as described in his book. So smart. Max has many flaws, but ignorance was never one of them.

I only wish he'd seen Antonio admiring me so that I could be prize-positioned, too.

What did all of that maneuvering get me instead? Rollins thinks I'm dating my murderous gigolo cousin.

But I really want to be able to X off a golden-rule box today. I'm thinking about the *Do Something Outrageous* one. My gaze falls to the twelve bags of cheesy puffs still in my cart. A plan starts to form.

On the twenty-second floor I start giving the cheesy puffs away. "You get an extra free one!" I say to my excited customers. I'll have to settle up with the Meow Squad powers that be, but who cares about obstacles like that when you're on the do-something-outrageous warpath?

I strategically work it out as only a delivery cat can so that I have precisely one bag left when I get into the elevator going up to his floor. One of the willowy, statuesque receptionists is riding with me; I'd hoped to have privacy for this part of my plan, but then again, it's not like people sit around staring at each other in elevators, right? Elevators are a zone of ignoring each other.

I retreat to the back of the elevator and pull open the last cheesy puff bag and stuff a handful into my mouth, allowing bright orange crumbs to cascade down my shirt. I stifle a grin, imagining Max's face after I tell him I'm out of cheesy puffs and he specifically sees them all over my front.

I shove another bunch in, kind of smashing them into my mouth so that they get into my hair a little bit.

It's right about here that I realize the statuesque beauty is watching me in the reflection of one of the slim, highly polished panels. She quickly looks away.

My pulse races. I think about saying something, but what? There are some instances when explaining an awkward thing will only make it more awkward.

Finally the elevator arrives at the top floor. She gets out first and walks off—eager, perhaps, to tell her willowy, statuesque co-workers the cautionary tale of the lunch-cart girl.

I keep Kelsey's faith in me in mind as I knock on Max's door wearing a cat suit full of orange cheesy puffs. "Meow Squad."

There's a largish puff right on the center of my chest, a bright orange badge of outrageousness. I'm so X-ing off that box.

"Come," he says.

I push in. "When did people stop saying *come in*? I don't know how I feel about *come*, just on its own."

Max has his jacket off again, his tie is a little bit loose, and his dress shirt is tight over his sternly crossed arms, creating a definite guns-n-stuff effect. Arm muscles ahoy. Just looking at him makes my head feel light.

He says, "I think of it as a Jean-Luc Picard from Star Trek: The Next Generation thing."

I snort, as if that's so uncool, though in my own personal hierarchy of pop culture references, Jean-Luc Picard beats Deckard from *Blade Runner*. Leave it to Max.

I pull his lunch from my cart. "I'm going to guess you want layout."

I go around without his telling me to. I flatten out the bag, feeling his stare, hungry and heavy on my skin.

"I've taken the liberty of ordering you a sesame chili salmon sandwich with kimchi fried rice today," I say. I'm thinking about the knuckles kiss, much as I'm trying not to.

He probably forgot about it by now. A brief knuckle kiss is just a drop of water in the vast ocean of Max Hilton's daily moves.

His arms are still lusciously crossed. I imagine flattening the shirt fabric over them, smoothing the shirt so that it perfectly outlines the contours of his muscles, and then I'd smooth some more, soft fabric over steely strength, like a party for my hands. And then maybe my lips could get involved. And then maybe my teeth.

"Am I ever going to get what I ordered again? You're not a very proficient lunch-cart girl."

"No, I'm not."

"Go ahead and play this sad little game if you want," he says, "just know that I don't like mushrooms, bacon, ham, or cilantro."

"Oh, I'm not the one playing a sad little game, my friend."

"What exactly is that supposed to mean?"

I place a napkin and knife and fork next to his new sandwich. He knows exactly what it means. Ordering from the Meow Squad. Requesting me.

"Who's your little friend out there?" he asks.

I still. He saw Antonio and me out there? Was he pretending he didn't see? "Out where?"

"Out where," he snorts. "The *strapping fella* in Hugo Boss out by your lunch-cart truck?" I get the sense he's going for lightness in the *strapping fella* bit, but it sounds slightly adversarial, too.

Is he jealous? Excitement surges through me. I've never been excited by jealousy before.

"Ah," I say with faraway eyes. "Antonio." I'm stoking it now. What's going on with me?

I continue my machinations, reveling in his covetous gaze. I set out his mustards with my usual flourish. He picks up a pen, moves it carelessly around in his fingers. His hands really are large. And warm and soft.

"*Please,*" he says.

"What?"

"*Ah, Antonio,*" he echoes, matching my intonation exactly. "He's a friend. You look at him like a friend. Like one of your galpals."

I give him a sympathetic look. "Poor Max Hilton. I think that's maybe what you wanted to see."

"I know what I saw."

"That was not a galpal face," I say. I set a bag of Lay's plain potato chips next to his sandwich.

"What is this?" He picks them up, brow furrowed. "Where's my array?"

"Can't you just go into your robot memory files and access the image of the last time I displayed them?"

He shakes his head.

"*Ungh.*" I go back to the cart and pluck out four bags of chips. I hold them up. "We have Lay's, barbeque, cool ranch, and baked sea salt."

"No cheesy puffs today?"

"I ran out."

He finally zeroes in on the bright orange cheesy puff crumbs on my front. "You're telling me you ran out?"

I show him the empty cheesy puffs box, quivering with maybe too much excitement. "The very last bag was eaten. Quite recently!" I bite my tongue—hard—applying intense, anti-laughter pressure.

He stands.

I'm fighting not to smile. Bite bite bite.

He's coming for me.

I back up.

He keeps coming. I'm a deer in the blazing headlights. If a deer ate the car's dinner. And the car is barreling down the road.

I'm backing up some more. I hit the wall. His hands hit the wall on either side of me.

My knees are jelly.

"What are you doing, Mia?"

I can feel his warmth deep in my chest—it's like he has his own personal force field.

His eyes bore into mine, and then he drops his gaze to my shirt.

My pulse pounds.

He picks a bit of cheesy puff off my chest and holds it between us, evidence of my impudence. "Who ate my cheesy puffs?"

Excited shivers rain over me. "I did," I whisper.

We both seem to hold our breath. It's like we're in some kind of strange limbo.

Sexiest. Re-enactment. Of Goldilocks. Ever.

His pulse drums hot and steady beneath the hard line of his jaw. I imagine pressing my lips to the tender skin there. Desire floods my veins. Something's melting in my belly.

"You think it's funny?"

"I don't know."

He drops the puff bit, his face lit with beautiful fury.

He brushes some crumbs off the center of my chest, off my shoulder. The feeling of his hand on me is electric.

And then he moves to my cheek, swiping it with his thumb, rough velvet on hot silk. There might have been a crumb there. Really, I don't care.

His chest rises and falls, seemingly in unison with mine. His expression is so serious. I remember it from that summer—it was the way he looked when he cared about getting something right.

I feel this rush of frustration. I want us to be different. Free of our factions and fraught history.

He slides his thumb across my lower lip. The urge to suck his thumb into my mouth is nearly unbearable. I would suck it so hard. I would suck the hell out of his thumb.

"Look at you." He reaches to my hair, brushes a possibly real or maybe imaginary crumb off, then slides a strand through his fingers. He watches his progress through lowered lashes.

I swallow with difficulty.

Again he slides my hair through his fingers, watching intently, as though he's really into making sure the crumbs are gone. The lightest sheen of whisker stubble glints on his cheeks.

He tucks another strand behind my ear. Then he brushes some more back.

I'm catatonic with lust.

And confusion.

What is Max doing?

He tucks my hair again, this time grazing the shell of my ear. The bright swipe of his touch ripples over my body. It arrows down between my legs.

My breath hitches.

I want him to press himself right into me and make me come. Coming like that is not a thing with me, but right now, it would be.

I want him so badly, I might burst into flames.

He draws his mouth close to my ear, right there where he tucked away the hair. His breath is warm velvet on my ear.

I close my eyes.

My entire skeletal system is turning into jelly at this point. I imagine gripping his shoulders, pulling him to me.

"There we go," he whispers, "there's your non-galpal face."

My eyes fly open. "Oh my god!" I push him away. "You are so full of shit."

He just watches me, amused.

"You think you're all that," I say.

He lowers his voice to a hard rumble. "You'll bring the cheesy puffs next time."

I snort. "Definitely not." I grab my cart and leave.

14

Only an idiot tells a woman what she wants to hear.

~THE MAX HILTON PLAYBOOK: TEN
GOLDEN RULES FOR LANDING THE
HOTTEST GIRL IN THE ROOM

Max

I try to make sense of the words on the screen as she closes the door behind her, but I'm too jacked.

Ah, Antonio.

Who the hell is he? A Wall Street guy? Hotshot exec? How does she even meet somebody like that?

No, she's not with him—I know it. Mia's gaze softens when she's captured by something. And that's not how she looked at Antonio. I saw her face only briefly, but it was enough.

Still. What was I seeing? He looked ready to haul her over his shoulder and carry her off.

I shake the whole thing out of my mind.

Also, eating my cheesy puffs? Letting the evidence of it sprinkle down her front? I'm sure she was laughing as she did it. Stuffing her face and laughing.

Did she deliberately place the one large puff on her front, hoping to draw my eye?

Yes, of course she did. Standing there trying to look serious. Mischief in her eyes; cheesy puff crumbs in her hair.

Damn, I wanted her. I wanted to press her up against the wall and peel that sexy little cat suit right off of her. I wanted to taste every maddening inch of her.

Except I discovered something better.

The satisfaction of watching her struggle with her attraction to me. Her supposedly indifferent sighs. She's come back to taunt me, this girl I could never have, but she didn't think it through, did she?

I happen to know, in fact, that she regrets it, now.

I found it out when I was passing by the front desk the other day—one of my assistants told me they still haven't heard from Meredith, but he mentioned that Meow Squad had contacted the desk at some point about switching delivery people.

I'd paused, trying not to look too interested. "They wanted to switch it up? What did you say?" I asked, casually spinning through my phone.

"I wasn't the one who talked to them, but they were told no," he informed me. "Delivery is Meredith's area. If she had notes to set it up a certain way, that's how it stays. She gets mad when people override her decisions. Unless *you* want to change it up..."

"No, keep it as is," I said simply, heading back to my office. I'd wanted details—when did they make the request? After which of her visits? But that would make it look like something more than it is.

Simply knowing that, at some point, the little vixen had tried to wriggle out of her own scheme—that made my day.

Did Mia figure out that she was out of her depth after one or two deliveries? Did she change her mind? I don't know how she got to Meredith, but she's not changing it now.

She made her bed; she can damn well toss and turn in it.

It's so like Mia to underestimate situations. To make rash decisions. To tilt at windmills. To decide that she's the cat delivery person who is going to taunt Max Hilton.

This isn't high school anymore—apparently she's figured that out. Yes, I was obsessed with her back then—this short, high-spirited spitfire with her dark curls and big attitude—but I'm not that horny, awkward, lost kid anymore.

Things don't affect me like they used to. *She* doesn't affect me.

And that's not about to change.

I lean back in my chair. My cocky, scrappy Jerseygirl with her fake sophistication and unflinching resilience. Her big dreams. Laughing at me. Too good for the robot.

You bring it, I think, taking another bite of the salmon sandwich. It is delicious, of course. It doesn't mean anything. She should know her own job, shouldn't she?

15

Open your eyes. Start seeing what's in front of your face.

~THE MAX HILTON PLAYBOOK: TEN
GOLDEN RULES FOR LANDING THE
HOTTEST GIRL IN THE ROOM

Max

The Maximillion Companies studio complex sits across the street from the main headquarters. It's a creative workshop, a refuge from the demands of running the company. Doing a round through there is the high point of my day—I enjoy finding out about my employees' projects on an informal basis. Hearing what's on people's minds.

I sometimes see Mia and her co-workers around the Meow Squad truck out on 8th, but she's not there today. Which means I may not see her today at all—I have an interview and a lunch event across town.

The studio complex was an abandoned eyesore across the street when we first took over the tower. After an unexpectedly good quarter—and against the wishes of our accounting team—we bought it and had it gutted and made into an open, colorful creative space with large and small work rooms honeycombed around the edges.

I love to walk around there and get the fashion designers, industrial designers, and marketing creatives to pitch me big ideas. Sometimes I pitch them.

It took a long time to get them to stop treating me like an owner, or worse, a celeb. To understand that I'm just a collaborator with extra juice. It took a few rounds of championing wild ideas and handing out bonuses even when things crashed to get them to relax around me. And Maximillion Companies is all the better for it.

I check on the apparel design team, and then I'm up in the photography studio talking about shots. The studio has windows that overlook the street below.

It's right before eleven when I see the Meow Squad truck pull into one of the fifteen-minute spaces.

Somebody is talking to me about a new series of images for the Maximillion body spray, but I can't stop watching the truck, wondering what she'll get up to today.

A young guy jumps out and opens up the back. A redhead with Meow Squad ears walks up—hers are lit with tiny lights, oddly enough. What is it with these delivery girls?

My photographer is talking about the color process, petitioning for a Japanese photo app that automates something or other. He drones on as more Meow Squad people arrive and get their pre-packed carts.

I nod, feigning interest.

And then *she's* there, ears shining in the late-morning

sunlight, standing straight and proud, making the most of her small frame. The stance is classic Mia.

That was her, all through high school. She'd hold her head high through every setback, going after her stage career with an urgency that wasn't there with other kids. It looked like urgency, anyway; I had this idea that it was a little bit about escape, too. We both wanted to escape in our own ways, I guess.

One of the few things we had in common.

I flex my fingers as she touches the young van driver on the shoulder, talking to him excitedly. Mia always had lots of funny, charming stories. Honestly, I think half the school was in love with her.

She pulls out her cart and arranges it just so, laughing.

Something lightens in me, seeing her laugh.

And then Antonio appears around the corner.

My mood darkens. How does he end up out there? Does he wait for her? Do they text?

Antonio's wearing another nice suit. He's young to know how to wear a suit so well. I'd think he was a model himself if not for his briefcase.

She seems happy to see him, but the way she looks at him—she's fond of him—no way is she with him. Or is she? Do I have my head in my ass here? She grabs his arm and says something, head tilted, just an air of mischief.

"Max?"

"Buy the app," I say, not wanting to tear my gaze from the scene unfolding below. "Send me a few shots so I can see."

"Okay. Thanks."

She's twisting her lips at him. It's her humorous and not-so-sure-about-this look. Playful scolding.

What am I seeing?

Now his hands are on her shoulders and he's regarding her with shock and joy. Very extreme emotions on this guy.

I'm reminded of a Facebook video I once saw of a deaf man who'd gotten some kind of ear implant and could hear for the first time. He listened to the ocean with this stunned, joyful, bewildered expression. Then he listened to some symphony music with a face like that.

Why is Antonio looking at Mia like that? Did she deliver some astonishing news? But she still has that fond scolding look. She reaches up and fixes his tie. Is she whispering to him?

My blood goes cold as he slides his hand to the side of her head. He leans in and kisses her.

I wait for her to push him away. Instead she shoves her hands into his hair, vigorously messing it up. Her hands grip his back. The kiss is getting dramatic.

I'm off, heading down to the lower level, my legs moving before my mind can stop me. I'm rushing down the stairwell, out the door.

My jaw is tight as I emerge onto the busy thoroughfare. I need to get to them. I don't know why. I don't need a reason.

Traffic is insane—I'm waiting at the light for what feels like forever. Finally it clears. The walk light flashes on and I'm stomping across the street. Around the corner. My brow lowers as I approach the truck.

They're both gone. There's just the redheaded kid. The driver.

"Can I help you?" he asks.

I take out my wallet and extract a fifty. "Who was that with Mia?"

The driver gapes at the money. "I can't take that."

"Why not? Did you take an oath of silence?"

"No, but...I don't want trouble with Antonio."

"Trouble? What kind of trouble?"

The kid looks up and down the street, as if he's worried

Antonio might jump out of the shadows. "He has a lot of darkness in his heart."

I frown. "What does *that* mean?"

"You don't want to know. Just leave it. And don't ask around about him—he's dangerous."

I get a little closer and shove the fifty into his front pocket. "I won't have to ask around if you tell me. What do you mean by dangerous?"

The kid lowers his voice. "Antonio would plunge a knife into your heart as easily as he'd cut a ripe tomato. *That's* what I mean."

I stare. Hard. "Are you being funny?"

Solemnly, he shakes his head. "You didn't hear it from me. Okay?"

My protective instincts kick into overdrive. "So this guy's some sort of criminal?"

"To put it mildly," the kid says. "The man is a killer from Italy who had very little to live for before Mia. He grew up selling his body on the streets of Roma and getting into knife fights. He's killed before. Sliced men to ribbons, and he thinks nothing of sleeping in pools of blood. And there are other things, too. Between him and Mia...it's very..." He shakes his head as he loads an empty cart into the back of his truck.

I frown. "Very *what*?"

"Unsavory. I'd rather not get into it."

"Unsavory how?"

He rushes around to the front and pulls open the door.

I follow on his heels. "Where is she? Right now."

"I don't know."

"Yes, you do," I say.

"The Hillman building. She has a quick route there, and then she's at the International Foods Center."

"Thank you." I turn and walk toward the Hillman building.

I don't like this. I don't like the boy's fear of this Antonio. I don't like that they kissed. Is this man in the mafia? Is that what the kid was getting at? Mia wouldn't have anything to do with somebody like that.

I go one block, two blocks, barreling past the dawdling pedestrians, ignoring the heads that swivel around in recognition.

I'm thinking about calling a friend on the force, a detective who's done time on an organized crime unit, and asking him what he knows about gang members newly arrived from Rome, specifically anybody named Antonio.

The Hillman building looms ahead.

I position myself to the side of the door, in the shade of a pillar, trying to collect my thoughts. I can't be late to this luncheon, but this Antonio situation feels all wrong.

I go over what I know: Roman male prostitute who graduated to knife fighting. He murdered several people. Sharp dresser. Model good looks.

And the way he looked at her, like a man in hell seeing an angel. And the way she gripped his back, the high drama.

I turn the thing over in my mind.

And then I just start laughing.

Mia's out the door moments later. She pulls her cart to my side.

"Max! What are you doing?"

"I heard some disturbing news about Antonio," I say.

"I don't think Antonio is really any of your business," she replies, eyes sparkling.

"He's extremely dangerous," I say. "Did you know that he sold his body in the gutters back in Italy?"

She looks bewildered. "Huh?"

"Antonio would plunge a knife into a man's heart as readily

as he would slice a tomato. He's killed before, you know. I'm thinking about alerting a friend on the force."

She looks pale. "A cop?"

"He bathes in the blood of his enemies. Though on the upside, tomato-slicing skills like that would make him handy around the kitchen."

Confusion fills her face.

I do my best not to smile, but I fail, and she sees it.

"Shut up!" She slaps my chest. "Screw off. I can't even with you."

I go to her, grip her upper arms, right there in the shade of the pillar, with streams of people on the sidewalk not ten feet away. She's warm and breathy, a beautiful, trembling confection.

What am I doing? I need to be across town. "That kiss. So fake."

A defiant gleam appears in her eyes. "Who are you to say what's fake?"

I lower my voice to a deep register. "I'm the man who's going to kiss you for real."

A slight movement of her nostrils is the only evidence of the sharp intake of breath.

I brush my lips lightly over hers. Our connection is electric. What am I doing?

"You think you're all that," she whispers into the millimeter of space between our lips.

That's when I lose it. I pull her to me. I kiss her with savage intensity, my lips pressing hers, moving against hers, devouring hers.

She makes a desperate little sound, fisting my jacket, pulling me close.

That's all the green light I need to deepen the kiss, edging my tongue along the seam of her lips, shoving in, consuming and mapping her inside and out.

She hums with pleasure, kissing me back, moving against me. Her pleasure is a drug. I grip her anew, I change my angle, kissing her with ragged energy.

Stage kisses are all style; this one's pure substance.

But then I remember myself. I slow.

Her lips curl into a smile against mine. Into the kiss, she whispers, "Three stars."

What am I doing? I force myself to stop.

I pull back and cup her cheeks, cradling them. I swipe my thumb over her perfectly plump lips. "Try not to eat all of the cheesy puffs next time."

I SIP MY LATTE, waiting for my pre-luncheon interview. Why did I kiss her like that? What was I thinking?

I'd vowed to stay away from her. And we were only semi-hidden. What if photographers had caught us?

But god, the way her eyes shone—burnt-sugar brown. Maddening, impossible Mia Corelli.

A shadow falls over the table, and there he is, Tarquin Millbauer, intrepid tabloid reporter. "I understand you've been kissing Meow Squad cats out on the street," he says, sitting down. "Leaving them stunned and breathless. I'm sensing a pattern. Wasn't that the same girl as before?"

I sit back. The last thing I want is for Mia to wind up in the tabloids with me. We may have some strange...whatever it is that we're doing, but I'm not out to destroy her career.

She'd hate being labeled as a Max Hilton girl—for good reason. It would ruin her credibility as an actress.

You never want to underestimate Tarquin Millbauer, intrepid Times reporter. You never want to give him anything.

"Kissing me is always a deeply religious experience for women."

Tarquin gives me a jaded look and orders a coffee.

"Come on," he says, "level with me. A delivery girl now? Do tell." Tarquin's doing a feature on me. The goal of a feature profiler is always to get something juicy.

I sigh.

"What would Lana Sheffidy say?"

"Lana's one of my best friends," I say. "I'd tell you if there was something going on. I promise you," I say when he protests. "Though she's threatening to design a men's fanny pack line for Maximillion." A joke. "Come on. Those are your questions? Kissing rumors?"

"I get to ask real questions now?"

"Do you have any?" I ask.

"Yes." He turns serious. He asks about a feud I have going with some industry asshole.

I give him a few irrelevant details. Information that costs me nothing.

Then he hits close to home. "Your family took a summer trip to Berlin when you were in high school. You ran away from home when you returned to the States. They filed a missing person report. You were gone for ten days. What happened?"

"Aren't juvie records sealed?" I ask.

"Usually."

I sip my coffee. "Doesn't every kid run away from home?"

He checks his iPad. "It was right after your elderly nanny, Annette O'Grady, died."

I stir my coffee. How did he think to connect those things? The narrative was that I was trying to get out of a concert.

"It was a big loss," I say. "Annette was a sweet, caring

woman. She'd been with us since I was a toddler and she was..."
Everything, I think. The one who kissed my skinned knees and sung me lullabies. The one who brought laughter to my grim childhood. The one who took the sunshine when she died.

I stare into my coffee. "Annette was full of life. Missed by the whole family. She loved custard, as I recall." I look up, pulse racing.

He's waiting.

"But I'm minimizing it. I was upset," I say. "I hitchhiked to the family cabin upstate. They didn't think to look there. I needed time to decompress."

This seems to satisfy him; he's back on his notes.

We discuss my upcoming pet project, Catwalk for a Cause. I give him some red meat on that one—warring factions in the fashion world. A juicy celeb cameo. I'll let him announce it.

We talk food. A restaurant opening we're attending. I tell him about the special-edition grilled whitefish sandwich from a food truck on Seventh. The chef with the Michelin rating.

How did she know I'd love the sandwich like that? Did it give her satisfaction to be right? She always did have excellent taste—that's something I remember from high school. She'd cultivated excellent taste and her own unique opinions on everything. Little Jerseygirl, scrabbling her way up. And she always, always wanted to show you that she was in charge.

Don't be part of the herd. Have your own unique opinions on things.

~THE MAX HILTON PLAYBOOK: TEN
GOLDEN RULES FOR LANDING THE
HOTTEST GIRL IN THE ROOM

Mia

I'm still fuming after dinner on the way to rehearsal.

He's a complete and utter jerk who loves to mess with me. One furious, utterly mind-blowing kiss and he thinks he owns me.

Why do I keep falling for it? Yes, it was a good kiss. Max is good at things. Ruthlessly so. And yes, I want him so badly, my heart gets all twisted into knots around him.

And my lady parts think they're rehearsing for Cabaret.

But I won't fall for him again. I know better. Make me fall for you once, shame on you. Make me fall for you twice, shame on me.

I fell so hard for him that summer. I really thought he cared. I didn't know he was playing me.

I spend the night rehearsing my new audition song with my old friend Glen, but the first full hour of it is me trying not to act weird, to get my head back in the game, which isn't easy after kissing my supposed enemy.

I should've told him to stop—he totally would've but it was the last thing I wanted.

Even though he's just playing me.

The piano music halts. "Mia? If there's a problem, just say so," Glen says.

"Oh, no, it's not you," I say quickly. Glen is as sensitive as he is talented, and he won't stand for criticism when he's being an accompanist. "I'm having a weird week," I say.

He frowns, still suspicious. I give him a pleading face and he takes it from the beginning of the verse.

I launch in. We run to the end, then back to the top.

Max really is playing me. I know it. I knew it during the kiss. So why was it the hottest kiss ever? It's not fair! It's not as if Max needs his head to swell any more than it already is! Also, there's the whole bringing-him-to-his-grovelly-knees thing. He's not supposed to be bringing me to *my* knees.

"Mia?" Glen says, poised at the keyboard, frowning. "Again from the key change?"

"Sorry!" I say. "Do it."

He launches into "How Could I Ever Know?" from *The Secret Garden*. It's one of the songs I'm doing for my audition for the role of Reno in *Anything Goes*.

You never do songs from the show you're auditioning for—it's a total amateur move.

I like this song because it shows off my high notes—word on the street is that they want somebody who can go ridiculously high, and I'm dead on for it.

I wouldn't usually bring in my own accompanist, but "How Could I Ever Know?" is really beautiful and complex with a zillion key changes; people will bring their own pianists in cases where the song is very challenging. At least in New York.

We're doing a trade where I'm giving Glen's cousin voice lessons. His little cousin is new in the city and not that polished. She reminds me of me when I came, except she has family behind her, and her accent isn't half as awful.

The end of the song is especially hard, so we've been hitting that—over and over and over. My concentration is a little bit shot, needless to say. Max has me unmoored. I'm still feeling him on my skin. His voice low and rumbly against my cheek.

Finally Glen stops. "I'm feeling like this is wrong. Should you just use their house pianist?"

"Oh my god, no! I can't do this without you. Again? I'll get it this time." Glen is always on the verge of quitting. It sucks.

"Or maybe cut our losses for today?" he says. That's something we say sometimes, you let certain days be the shitty days that your good days are built on.

"Maybe you're right," I say. "I don't want to waste your time. I really am so grateful you're in this with me."

Glen shuffles together the music. "I appreciate your help with Jenny."

I grab my phone and my coat. "So you'll never guess who I'm delivering sandwiches to now," I say. "And I can't get out of it no matter how hard I try. It's somebody we both know."

"Hmmm. Somebody we both know. Is it someone from high school or after high school?"

"You won't get it. Maxfield Miller—excuse me, Max Hilton."

He furrows his brow. "What?"

"I know!" I grab my bag. "Every day. And you know he's enjoying the shit out of it."

"Mr. Roboto ordered sandwiches just so that you have to deliver them?" Glen asks, incredulous.

"Can you even?" I say, surprised my nickname for him is still sticking.

"Unbelievable," he says. "He was always so above everyone. But to make you be his delivery girl."

"Well, what is it that his book says? Women are like dogs, they enjoy knowing you're in charge."

"Hmm," Glen says as we head down the hallway, past the row of doors, every few steps another rehearsal studio where you can hear muffled music. "Didn't *you* use to say something like that?"

"What are you talking about?" I ask.

"During *Evita*, remember? You were saying that all the time. There were all those problems with soldier guys, with the blocking, and you were always telling them where to go, and that's what you said. Guys are like dogs—they like somebody to tell them what to do."

I frown. I don't remember that at all, though I do remember a lot of guys not paying attention and needing to be ordered around.

"Anyway, that seems a little...petty?" Glen says. "What an asshole."

Something unpleasant rises up in me at his calling Max an asshole. I'm the only one who gets to insult Max. "It's just...strange."

He shakes his head as he locks up.

Outside, the holiday lights are still in full flare, white lights in the trees, decorations blazing out darkened windows, flurries high above twinkling in the streetlights.

We head down the block toward the subway station, right on time for my eleven-ten.

I can't stop thinking about that kiss. It felt so real. Am I being a total fool?

17

Show your sense of humor—you never want to take yourself too seriously, and you definitely don't want to take her too seriously.

~THE MAX HILTON PLAYBOOK: TEN GOLDEN RULES FOR LANDING THE HOTTEST GIRL IN THE ROOM

Mia

Sienna is at the meeting spot the next day, posed next to a fire hydrant. She has pink fur on her ears and a pink feather boa. She springs up and hugs me. "I should give you the two hundred dollars extra I made yesterday from your idea to pimp out these stupid cat getups. But I need it for rent. Thank you."

"You're welcome. It wasn't really my idea," I say, eyeing her boots. "I adapted it from Max Hilton's playbook. You know, that pickup book?"

"Seriously? Why would you read that?"

"I deliver to his tower. Always be prepared, right?" I explain alpha-signaling.

Sienna is just laughing. "The playbook. Thanks, Hilton," she says. "What else are you doing? I want more tricks."

I cross my arms. "Here's another: Be playful and outrageous. You need to show you just don't give a shit. Like, give people funny nicknames and boss them around."

"Seriously?"

"For instance, if there's any sports stuff in their office, you call them that—like Bengals or Cubby if it's Cubs. There's this guy with *Blade Runner* stuff in his office who I call Blade. Or if they order something unusual, like Shasta, you call them that."

"You just say, here ya go, Shasta?"

"Or Dr. Pepper. Whatever."

"I could do that," Sienna says.

Rollins arrives with our go-sheets. I grab mine to see what Max ordered.

Nothing. No order from the twenty-fifth floor. *Again.*

My heart sinks. But it's for the best. I'm supposed to be fighting for my friends, not kissing Max Hilton, king of careless trysts and liquor carts, the player responsible for Kelsey's misery.

I head out to my financial building, delivering meals, trying to be bright, calling people by their fun, new nicknames and playfully bossing them.

I hit my next building, then the next, and then I'm at Maximillion Plaza.

The people are upbeat. It seems like a good place to work. Blade, in particular, is all smiles.

"What's up, Blade?" I ask.

He launches into some funny story—not from Max's book. But still. I give him a sideways look. Is he flirting with me?

He says, "I know this is last minute, but what are you doing Saturday night?"

My mind goes blank. Not only flirting; he's asking me out.

"It's the Maximillion New Year's Eve party," he says. "I want you to feel free to say no and know that I'll never ask you out again or be weird, and I don't want you to feel any pressure to say yes because I'm a delivery client," he adds. "But before you answer, let me add that it's one of the hottest parties in town. Because of the scavenger hunt. Have you heard about it?"

"I thought people hated scavenger hunts."

"They don't hate them when there's actual treasure to be scavenged—like cruises and thousand-dollar bills. And there's a trivia component and you seem to know a lot of useless music trivia and I know sports. We could clean up."

"What was that, mister? *Useless* music trivia?"

He pulls open his chips, which he in no way gives me a hard time about. "*Seemingly* useless..."

"I don't know," I say. I'd feel...weird. Even though it would be hugely effective as prize-positioning. "I'm not technically available at the moment."

"That's fine. We'd do it as a friends thing. Seriously. The prizes are insane."

"I'll think about it," I say, and I give him a silent meow, just because that feels appropriate.

18

Never let her smell blood in the water.

~THE MAX HILTON PLAYBOOK: TEN
GOLDEN RULES FOR LANDING THE
HOTTEST GIRL IN THE ROOM

Max

Parker and I are hosting the Catwalk for a Cause steering committee luncheon over the noon hour.

Laughing and brainstorming with some of the most fascinating people in the style and design world is something that would've been a welcome break from the stress of my routine just weeks ago. But now? I wish I could be back in my office.

I straighten up, wiping that kiss out of my mind. It's good that I'm at this meeting. I need to remember who I am.

I need to remember that she doesn't get to consume my thoughts. Those days are over.

The topic is music. Parker's at the head of the table with a lot of opinions on the subject. He loves music. Lana's next to me, bending over the proposed schedule that I've worked out, practically on my lap, and Brazilian supermodel Zera Valsano, who hates costumes, is playfully wringing my neck over my suggestion she walk out in a whale costume, and I'm laughing.

That's when Mia appears.

I stiffen. What does she think she's doing here? She thinks she can barge into my life? Into this meeting I've been looking forward to? There's usually a caterer for these things. How did she arrange this?

She smiles as she looks around but it's not a real smile.

I feel darkly satisfied. She doesn't like my office wall photo of me with beautiful women, and she really doesn't like it being re-enacted in front of her.

Well, maybe you shouldn't have come at me again, I think at her. *This time you will not win.*

She pushes her cart to the edge of the room, proud and aloof, with that slight air of danger.

How did she engineer this? Parker's assistant usually arranges the catering on these things, but then, Mia always was hugely resourceful. She has some kind of inside contact, that much is clear.

"I have seven low-carb salmon bowls, five keto pork, one vegan veggie, two teriyaki steak wraps, and a roast beef and swiss croissant sandwich." This last in a tone dripping with loathing.

Our gazes lock. The sparkle of anger and aliveness in her expression hits something deep inside me.

Mia's beautiful even in her hatred. Not that it will help her.

Zera still has her hand on my shoulder, but it's Mia I'm watching, Mia's hand I'm imagining.

My girl goes through the layout with confident movements, never giving me the satisfaction of seeing her sweat.

"Now where were we?" Parker says, squeezing mayo onto his sandwich. "Lindsey, let's have the media schedule."

Lindsey launches into a spirited rundown of the schedule. She always talks like things are exciting and slightly confidential.

Mia just smiles sweetly at me, but I can see the devil in her eyes. What the hell does she think she's doing? She puts down the napkin and sets down the sandwich.

"Mustards, please," I say.

She sets down the mustards. Energy flares between us. It's all so wrong. And then she sets down the cheesy puffs.

"What other chips are available?" My voice sounds hoarse to my ears.

Her cheeks go pink. "Cheesy puffs were specified."

"You were out of cheesy puffs the other day and I recall having something else that was really delicious," I say.

She narrows her eyes. "That choice is no longer available to you, I'm afraid. It'll have to be a fond memory. Never to be repeated."

"No? Are you sure about that?" I can feel Parker staring at us—probably wondering what is up. I'm so far from caring.

"Oh, I'm sure," she says, opening the chips and arranging them just so, at a specific angle like she does when she's trying to annoy me. After that she positions the mustards.

"Thank you," I say. At least it sounds like a thank you to the people around the table. It's really just a tug on the rope between us.

Mia spares me a burning glance.

I look right back at her, meeting her energy.

She looks back down at her work. She's doing her fussy repositioning of my sandwich. I stifle the impulse to kiss her. I'm going mad.

"Wait, it's not quite right," she says sweetly.

Is this her plan? To try to annoy me with all of this fussing?

"It looks good to me," I say, breath speeding.

"No, there's something missing," she says.

Our weird interaction has everybody's attention now. I'm so beyond caring. "I think this is all very impressive, Mia. Thank you for all of your hard work."

"Wait, I know what's missing," she says.

"What?" I ask, rapt.

With the economical speed of a boxer, she punches her fist down into my sandwich.

Thump.

Her fist hits meat and pastry. The *thump* resounds through the hush.

Gasps rise up from the table.

I stare at the sandwich in shock. My pulse races.

She's smashed a crater into the middle of it. Bits of roast beef and swiss bulge out the sides of the misshapen croissant.

She straightens. She smiles at me. "There we go."

My people watch me, aghast. The lunch-cart girl just smashed her fist into my sandwich. What will I do?

Everything falls away but her. She just doesn't give a fuck—she never did. Even back in high school she was like that.

"Odd," I say in the cool and emotionless tone that drives her insane. "I don't recall ordering a panini."

"My bad." She smiles sweetly.

Everybody turns back to me, waiting for the famous Max Hilton retort. I always have something clever to say. I've never needed something clever to say more than now. But my mind is whirling.

"Anything else? No? Okay, then. *Bon appetit.*" She pushes her cart out.

I stand. "I'll go see if everything's..." I mumble something that includes the phrase *clearly distraught.*

Nothing in that room is important anymore. I head out after her, down the hall.

I have this fuzzy idea that I need to *show* her, once and for all. Show her that things are different, now. Show her that I could break her if I wanted. I round a corner just as her cart disappears into the elevator.

I slap my hand over the door and push it back open. "You seem a bit disgruntled," I say dryly, knowing the word will annoy her.

"Disgruntled," she sniffs. "I'm far from disgruntled."

"A disgruntled employee," I add.

"I'm not your employee," she snaps.

"No?" I give her a cool smile.

Her nostrils flare. "You think you're all that. What with the models. Please."

I'm in the elevator. The doors close behind me with a muted *clunk.* "Do you have an apology for me?"

"Nope," she says.

"What was that?" She's standing on the side of the elevator, and I cage her there with my arms. Pure lust courses through my veins. "No? No apology? That won't do."

"Okay, let me adjust that answer." She grabs my lapels, goes up on her tiptoes, gets right in my face. "*Hell, no,*" she says.

"That's not an apology," I whisper. But really, it is better. It's way more of a Mia answer than a simple no, and I'm on the knife-edge of need, of raw desire. I never could resist her.

"*I don't have an apology,*" she grates out. "Is that better?"

She's still in my face. The air between our lips dances with electricity.

"You're like a little pink cupcake when you're jealous," I say.

"I'm hardly jealous," she breathes. But right there I hear it—it's there in her tone. I'd recognize her line-reading tone any day of the week. She's lying. She's jealous as shit.

I feel my power surge back, and along with it, this dark need to make her beg, to end this once and for all.

She may have my number, but I have hers. And god, I want her.

My gaze falls to her pulse, drumming in her neck. "You're an agitated pink cupcake I might want to take a bite of," I rumble.

"Screw off with your Max Hilton crap. There's nobody in here but me, and I know what you are—the biggest fraud on the planet."

"Is that so?" I lean in, out of control, drunk on the primal fuel raging between us. "And you can't get enough, can you? You had to come back for more."

19

Never ask a woman what she wants. Tell her what she wants.

~THE MAX HILTON PLAYBOOK: TEN GOLDEN RULES FOR LANDING THE HOTTEST GIRL IN THE ROOM

Mia

He slides his hand around the back of my neck. His fingers seem to tremble—there's something so raw about him now, the way he stares into my eyes. He looks furious and beautiful and I want him like crazy. I shouldn't want a heartless, careless, calculating man like this, but I do.

I should leave. I should push him away and tell him to screw off.

But I can't.

Being with him in this small space is putting my hormones into overdrive. Lighting my skin with electricity. I've always wanted him. It hurts how much I want him.

He knows how to crumble my defenses. He's doing it now.

"What's wrong, Mr. Suave?" I ask, trying for indifference. "Did your software for simulating a heart go offline?"

"Fuck," he says raggedly, right before he closes his mouth over mine in a bruising kiss.

My hands are sliding around the bulk of him. My hands are treating themselves to generous helpings of his cashmere suit coat, pulling him to me, rampaging across soft fabric and hard muscle.

He kisses me—furiously, passionately. He hauls me up to him, closer, harder. His chest is a flat plane against my breasts; his cock at the V of my legs a delicious presence.

"Damn," I say into our kiss.

He peppers hot kisses over my neck while I pant and melt. He's a spy in the night, stealing over enemy lines, going deeper, taking territory.

Meanwhile, my fingers have hit warm skin under his white shirt.

And I don't want to stop. I want Max like there's no tomorrow. Like there's no chart on our wall that's a service to all womankind.

The elevator starts to move.

He lets out a shuddery breath. He digs into his pocket and with one fast, brutal movement, he shoves a key into the panel. Even that is hot, somehow.

"Where are we going?" I ask.

"Nowhere," he says, twisting my hair in his fist and pressing kisses onto my neck. "Does that work for you?" he asks.

He sucks in a small tag of skin. It bites with pain in a way that feels deeply satisfying. I'm going to have a hickey. I want it. I want him to mark me.

"Yes," I gasp. I'm losing my bearings completely now. I'm not talking about the elevator anymore. He knows it, of course. "Yes," I say again.

He slides his hand slowly down my front, passing over one electrified nipple on his way to my pussy. "Yes, what?" He shoves my apron out of the way and his whole hand is between my legs, cupping and kneading me through the warm fabric.

"Omigod," I breathe.

He's on the move again. He found the hidden elastic waistband of my cat suit pants and pushes his hand in. I hiss as he makes contact with my wetness.

He keeps hold of my hair, gazing into my eyes. "Such a little vixen," he grates, rubbing a heavy finger across my swollen nub.

"Whatevs," I breathe, trying to act self-possessed even as my body hums in response to his confident strokes. He's ratcheting up with pleasure. Everything is so surreal now, maybe I can fly.

But I wouldn't want to fly. I want to stay.

He slides a wide finger along my seam and my eyes drift shut. I'm in some delicious agony where Max is owning me and I'll probably regret it but I don't care. I'm a junkie who will give up her world for what his finger is doing.

He kisses me at an expert angle that feels like heaven, nipping my lip. I'm panting out words that don't make a lot of sense unless you understand that every word I'm saying right now means *more*, which Max seems to fully understand at the moment. Because he gets me like that.

He's pushing down my leggings. "You want your oldest enemy to fuck you, don't you?"

"Ungh," I say.

"It's all you can think about." He presses me against the wall. "You want me so bad, you're seeing stars."

Blue eyes meet mine and I gasp sharply as I feel his fingers press into my core.

He asks, "Did you get yourself off thinking about it? Thinking about the way I can make you feel?"

"Don't tell me, let me guess," I manage. "What is transference?"

He's kissing me. "Say it. You want me to fuck you."

He has two fingers in me, and while he's pretty much fucking me right now, I do want him to really fuck me. Right about now, I'll die if we didn't fuck. I've never wanted somebody so badly. It's always been him.

"Say it," he gasps. "Beg me to fuck you."

"Please, I beg you—stop being such a jackass and fuck me already," I manage.

He's doing me with his finger, pinning me to the wall. "Beg," he whispers.

He takes my hand and puts it over his cock. I close my hand around him, huge and heavy and warm, even through fabric. I feel a little dizzy, because he's perfect and huge. Dizzyingly perfect.

"Please," I say, squeezing, "god, please already!"

"Do better," he whispers. "Beg me."

I burrow my fingers under the belt of his trousers. Feverishly I pull his belt from the loops. "Please, Max, stop being such a loser."

He has a condom, of course, seemingly produced out of thin air. In the next moment he's wearing it.

Maybe that's in the advanced training he gives his minions of losers. I'm about to say that, but he has one hand under my knee, and he's got my leg lifted, and he's pressing himself into my entrance, thick and hard at my seam, pressing in slow, and it's the hottest thing ever.

I make a desperate little sound, full of need.

"Mia. Take me, Mia." He says it almost like he cares. Max Hilton saying my name like he cares sends me nearly over the edge.

I nudge at him with my hips, rocking him in a ways. My skin is too tight. I feel like I might explode if he's not all the way inside me soon.

"Baby," he grates. He enters me with one smooth hard thrust and has me seeing stars from another dimension.

"Ahhh!" I sink my nails into his back.

"Yes," he says. He's fucking me and I'm gasping from the goodness of it.

I pull him to me. I'm giving him everything. I can't stop myself.

He's got hold of my thigh, fucking me against the elevator wall, filling me. It's so wrong and so good.

He whispers something that sounds like, "Jesus, Mia." He whispers it in an accusatory way, as if I'm doing something really outrageous right now. Like me and my body and my panting ways are an offense to everything an angry robot stands for.

Body parts slap against body parts. Hands claw flesh. Tongues seek lips. My shoulder blades press into the elevator wall. I'm fucking Max, and it's so forbidden and wrong and good.

Out of nowhere, he sucks in air like he used to when he'd play. And I think I see that vulnerable boy I knew that summer.

I'm going to come.

He made me beg, and I'm going to come.

"Not yet," he says, hungry hands sliding up and down my body. But it's too late; I'm coming—wildly. I'm coming with abandon. I'm coming with the horsepower of ten trains.

He's coming, too. I feel him coming in me. There's that little suck of breath. The quiver of his cock. A last, delicious, desperate shove.

And then we're just balancing there against the wall, partly entwined, breathing hard in the silence of the elevator.

Reality shifts back into place.

I blink, overcome with something that feels like grief. I'm completely cracked open to this man. God, why did it have to be so good? Why do I have to keep falling for him?

Eventually he pulls out. He releases my leg.

I start to assemble myself, like it's all no big, but really, I'm cracked open. Only Max can do this to me.

Only Max.

I should say something sassy and give him three stars or something, but somehow I can't. Still, I try. "Let's see..." I begin in a sassy tone.

A strange expression crosses his face as I utter those two little words. I see right when his face changes, or more, hardens. He seems to come to his senses.

He puts on his cold suave smile, ice crystals sparkling in his blue eyes. Like he was his old self for a second—that self I knew back in that production of *Oklahoma!*—and then he remembered he's not that guy.

"What?" I ask.

He swallows. "I find sex greatly improves an otherwise dull elevator ride, don't you agree?"

"What?" I gasp.

His eyes twinkle. "I should find a way to get room service in here one of these days," he continues. "Or at least a liquor cart with a selection of mixed nuts."

His words are a knife in my chest. And that's the end of my strength. The end of my sassiness.

With shaking hands I start to pull my cat outfit back together. "Please, Max," I whisper softly, adjusting my apron. I really am begging him, but not for sex. I'm begging for him not to hurt me anymore. I've got nothing left.

I just need him to stop hurting me.

"What?"

"God, Max, really?" I gather myself up, steeling my spine. "It's not enough for you to mock me and ridicule me? Make me feel two inches tall? I get it," I say. "You won. You have everything. You can destroy and twist apart my heart whenever you please. Toy with me and throw me aside like garbage. Happy?"

"W-what?" He looks confused.

"Your little demonstration?" I punch the lobby button. Nothing happens. I turn the key that he used and the elevator lurches to life. He's saying something but I'm talking over him. "You still got it, buddy. You can still hurt me. Reduce me to nothing. You want another award?"

"Mia, what are you talking about?" He reaches out.

I shove off his hand. "Can't you just let me be for once?"

The elevator slows, nearing the next floor.

"I hope you enjoyed your little game." I grab my cart and put it between us, trapping him at the back of the elevator.

"Mia—"

"What now? You want me to grab one of the plastic knives out of my cart and saw out my heart? Would that make the great Max Hilton happy?"

Dark brows furrow. Is he really going to pretend not to understand?

"Oh, please! Leave it," I hiss. I give him a murderous look just as the door behind me opens.

The door opens on the lobby floor. A group of chattering professionals part as I pull my cart backwards out of the elevator.

Max is held up. Good.

I get out and manage to pull my cart into a different elevator.

The doors shut. I stab a bunch of buttons.

I stand alone in there, panting. Bringing me in to wait on him and then seducing me? Rage clouds my vision. This is a victory lap, and I'm such a fool!

I hit the button for the twentieth floor. When I arrive, I leave my cart in the hall and burst into Blade's office. "Let's do it. Let's kick some scavenger ass."

He looks surprised.

"The New Year's Eve party?" I say. "Is it still this weekend? You still want to go together?" And then, because I'd never lead a guy on, I add, "Our friends date?"

"Really?" he asks.

"Yes, really," I say. "If you're still looking for a scavenger hunt partner."

I've decided I'll go have fun in front of Max with another guy. I'll put on my best dress and eat and drink on his dime, hopefully win prizes, and then he'll never see me again. I want the last image he has of me to be something other than the distraught girl running from the elevator.

I need that for myself, too.

If there's one thing any actress knows, it's how to make a big, splashy exit.

"Of course," he says. "Let's do this!"

"Okay, Blade, we're on."

"I'll text you the deets," he says.

Max texts me that night.
Repeatedly.

Max: We need to talk.

Me: Don't text me again. Can you please just leave me alone for once?

Max: I think I screwed up. I didn't understand what was happening. Honestly, I didn't set out to play games.

Me: Liquor cart? Room service? Screw off!

Max: Can we do this in person?

Me: I'm going to be requesting not to do your building anymore. Have a little decency and let it be.

Max: I need to see you.

THAT'S when I block his number.

The next day, I trade routes with Sienna. We're not supposed to do it, but I talk her into it. I lure her with stories about my sky-high tips there, and I promise her that if anybody complains, I'll take the heat—I'll say our manager okayed it. She makes me write her an email saying our manager okayed it so that she has a trail of evidence if we get into trouble. I do it.

I'll be seeing him exactly one last time, and it'll be on my terms only.

20

Never ask a woman if you can kiss her. She should be asking *you*. Better yet, she should be begging you.

~THE MAX HILTON PLAYBOOK: TEN
GOLDEN RULES FOR LANDING THE
HOTTEST GIRL IN THE ROOM

Max

People start streaming into the four-story atrium, everybody in their finest. Oscars-night shit. I shake hands and exchange New Year's wishes with guests.

I'm not a fan of New Year's Eve, but I'm proud that the Maximillion holiday ball is such a hot ticket, all tuxedos and cocktail-length gowns. Never underestimate the draw of a dress-up party with a large Instagram component.

Or, usually I'm proud. There's a stone in the pit of my belly. I can't stop thinking about Mia.

I fix my bow tie.

Parker's sitting on the edge of the stage, holding court with a glittering group. I catch his eye and salute him. He smiles huge and salutes me back. You couldn't want a better business partner.

The professional scavenger-hunt designers—yes, there is such a thing—come over to consult with me about some last-minute decisions. They've been hiding prizes and clues in the blocks between the park and Midtown. You have to take selfies with the clues when you find them. They've done an amazing job.

The party is also beloved by my employees, thanks in part to the massive loot that's involved. The socialites and industry people tend to play for charity. The PR and social media buzz we get off it is worth ten times what we spend on the thing.

My heart is not in it. All I can think about is Mia. Mia punching my sandwich like an outrageous goddess. The way she felt in the elevator, soft and hot in my arms. Mia's face at the end.

What happened?

Maybe I should've tried harder to follow her, but I'm not in the habit of following women who say *leave it* as energetically as Mia did.

I tracked down her number and texted her a few times, and she promptly blocked me. I got her address, and I gave serious thought to sending something nice, or even going over there. I'm going to figure it out after this party.

I need to make her see that she's not a notch in my elevator bar.

I've never felt such an intense connection with a woman—not even close, except maybe that summer with Mia.

I grab a champagne off a passing tray.

The string quartet plays a festive arrangement that has its roots in folk songs—the key changes feel Slavic. Russian, maybe.

They've got an excellent fiddler—somebody actually trained. Enough that I have to wander near to get a look.

I stop short when I recognize the lead violinist. He's from the Shiz—DJ Barnes.

I'm not loving that DJ Barnes is here. A lot of the people from high school are jobbers now, sitting in on musical groups and bands and orchestras. It's inevitable that I run into them at events. Still. High school was a miserable time, and I don't like seeing people from then. Except Parker. And Mia, of course.

DJ looks over and smiles. I give him a friendly nod.

They start up something new—a demanding number designed to pluck annoyingly at the heartstrings, and they're putting their all into it.

Hearing him play his heart out, it sends a feeling through me that's not exactly pleasant.

As if on cue, Tarquin Millbauer is by my side with his photographer. Still working that profile. He's the last person I want to see. "I appreciate the invite."

I raise my glass with a smile. "You find your angle yet?"

He gives me a look I can't quite read. "Are you playing this year?"

I frown, stiffen. "Playing?"

"The famous scavenger hunt? They say you sometimes do it."

"I play when there's an odd number." I shrug. "I hope you're getting in on it. You're perfectly welcome to."

"I'm on the job. I'll stick with you."

Of course he will. All the better to ruin my party for me. Not that it isn't ruined already, because I can't stop thinking about Mia.

Lana comes up and links arms with Tarquin. I give her a grateful look.

My attention drifts back to the quartet. *In your dreams,* she said.

Except she was right there with me before that. My blood races. She thinks I'm toying with her?

Tarquin's addressing me now. He's broken away from Lana, who shrugs helplessly behind him.

I give him a charming smile. An in-on-the-joke smile. People want a lot of things from me. Tarquin wants his angle, yes, but he also wants to feel like part of the in-crowd. One of the beautiful people. I have created this empire by knowing what people want. Specifically what men want.

A new song. A musical arrangement that's new to my ears. I feel his eyes on me as I zero in on the contrapuntal voice of the bass. "Question?"

"Who picked the music?"

"Planners."

"They're good. This quartet."

I cock my head. "Can anybody really tell? With classical music?"

"But you went to The Soho High School for the Performing Arts. You studied music. Surely you know. Surely you'd have an ear."

I lean in to him as if I'm about to share a confidence, to give him a piece of Max Hilton. "Did you take a language in high school?"

"French," he says.

"Tell me this—" I dip my head closer to his, deepening my confiding tone. "Can you watch a French movie without subtitles and understand what the fuck they're saying?"

He snorts.

I smile. I slap his back. We clink glasses.

"And please. Don't call me Shirley," I add. He laughs at the ridiculous reference. I take another glass. I have him back under control. We talk movies and he takes notes on that.

People stream in, peacock colors across my periphery.

My attention drifts to the east doorway and everything in me goes hot.

I blink, unsure whether I'm seeing right. But I'd know that posture anywhere. It's Mia in a sky-blue gown that hugs her curves and sets off her dark hair. She stands out from the crowd, so self-assured and heart-stoppingly beautiful.

Something in me surges to attention.

What is she doing here? The crowd shifts and I see him there on her arm, Ryan, I think his name is. From marketing. Heat fills me.

She's with Ryan? She waves to somebody. She turns to say something to Ryan and he laughs. She's animated. Relaxed.

You can't be with him, I think wildly.

Tarquin is saying something about *Airplane Two.* Family anecdote. I tune back in. "Funny," I say, and from his face, I see that wasn't the right answer. "I mean, the franchise."

"Yes," he says.

I swallow and look back at her. People are coming up to her, but Ryan keeps ahold of her. I want to storm over there and pull her away from him. I want to wrap her up in my coat and take her home and kiss every inch of her.

"Who is that?" Tarquin asks.

"Who?"

He gives me a strange look and nods. "The couple you're staring daggers at?"

"I do believe..." I furrow my brow. "I do believe one of my employees has hit on our poor lunch-cart girl. Meow Squad or something."

"Wasn't she the one running from your office a week or two

back? Wait, could she be the one you were spotted kissing? The newest Max Hilton girl?"

Cold goes over me. I don't know what's happening between Mia and me, but one thing I do know: making her out to be a Max Hilton girl wannabe would destroy her career completely.

I won't have it.

"They all look so different without their ears." I drain my drink, hand it off, pull out my phone, and start trashing emails, as if clearing my Gmail deck might magically translate to clearing the snarl from my mind, which, for the record, it doesn't. What does Ryan think he's doing, bringing her? Why would she come with him?

I look back over. They're laughing together again.

"You have a policy against fraternization here," Tarquin says. A statement, not a question. "Does that extend to vendors?"

Unease twists through me. "No, it wouldn't be against the policy. He's free to ask a delivery girl out," I say, wishing Tarquin would leave it already. I hate that she's here with him.

Parker comes up and points out my jacket to Tarquin. Tarquin feigns interest, but he's sensing red meat elsewhere. "What's her name?" Tarquin asks.

I frown. "The lunch-cart girl?"

Parker gives me a strange look.

Tarquin's not letting it go. "Maybe she's the next Max Hilton girl."

"Dude," Parker says, reading my mood. "Sometimes a lunch-cart girl is just a lunch-cart girl. On the other hand, speaking of Max Hilton girls..." Parker drags us over to Britta and Veronica, two of the nerdiest models you'll ever meet. I encourage Veronica to show him images of her stamp collection. That will trap him for at least twenty minutes.

I watch Mia out of the corner of my eye as she moves

around the edge of the place like the fucking queen of England, with Ryan gazing at her like a besotted serf, utterly outclassed. A grim smile tugs at my lips. He probably thought he was getting a bit of bling on his arm only to have her outshine him like the sun.

"Excuse me," I say, extricating myself from the three of them.

I wander toward Mia, greeting all the people who want something from me—favors, promotion, proximity. Usually I try to talk up this year's charities, trying to goose the donations. I force myself to do it now.

I draw near enough to her for her voice to burn. I'm agitated, flustered, hurt, angry. I catch shards of the accent she buried like a violet in a snowstorm. I'm shaking hands, talking with people, her laughter invading my awareness. Finally I reach them.

Her gaze skitters over my tux before snapping back to my face.

I give her a significant look. I want to cut through everything. I need it to be just us. Or something.

She grabs Ryan's arm, observing me as she would a stranger.

"Finally free from the ears," I say.

"I was going to wear them, but people would expect sandwiches."

Ryan laughs, gazing at her like a puppy. I turn to him. "The lunch-cart girl," I say.

He can't seem to tear his eyes from her. "Mia. Her name is Mia."

"Oh, don't worry, he knows," Mia says. "We went to high school together, didn't we, Max? The Shiz."

"The Shiz," I say, holding her gaze.

"*You* went to an arts high school?" Ryan says to me.

"Yes," I grate out.

Ryan looks amazed. I don't publicize it, but it's on Wikipedia. Did he not look at my entry? I make a mental note to check with his supervisor about his fitness for whatever role he plays in marketing. "I guess I can't imagine you in a performing arts high school."

"He was quite the piano virtuoso at one time," Mia says.

"You play piano?"

"Played," I say, wondering how many times tonight I'm going to have to have a conversation about the Shiz. I turn to Mia. "You might see somebody familiar in the string section over there."

She puts a hand on Ryan's shoulder and goes up on her tiptoes, craning her neck to see the band. "DJ! DJ Barnes!"

"Break out the party hats," I say.

"A piano virtuoso?" Ryan still can't get past that one.

Mia's shining eyes meet mine. "Max could play anything. He could certainly dazzle."

There it is. I turn to her, my gaze every bit as bright as hers. "I tend to succeed at whatever I put my hand to."

She stares daggers at me. My blood runs thick with lust, and there's a strange energy in my chest. Everything feels too bright. The room feels hot.

"Do you still play?" Ryan inquires from somewhere out on the nowhere fringes.

She turns to him. "Blade, did you play an instrument?"

"*Blade?*" It's out of my mouth before I can stop it.

"Yes, that's my nickname for him." She grabs his arm. "Blade." She says it kind of badass, like they have a dirty inside joke.

What? She calls him *Blade?* Why would a woman call a man Blade? Why would a woman call *this man* Blade? It's like calling a Chihuahua *Killer* or something. But he seems to be in on it. Does he carry a blade? Is he thuggish in bed?

An unpleasant heat prickles over my skin. "Interesting," I bite out.

"We're both *Blade Runner* fans," he explains.

"Mmm," I say, still not liking it.

She glares back at me. "Yes, he has one of my favorite stills from the movie up on his office wall." She turns to him. "We share a passion for that movie. It's good to have *genuine* passions."

"That scene is your favorite?" Ryan says to her. "I would've guessed the street walk scene. That's usually people's favorite."

"But isn't that one so obvious?" she says. "A lot of steam is coming up from grates."

"Steam coming up from grates is awesome!" he says.

I gaze over at her and she itches her nose with her middle finger. FU. Everything in me swells.

"Is everything okay?" Ryan says. "This isn't..." He motions between them. "This isn't against policy, is it?"

"Of course not," I say. "You can bring whoever you want outside of the company."

"Don't pay any attention to Max," Mia says, giving me a challenging stare. "He's just crabby because we're discontinuing cheesy puffs. I'm sad to say that there will be no more."

"Oh, I've heard that before," I say.

She sets her jaw and straightens up, a posture I came to understand, over long hours of watching her, as her *strong-against-the-world* posture. The stance she takes when she means business "This time it's true."

"They really are my favorite." I lower my voice. "Nothing else compares."

Her cheeks go pink.

"I have to admit, cheesy puffs *are* good," Ryan says.

"Well, you can't have any," I say to Ryan, though I'm still looking at Mia.

"I don't know, I might scrounge some up somewhere. For Ryan."

"Uh, that's okay, there's plenty of food here," Ryan says.

Mia sniffs. "You know what this stupid conversation needs? A nice liquor cart stocked with pure-grain alcohol, because it's making me want to kill all my brain cells."

I want to drag her off. I want to tell her I didn't mean to say that shit in the elevator. I want to kiss that smart mouth and peel off that gown and worship every sassy inch of her. Never have I felt such absolute, primal desire for a woman. My gut twists with the force of it.

And then my phone buzzes. Again and again. It's here I realize the band's stopped. When did it stop? Parker would be the one buzzing. I have a speech to make, but I'm feeling crazy. Mia can't be with Ryan.

I look over at Ryan, who gives me a faltering smile, and I smile back. This isn't about him and I can't blame him for wanting her. *Just don't fucking touch her again,* I think like a man possessed.

"Speech time." I head up toward the stage on autopilot, doing the Max Hilton walk, cool as a cucumber in my designer tux.

I grab a glass of champagne from an assistant and climb the three steps, sauntering over to the podium like I own the place, which I do. I smile, holding my glass in two careless fingers, trying to find her in the crowd, but the lights are dimming.

I gaze out at the crowd, like, *what the hell are you all still talking for?* Some people laugh. More look up at me.

Eventually everyone's with me without my saying a word. Because people want to be with me. I'm the playboy with a glass in his hand and a sparkle in his eyes, the man who makes them feel like they're part of the glamorous, carefree, lux life that exists in the lifestyle ads we pump out like useless dreams.

I start the speech, forcing my mind to timing, delivery. I try to forget her, to concentrate on the lift of the audience coalescing around me. Performing arts high school wasn't a total waste.

Parker comes up and we give each other shit like we do every year, and then we talk about the charity. "Give a bit to a cause," I say. "Who cares, it's only money. What's the use of money when there's a champagne fountain?"

Parker gives me perfectly scripted shit about that. I loop an arm around him and we clink glasses and wish each other a happy New Year.

I thank the caterers and the band. Fifteen minutes to hunt time. I remind people of the rules.

The quartet strikes back up.

Parker hops down.

I move to the edge of the stage and hand the mic back to the audio guy. I ask him a question about the acoustics of the place, knowing he'll spin on it for a bit.

She's brilliant in that blue. Did she wear it for him? I bristle as he touches her arm. *Blade.* Does he think he's a tenth of a match for her?

I watch her circulate. She seems to have close personal relationships with every last one of my employees. Mia, beloved by everybody, just like old times.

Lana's up with the scavenger-hunt crew, comparing clipboards. They have directions for me to read off clipboards after people drink some more. This is a group that loves clipboards.

The music stops just then. I look up, confused. I'm not ready to kick off the hunt, but I see the problem. Mia. The inevitable reunion with DJ Barnes.

Tearful hugs. I shouldn't watch, but I can't look away.

They're arguing, or more, bantering. Mia is turning back and forth between Ryan and DJ. She's lit up with energy. It's a form of her I remember, laughing and arguing. Mia pokes a finger into DJ's chest. The oboist is shoving a microphone at her. Shivers cascade over my body. They're asking her to do a song.

No, I think.

I stand, immobile. Parker's back, talking. Parker's saying my name, somewhere at the fringes of my awareness.

She's going to sing. *Something, something wrong,* Max? Parker again.

I can see plainly where DJ places his fingers on the fiddle. He scrapes out the first strains. *Many a New Day.* That's what she's going to sing. One of her *Oklahoma!* solos.

Not in front of all these people, I think. Because it's ours.

"What's wrong?" Parker asks.

Wrong. Wrong doesn't come close.

I need a bigger word, the kind of word that the Germans might invent. A word that means that you're dreading something that will be painful, but you also very much want that thing to happen.

And that painful thing you dread and want would involve longing for moments you can never have again. And it would involve a bursting, shouting feeling inside your chest, and all the while, your teeth are clenched. *Dreadshockjoy* or something.

She takes a breath, and I breathe, too, because that's what Mia Corelli does, she reaches into your chest and pulls your breath out. Mia Corelli, always longing for more. Fighting for more. All brave and beautiful and tragic, but yet always somehow out of reach. Like a not-quite-remembered dream that floats away as soon as you grab for it, laughing as it goes.

Back in your life to bring it.

She starts in, high and strong and full of emotion. Voice clear like a bell. My dreadshockjoy swells. She's really doing it.

She looks across the room at me, eyes colliding with mine, show tune like a cannonball.

Parker's still there. "My bad," he says.

"What?" I say.

"I thought you'd have fun seeing her again. Delivering your sandwiches and all. I didn't think you'd get all twisted up about it."

I turn to him. "You arranged it?"

He holds up his hands in mock defense. "I thought you'd get a kick out of it. You've always had such a spark around her."

"So you arranged for her to deliver my sandwiches? Directly to me in my office? And didn't see fit to tell me?"

"Well..." he stammers.

"Never mind." Everything I understood about the situation reshuffles in my mind.

I thought she'd somehow engineered it. And she thinks I arranged it...in order to what? Taunt her and boss her around? Punch down and seduce her? Of course that's what she'd think. Why not?

God, what a dick move. And of course it's what she thinks.

The song's over. She's smiling. She looks at Ryan. He smiles at her. People will start setting off with their clues. *No,* I think. *You can't have her.*

My feet take me back to the scavenger-hunt people. I tell them I'm changing it up. We'll make it random.

"You're not letting them pick their own partners?" the guy asks.

"Random partners are better for team building," I say, on full Max Hilton arrogance mode. I take an iPad. I redo the numbers, putting Mia and me together. It shuffles all the rest of the partnerships. I hand it back. "That's how the partners go now. Send it out."

They send out a new list based on my idea.

21

You have high standards. Let her know that it's up to her to meet those standards.

~THE MAX HILTON PLAYBOOK: TEN
GOLDEN RULES FOR LANDING THE
HOTTEST GIRL IN THE ROOM

Mia

"Usually they let you pick your partners," Ryan says, frowning at the app. "I can't believe you're with Max."

I blink at the list. "What happened?"

"I'm seeing some comments that the partners were shuffled for team building and community building or something," Ryan says.

Heart still thundering in my chest, I gaze across the room at Max, cold and beautiful and perfect in his tux.

Community building. *Riiiight.*

Seriously, Max should've been a spy. He'd be an amazing

spy. He changed the entire course of the party and created a disinformation campaign in one fell swoop, just to ruin my date.

I should be annoyed. My face is annoyed, but inside there's this spark of forbidden excitement.

And really, I shouldn't have sung the song. I told myself I wanted to get some control back, but it was a lie. I wanted some connection. To rip down his cool façade. It's crazy behavior.

"I'm sorry," I say.

Ryan smiles. "Not your fault."

Partygoers in their glamorous garb are heading out to take selfies. People have brought awesome coats, because some of this takes place outside. That's how you collect the clues, you do a selfie with your partner with an Instagram tag. There's even a special glam black-and-white filter for the party that nobody else gets to use.

"A lot of women would kill to do the hunt with Max," Ryan says unhelpfully.

"I would kill to *not* do the hunt with Max. Does that mean we can have peace? Or does everybody have to die?"

Ryan smiles. "You are so funny."

Ryan's partner comes up. She's a perky redhead, an intern who is super pumped about the game. She reads their first clue off her phone and tells him her theory. Everybody's clues are different because this is a scavenger hunt created exclusively for this party. Max probably flew in a team of turtleneck-and-mono-cle-wearing Viennese game designers.

"We should go," she says.

I smile. "Good luck."

"Thanks," Ryan says.

The intern isn't listening; she's staring at Max, strolling toward us, a tiger in a tux, New York's most eligible Prince Charming.

I'm angry, but there's something else—this warm buzz of familiarity as he nears.

People head away, leaving us standing there, an island in the ballroom. "Ready?" Max says.

"What do you want from me? You think you can control me. You just think you can control everything."

He hushes his voice like he doesn't want anyone to hear. "Let's go."

"To play the game? Which game is this? The one designed to ruin my date? Because it looks like you won that one already."

"I'll explain."

"I get it—you're in charge, not me. You really had to change the whole game to prove it?"

"You think that's why I changed the game? To prove a point about who's in charge?"

I raise my brows. A *yes*.

People are coming up. Max is a magnet for people. "Let's get out of here," he says.

I narrow my eyes.

"Hear me out. Please?" His tone is serious, like this is really something. It's new. Maybe that's why I don't notice the man who joins us. I can tell by Max's expression that he's not thrilled. "Tarquin," Max says.

"Tarquin Millbauer." Tarquin sticks out his hand. I take it, shake it. "And you are..."

"Tarquin is with the Times," Max adds. Now I see why Max was so cagey.

"I work in the building," I say. "Sometimes."

"Did I hear somebody ruined your date?" Tarquin says to me.

I shrug. "Not if I win a vacation I can take him on. Let's do this. I expect you to know the answers, Max. Ryan and I want the Bali vacation, if possible."

"We'll see," Max says. "Everybody has an equal chance."

Lara, Max's supermodel d'jour, comes up just then. She links arms with Tarquin. "Ready?"

"I'm not playing," Tarquin says.

She frowns and shows him their names on the app.

We grab our coats and head toward the elevator with the mob, but luckily not the press guy.

"The Times? Are you kidding me?" I say.

In a low voice, he says, "We're getting out of here, and then we'll talk." His fingers on the small of my back seem to radiate across my body.

We ride down with a crowd of rowdy partygoers. People are talking to him, jokingly trying to get him to give clues. A few of them have bottles of champagne, and the mood is jolly.

He tells them that he didn't create the game. "We're all on equal footing," he insists.

It's not the elevator we banged in, but it's the same décor. I give him the side eye.

Eventually we all spill into the lobby and out onto the sidewalk in front of Maximillion Plaza. It's a magical night; snow falls in thick, lazy flakes, frosting the dirty pavement in sparkling white. The air is warm-ish, almost balmy, and the traffic sounds are subdued.

Max looks up and down the street. More people are talking to him. The partygoers want a piece of him, or at least a selfie.

I turn to him during a rare hush. "A Times guy? What's up with the Times guy?"

"Nothing. He just wants to do a profile, and I don't imagine you want to appear in that."

"Me? In your profile? Like I'm a Max Hilton girl or something? Oh my god," I say, horrified.

"It's under control," he says, all Max Hilton confidence.

"Don't worry." More people come by. He chats them up and sends them off.

He has his phone out. He's texting, leading me around the corner.

"Don't worry?" I say. "I am worried. I need to get out of here."

He fixes me with a serious look. "We are getting out of here. And we have to talk."

"I'm grabbing a cab," I tell him. "I think I've had enough."

"Please," he says. There's something achingly real about him right now. He feels genuine; raw, even. "We'll talk and then I'll take you wherever you want. I need to tell you something and..." Somebody else waves.

A limo slides around the corner. "Come on, then. Come on before he gets down here."

We round the corner and slip into the back. He gives an address that sounds vaguely familiar. The limo takes off.

I say, "Do you know how long it took to curate my Google results page to show my achievements? To show casting directors what a hard-working and respectable artist I am? If a casting director Googles me and all he sees is dozens of pages of Max Hilton girl drama, they'll think I'm not serious."

"I'm managing it," he says as the limo turns west.

"So there's something to manage?" I say. "Please, Max. I'm going out for *Anything Goes* and if I can get it, it'll be my big break. Don't let him write that I'm a Max Hilton girl. Even if I nail my audition, they would never cast a Max Hilton girl."

"I'll deal with him."

"This is important.'

"Jesus, Mia, it's the last thing I want," he says. "Okay? I got this." Then, "Are you going out for the part of Reno?"

I nod.

"You'll be perfect," he says.

The neighborhood is looking more and more familiar. "Where are we going? You should just take me home."

"We're almost there." The limo pulls around to the back of a large office-looking brownstone and down an alley. He gets out and reaches in.

I take his hand, let him pull me to him. "If you think this will be a repeat of the elevator," I say.

He leans down and says something to his driver. Then he unlocks the back door of the building.

"What is this?" I ask.

We head in and he unlocks another door.

Going against my better judgment, I follow him into a hushed hallway. "What is this place?"

"A secret from the pap," he says, meaning the paparazzi. We head down another short hall to a small elevator. "We can't go out somewhere, or to my place." He hits the button. There's a building directory and I catch sight of the words Namaste Way.

"Wait! I'm not going with you to some kind of sex den of yours," I say.

"What would give you that idea?" he asks.

"Umm..."

The doors open and we get in. He pushes the button for the fifth floor. "We need to clear the air." He turns to me, eyes serious, no ironic twinkle. "I need you to know something—I didn't arrange the Meow Squad deliveries. I didn't have anything to do with them. I wouldn't do that to you, Mia."

"Wait, what?" The elevator inches upward. One floor lights up, then another.

He fixes me with a serious look. "I need you to know, I didn't arrange the deliveries. I know you think I did. I don't blame you. It was Parker. I just found out."

"Parker? So you didn't..."

"Make you deliver my lunch? What kind of asshole..."

"I totally thought you were behind it!"

"Mia." One word, a low rumble. "You think I would do that?"

I don't know how to answer that question. My preconceptions about Max have been getting scrambled around.

"Actually, I thought *you'd* engineered it," he adds.

I laugh. "Me? Why would I engineer something like that? Like as some sort of twisted boo-yah? Like, ha-ha, I'm a lunch-cart girl, and you're just some jerk sitting on a gleaming empire! Ha-ha, I'm glorious."

"You would've pulled it off. You *are* glorious."

My heart skips a beat. I know what to do with cold arrogant Max who makes me deliver sandwiches, an asshole on a victory lap, the author of the world's jerkiest pickup guide. I don't know what to do with sweet Max. Sweet Max makes me feel dizzy. And a little bit scared.

The elevator car bumps to a stop and the doors open.

I follow him down a hallway to the end of a hall. The sign next to the door says Namaste Way. "He only just told me back there at the party," he says, unlocking the door. "I couldn't believe it. Making you be my delivery person like that? He thought it would be funny. I would've never—"

He pushes open the door.

Across an expanse of hardwood floor are mats in cubbies. He heads toward a little seating area in the corner. "So this is...a yoga studio."

"For a few hours a week. And a ballet studio. The rest of the time it's mine. It's really just mine."

I look all around. Mirrors line the far side, with a ballet barre running straight across. But that's not what I'm looking at. I'm looking at the baby grand, glinting in the other corner. I go to it.

"Come on over."

I ignore him. I go to the piano. I run my hands over it.

"What is this?" My accusation is a whisper with sharp edges. "This." I set my hand on the piano. A Bösendorfer 155. That's the kind Max would prefer. I sit. I plunk a key.

He comes around and stands behind me. "A piano."

"I can see that. You still play?"

He makes a noncommittal noise.

"Still with the Ligeti?"

"That's not the kind of music I play anymore," he says.

"Don't tell me you play pretty music now."

I look up, catch him shrugging.

"Oh my god," I say. "Seriously? Why not have it in your home?"

"You know what they say about people who decorate with grand pianos."

I snort. "I can't believe it." But that's a lie. I *can* believe it deep in my bones. *I know you,* I think.

"Protecting my investment. All that practice time—"

I play half a scale. I can feel him cringe. He used to play even scales with artistry.

"Why would you play in secret?" I spin around, sit on the bench backwards.

"Mia." One word. My name. *Mia.* The low rumble of it pulls at something inside me. And I'm so acutely aware of us alone in this space. "I don't want to talk about music. Do you believe me? That I wouldn't have brought you back into my life like that?"

I spin around and look up at him. "Can you punch Parker for me? Also, it's just funny you thought I was doing lunch deliveries in a cat suit as my plan of vengeance. As evil master plans go? D minus."

He kneels in front of me. "You think you weren't getting to me? You were driving me crazy. I could barely concentrate on anything, just waiting for those deliveries." He grabs the bench on either side of my thighs. "Your deliveries were destroying me, Mia."

He's saying some more words, but his head is in the zone of my lap, now, and it's hard to concentrate. I imagine my lap lined with lights, like an airport runway, highlighting the forward route his face needs to travel in order to land in the safety and comfort of my pussy.

My breath quickens. He's talking more. Something about the sandwiches.

"I don't like how this happened," he continues. "I'm tired of this bullshit between us, just like before." *High school*, he means.

"Let's not think about that," I say.

His eyes go dark, and I'm stunned anew by how beautiful he is. "We need to think about it," he rumbles.

My hormones are little luggage trucks, driving in furious circles, *beep-beep-beeping* excitedly. "Do we, though? Right this minute?"

"I didn't bring you here to fuck," he growls.

I have this sense that it's not me he's growling at—it's more like he's growling at the part of himself that also wants to fuck. The really primal and base animal part that might grab my hair and press me against a wall.

"And yet..." I whisper.

"Fuck, Mia." Again his eyes rake up and down me, and suddenly his hands are heavy on my thighs, all harsh gravity through the delicate silk of my dress.

I exhale a breath I didn't know I was holding and I settle my hands onto his, slipping my fingers suggestively under his cuffs. I meet his feral gaze with a sassy little smile.

Right then, it's as if the floodgates let loose. "God, Mia." He's pushing his hands up my legs, taking the silky fabric of my dress with it, motions getting more frantic the more stocking he uncovers. He gathers my skirt in his fists, shoving it up over my knees.

I lift my butt, giving him an assist. Dimly I remind myself of my girl squad. Yes, I had it wrong about him ordering the deliveries like a jackass, but my friends are all mad at him—for good reason!

He shudders out a breath when he finds bare skin over thigh-high stockings. He kisses the inside of my thigh, then he rubs his whiskers there, hungry, wildly, as if to mark me.

"Fuck, yes," I pant, forgetting about the book. Forgetting about my friends.

He presses a thumb to my core, wet through silky undergarments, and moves it, slides it, stoking waves of pleasure while he attacks my other thigh with his hungry face.

It's silk and sandpaper.

My breath catches. My toes curl.

He rumbles against my tender skin.

I squirm, whimpering with need.

I shove my hands into his hair. Air traffic control to Max!

And just like magic, he's shoving my legs apart and kissing my pussy, the hot tenor of his breath against the silk that covers my clit. I hold his hair, holding on, loving him there.

He kisses me again. I'm diffuse with pleasure. My clit stands at attention, a tendril of need. The blunt pressure of his lips drives me nearly over the edge. Then his tongue is gone. He scrapes his teeth gently over my core.

I cry out, meeting his gaze.

"Need you bare," he growls.

"Do you want me to..." My mind races with the logistics of the strapless bodysuit I'm currently wearing. "Um..."

He's pulling at the fabric, shoving his fingers clear through the lacy part above the crotch, and then he just rips it down.

Cool air invades my hot, wet pussy.

"Taking it as a no," I gasp.

He's not done. "Need you spread out for me." He pushes my legs wide. I'm about to protest, except his tongue is there, warm and thick against my core.

"Ohmigod."

He licks up once, again.

My breath comes fast.

I'm so exposed to him, it's madness, and the sexiest thing ever.

He grips my thighs, holding me apart as he licks me. He's holding me in place as though he has me right where he wants me and he won't be letting me go. He's my roller coaster and my seat belt.

Mercilessly he licks me until I'm at the point of no return, the tippy-top of the arc, suspended before the free fall.

He draws his tongue roughly along my clit one more time. Pleasure explodes over my brain, bright behind my eyes.

I'm weightless. I'm crying out.

Max's rumble is a merciless vibration between my legs. I tighten my grip on his hair. "Slower!"

He's already there, following my cadence like the musician he once was. Still is.

Suddenly I'm laughing. It's the release of pressure, and how crazy good that was, and how fast I came, and a little bit the sounds I made.

He kisses my belly, and then gazes up at me in wonder.

"Need you inside," I say.

Slowly he presses a finger into me.

My body shudders around him.

He doesn't reply; he simply adds a finger.

"You," I say. "You, Max."

There's something shattered about his gaze. He kisses the

inside of my thigh, and then the other side for symmetry. And then he carries me over to that couch in the far corner, sets me down with my legs over either chair arm.

"Stay like that," he rumbles, undoing his bow tie in the dim light of the city, a pale wash of yellow.

"This is dirty," I whisper.

"I'm sorry I wrecked your undergarments, but you waiting for me like this...so hot."

"In other words, you're not sorry at all."

"Not sorry. I'm gonna take you just like that." He whips off his bow tie and then he's undoing his buttons. "You are so hot, it blows my mind." He rips the rest of his shirt open, not bothering with the buttons, then skips to his pants.

"Cheating. One demerit."

A wicked light shines in his eyes as he yanks off his belt. His pants are off and his cock juts upward, so thick and hard, it's nearly against his belly. I've never seen his cock uncovered, but somehow, it's so him. He has a condom.

"No, no, no." I undo my sex-ready position and stand.

"Hey."

I go to him. "Let me." I want to be in on this with him. I kneel in front of him, wrapping my hand around him, marveling at his cock.

"What do you think you're doing?"

"I love the shape of you," I whisper, "how you're slightly wider than round." I kiss him and he groans. "I love this vein here." I trail the side of him with my fingers.

"Mia," he gasps. "I'm not an art exhibit."

No, he's something better. He's undiscovered territory, wild and exotic, yet achingly familiar. So perfectly him.

I lick the underside, and it jumps. I do it again, reveling in the salty, musky maleness of him, and then I press my cheek to it.

"Mia." His voice sounds strained.

I put him in my mouth, feeling the whole shape of him with my tongue and lips. I wrap my hand around his thick root and explore him. I don't want to stop.

With other guys, I try to stage manage. Maybe set the scene with flower petals and candles. Or juice things up with breathless oohs and aahs, but Max and I are beyond that. We've been through a war together.

I pull him from my mouth and kiss just his tip.

Suddenly he's out of my hand. He kneels in front of me. "You're too slow," he whispers.

"You're too perfect," I whisper.

"You're too hot," he says, watching my eyes.

A condom wrapper crinkles at the edge of my awareness.

My heart pounds. We're kneeling face-to-face in this empty secret yoga-slash-ballet studio in the middle of the city, me and my enemy who I know like the back of my hand, and all the walls are coming down.

"You're too terrifying," I finally say.

The light flooding in the windows is a faint dot of white in each of his eyes. "So are you," he says.

I kiss him. I press into him because I want my chest against his, because my heart feels raw, like there's a hole there that can only be plugged by his chest.

"Mia," he rumbles into the kiss. He stands, pulling me up with him, never once breaking the kiss. I fling my legs around him and kiss him. He holds me aloft, kneading my partly silk-clad butt cheeks. He lays me down on the couch.

"You're gonna make me come again."

"That's the plan."

My eyes drift closed.

"Look at me," he rumbles.

I look at him as he puts himself at my entrance, sliding his condom-clad cock around, picking up juice. "Your enemy of yore is gonna fuck you now and it's gonna be unbelievable."

"Please," I beg.

He pushes a little ways in, stretching me. "God, it already is unbelievable."

I grab handfuls of his shirt, holding him, rocking with him.

His gaze falls to my lips. He leans in, nips my lower lip, just softly.

I suck in a shaky little breath, trying to be quiet about it. I don't want him to know how he shatters me. How much power he has over me. How much I want this.

"I love when you do that," he says.

"What, when I breathe?" I joke. "You need to get out more."

"I love when I touch you, and you try to act like it's nothing."

"Are you calling me a bad actress?"

"You're a great actress—you know you are." He pushes in deeper, rocking gently, in and out. "But when you secretly melt like that, you have no idea how sexy it is. It's a gift," he whispers. "Something only for me."

My eyes drift closed again as he moves deeper, filling me fully. The shock of him so thick inside me makes me shudder with pleasure.

He rocks into me again, breath erratic. He's fucking me. Owning me. It's beyond anything.

My hands are all over his chest, hungrily smoothing over hot skin and cool shirt. I push his shirt off him. I kiss his sweaty chest, learning the shape of his shoulders with my palms.

I'm the queen of the cats, plundering the catnip storeroom.

"Max—"

"What, baby? Anything." He does me slowly, grinding against my pussy. "Anything." He says the word in time with the roll of his hips. "Anything. Anything."

"Like that," I say.

He replies with nonsense into my ear. The music of his voice is familiar, but this is a new key.

I can feel him quickening, lost in a primal rhythm, old as the hills. "Anything."

I grab his thumb and press it to my clit. "Right here," I say.

"God that is so hot." He does my clit while he fucks me. "Like that?"

"Faster," I gasp. He's grinding me and rubbing me. I'm lost in us.

An orgasm explodes over me, white-hot behind my eyes. I grip his arms as he cries out, a pleasure-pain sound that's so Max-ish, I want to die.

He stays in me a long time, forehead to mine.

I bring my palm to his cheek. "Max," I say.

"Oh my god, Mia," he finally says.

Neither of us say anything. There's just the sound of our breath and the press of our sweaty foreheads together.

And then I just laugh.

"What's so funny?" he asks.

"Us," I say.

"Right?" He pulls out. "We deserve an award for...I don't know what."

"My mind is too offline to think of what."

"Here." He whips a monogrammed hanky from his pocket and shoves it into my hand.

"I could just use...a paper napkin."

"I insist."

"It's monogrammed."

He rips it from my hand and swipes it between my legs. "And now it's the most fucking perfect hanky in the world." He tosses it in a nearby garbage can.

"Is it too perfect for the world, and that's why it must die?"

He rolls off his condom and gets rid of that, too. "Yes."

I slide my hand over his whiskers. I love the force of him. The confidence of him.

I stand up and pull myself together...as much as I can with ripped undergarments. I smooth down my dress. I even put my shoes back on. Then I stroll over to the piano. I sit at the bench.

He comes and sits next to me. He brushes back my hair. "I'm going to make Parker apologize. That was so out of line. You must've hated it."

"At first."

"But you launched right in, taking no shit."

I should talk about the book here, but I don't know how to start it. "You don't have to make Parker apologize," I say.

"He thought I'd get a kick out of you turning up with sandwiches. That's not okay. You're not entertainment."

"Dude, it's my whole goal in life. To be entertainment."

"You know what I mean. And while we're at it, Mia. The way things happened after the summer of *Oklahoma!*?"

"Please. Can't we leave what happened in high school back in high school?" I press my fingers to his lips. I don't want to think about the worst time of my life.

He pulls down my hand. "The way things went so bad between us, I know it started with me, the way I came back. I was shut down, and I know how it looked to you. When you did that whole spaghetti-on-your-shirt pratfall? I left you hanging. I was shell-shocked, really, and I was too numb to react. I watched myself sit there."

"I don't understand. What happened?"

He looks down. "I'd lost somebody close to me. While we were in Europe. They took me away because this person was dying and it messed me up."

"Oh my god," I say. "I didn't know."

"How could you?" he asks. "I didn't tell you. I didn't tell anybody. I didn't know how to do that."

"I'm so sorry," I say. "I was so hard on you after that. I felt so humiliated, I couldn't think straight."

"You thought I was that guy. That cold, hard, ruthless musician that everyone thought I was." He pauses here, and I sense worlds in his pause. A place he doesn't want to go, and I want to respect that. "I didn't tell anybody. I was hurting, and it felt good to be cold and hard."

Something melts inside me. "But you tried to apologize later."

"And you told me to fuck off in front of everyone," he says. "I deserved it. It was too little too late. Everything between us was so out of control by then."

"All I could hear was that laughing. Running out of there with spaghetti all over the shirt that I'd worn to impress you."

He takes a curl in his fingers, knuckle brushing my cheek. "You always hated people laughing at you."

"It wasn't just that. I thought maybe it was never real—how we were in *Oklahoma!*"

"It was real to me," he says.

"You tried to apologize twice. Why didn't I believe you? Don't answer that. I did think you were that guy. Like you were too good for me."

"That would never be a thing," he says. "It's not your fault. I was an asshole to everybody. I mean, I was sullen before that summer, but I came back colder."

"And then I went around ruining your dates. I was so angry, but I also didn't want you with anyone else."

"I didn't want you to be with anybody else either," he says. "But you were a more creative date ruiner. The Max Robot impression you put on YouTube?"

"And then the song about me?"

He winces.

"It was both brilliant and diabolical. And my accent—the highlight of your day was in pointing it out when I slipped up. You hated it."

He takes my hand. "I loved your accent. I loved your laugh. I would hunt for the Jerseygirl in your words. I would hunt for that girl."

"Nobody wanted that girl."

"I wanted that girl."

My heart skips a beat. Max kisses my finger.

I give him a smile. "And you are *still* ruining my dates."

He seems to snap back from wherever he went. "I hated you walking in there with Ryan. I hated him putting his hands on you."

I probably shouldn't love that. I definitely shouldn't want to climb all over him for it. "We're just friends," I say. "And now your shirt has no buttons."

"I have an extra shirt here. A T-shirt."

"Max in a T-shirt playing the piano. That's so off brand."

He grins. "Right? And I play pretty songs now. Nice songs."

"Wuuuuut?" I say.

He grins. He's letting me into his private world. It feels huge. Scary.

"I don't know how this works where we're not enemies," I say.

He slides his hand to my heart, resting it there on my chest. It's the most intimate thing he's done to me yet, because I know he can feel my heart pounding. And there's no fucking to take away the attention. I feel naked to him, bare to him. "How it works is that I'm in your corner," he says, "and I always have been."

"Okay," I whisper.

He positions himself on the bench and plunks a note. "What songs are you preparing for *Anything Goes*?"

"'Wonderful' from *Olympus on My Mind* for my comic one. It's a little risky. Bawdy."

"I love that for Reno. A big personality piece."

"I have that one down cold, but my challenge is 'How Could I Ever Know?' from *The Secret Garden*. It's tricky."

"I know that one. It would show off your high notes like crazy."

"Right? It goes up to F5."

"You know you can nail that." He plunks a few notes of it. At least the refrain. Then he plays a few chords.

"You really do know it," I say.

"Not enough to play, but..." He grabs his iPad and looks up the music.

"You're going to play it?"

"I want to hear you sing it, and I'm thinking that's the only way that happens." He's got the music up. My heart pounds.

It's a marvel to watch him run through enough of it to get it down. I'd forgotten how well he can sight read, just a few stops and starts to get it in his bones and he's on his way, making it his own. His phrasing is everything. Like he's discovering the heart of the song. He could always do that.

"You've been playing a lot," I say.

"No more chat." He goes to the top, giving me my way in.

My chest feels light—I'm not sure if it's fear or excitement. We're doing music together. I want to jump in, but something stops me.

"Train's leaving," he says, repeating the prelude, a musical question he knows I have to answer.

We're two pieces of a puzzle. We always were.

He goes back to the top. I watch his face.

He glances at me and groans and starts again. It's a leap

what I'm about to do—more intimate than fucking him. He knows it. He's pulling me.

I stand. I launch in. The first verse lyrical and sad—the whole song is. I sing it like I've been practicing.

It was good how I did it, and then I look at him and his eyes are smiling. Shivers go over me because he's right in there with me.

He comes back at me with the next verse. Max makes it seem easy. Max has a distinct piano voice, but he knows how to use it to support my voice. We sang together that summer and he knows how to make me shine. The perfect tone to enrich mine.

We head into the song, like heading into the wilderness together.

And then everything falls away, and it's just us, meeting in the music. The song is heartbreaking, and toward the middle it soars operatically.

When we come to the end, he moves his finger in a circle to show he's circling back to the beginning. I head in again and we're off.

Flying again. Back in that magical summer, but so much better.

He pauses when I falter, returning to just the right point to get me back. We go again and again and then back around to the front. Like if we never stop the song, this doesn't have to end.

It's so beautiful and right that at one point this wave of grief washes over me. All the years of being stupid.

He stops. "Where did you go?"

"I feel sad." Like sad could even begin to describe it. "We really do deserve some kind of an award. For friggin' bone-headedness."

He looks at his hands, poised over the keys. Does he feel it?

"You want to stop?"

"Hell no." I sit next to him on the bench and show him on the score where I'm thinking of trying something new.

He starts back a few bars, posture erect, color high. He's the opposite of the Max Hilton that's offered for public consumption. He's the old Max. Genuine. In my corner.

I try the new thing. He goes back again and again. I feel like we could play forever. I want the shine of our music to push away reality. But finally I have to stop or I'll burn out my vocal cords.

He looks over at me.

Smiles.

Not his Max Hilton smile, but his goofy smile. "You are gonna kill it," he says. "And the role is for you." He's up, crossing the room to a small refrigerator. He tosses me a bottle of water. To soothe my throat. "You hungry?" he asks. "I'm hungry."

"If you're hinting that you want me to serve you a sandwich, you can forget it."

"We could grab a bite. Except..."

The Max Hilton girl thing. And what about my friends? The whole mission regarding his pickup book?

"Come over," he says.

22

The world is your cocktail party; never forget it.

~THE MAX HILTON PLAYBOOK: TEN
GOLDEN RULES FOR LANDING THE
HOTTEST GIRL IN THE ROOM

Max

I call Parker from the limo. He's handling the party—he'll award the prizes. The beginning is the important part for me to be at. Mia clicks off her phone. "Ryan's having a blast without me. I think he likes that intern. Don't tell the boss."

"I guess the boss can relax the rule against workplace romances just this once," I say, relieved to keep Mia all to myself for the rest of the night.

The limo parks in the underground space. We head over to the elevator bank. I hit the button for my penthouse in the dim garage, safe from the prying eyes of the world. The elevator doors shut us up inside, and she leans back, hands on the rail behind her, luminous in her blue dress.

"Nice elevator. There's just one thing missing," she says. "What could be missing?"

I go to her and cage her with my arms. I love being back with her—it feels like we never stopped being together. I loved singing with her. I love her sassy smile. I love that she gives me shit about the Max Hilton lines.

"What could it be?" she teases.

I shut her up with a kiss. She grabs my shirt, pulls me in hard. I'm stunned all over again at how well we fit. The more time I spend with her, the less I want to let her go back to her apartment, her job, her world.

The door opens and we're there.

She turns. "So this is where you live."

"When I'm in the city."

"Ah, of course." I can hear the smile on her lips as she says it. More Max Hilton mockery, but she likes that I've built this. Mia loves competence. She always has.

I hang behind and watch her look around. "Where are the giant freak lips?" she asks.

It takes me a moment to realize what she's talking about—a massive posterized image of lips that was above the fireplace once upon a time. My designer hung it as a favor to the artist for the magazine shoots.

"Somebody is obsessed with me. Did you collect all of the articles ever written about me?"

"You're inescapable," she says. "You're even on the sides of the busses. Somebody loves his own face." She goes to the window and peers out over the park.

I go up behind her. I move her hair aside and kiss her neck. "I think *you* love my own face."

She turns around in my arms. Her look says, *aren't you so*

full of yourself? It also says, *I do love your own face.* She kisses me and pulls away to continue her self-guided tour around the living room.

I love the sense of ease between us. I never brought a woman home into my private space. Never introduced a woman to my driver, and I never ever played for a woman.

But Mia is like no other woman.

She runs her hand over the nubby blue couch, slides a fingertip over the antique lamp.

"This isn't at all what was in the magazine. It's so much more..." She turns around and looks at the painting above the fireplace. I bought it at a flea market in Amsterdam. It's a crow in a tree, done in bold, heavy black strokes on a bright blue background. It's not at all realistic, but there's something I just love about it. I want her to love it, too.

"It's so you," she says.

"A crow?"

"It's so straightforward, just the lines of it. Energetic and watchful. People think crows are carnivorous and mercenary, but in truth, they're fun and smart and playful."

"Are you saying people think I'm carnivorous and mercenary?"

She looks at me strangely. "Maybe."

I don't love that she'd say that. We've been trying to modulate that image lately. Not enough to defang the brand, but corporate responsibility is a thing with me these days. It's a lot of what Catwalk for a Cause is about.

She moves on into the dining room. "It looked so different in the *Architectural Digest* article. This is much more human."

"I'm still on the carnivorous and mercenary thing."

"Well..." She trails off thoughtfully, as though she has something more to say.

"What?"

I think she's about to tell me, but then she spots the hot tub on the porch. "Look, Max, there's steam coming out of there." She points to the corner of the cover where steam leaks up. "Is that thing functional in the wintertime?"

"Maybe."

"That is so decadent."

"Decadence is the spice of life, baby."

She gives the Max Hilton line an eye roll and I go to her, slide a hand down the smooth silky bodice of her dress. I'm imagining her naked in there. "It's amazing in the winter. You want to go in?"

"Would we need suits?"

"I have a no-suit policy for you."

She gives me a sassy smile. "Oh really?"

"I'm sorry, but it's a strict no-suit policy that I enforce in only the harshest way." I slowly unzip her dress, kissing my way down, unwrapping her like an erotic confection. "I'm afraid I'll have to enforce it."

Her breath speeds. I love that I can affect her this way. I plant kiss after kiss along her spine. My cock is rock hard as I push her dress down in front of the panorama of the park. Her whole body shudders as I pull down her panties, get her to step out of her clothes. "Bra off," I grate.

She takes it off and flings it in true Mia style. It lands on the couch.

I stand, running my hands over her hips. "So beautiful."

She gives me a wicked look over her shoulder, and I'm so overcome with affection, I forget how to breathe. Just her standing there naked is all my fantasies from that lost summer coming true, but so much better. She goes to slip off her shoes, but I stop her. "No, no, no, no. Keep the shoes on," I growl.

"I can't wear shoes in there."

I wrap my arms around her from behind, slide my hand

down over her pussy. One stroke and her whole body quivers. In her ear I whisper, "Bad news. We're not gonna make it that far."

She gasps as I stroke again.

I hold her more tightly. "You're so wet for me," I say. "I love how you get wet for me so fast. Almost as fast as I get hard for you. Almost." I finger her some more, waiting for the feeling of her melting in my arms.

"See that table over there? I'm going to bend you over that table, and you're going to let me do what I need to do."

She turns all the way around now, with a hazy look in her eyes. "Yeah?"

I lower my voice. "You want me to describe how I'm going to fuck you?"

"Yeah, Hilton." She pushes my jacket off my shoulders. "I want the details."

I kiss her the way she seems to like—soft and slow, though there's nothing soft and slow about how I want to take her.

"I'm going to hold your hair in my fist and press you right onto that table. It's cool marble, but you'll warm it up with your sweaty little body, because I'm going to be working you so hard."

I slide my hands over her chest, her hips, learning her curves, the silky warmth of her skin.

"I'm not just gonna fuck you. I know you like a little something extra over your clit, and it's the perfect position for that. I'm going to make you come so hard you'll forget how to meow."

"That's a tall order," she whispers huskily.

I hoist her up; her legs lock around my waist like it's the most natural thing in the world, like she was always meant to be flush against me. I carry her over to the table and put her down, threading my fingers through her soft curls before I fist her hair at the nape of her neck. Her eyes go unfocused as I tighten my grip.

"Undo me," I whisper.

I kiss her while she fumbles at my pants. I want her hands on me again. I loved the reverent way she touched my cock. The way she kissed it.

She takes me in her hand and squeezes.

"So good," I whisper. "That's how hard I am for you. I'll get even harder once I'm inside that pussy of yours. I'm gonna make you come so hard, your knees might give out. But I'll hold you. I need you upright for how I'm gonna do you."

I spin her around. There's nothing gentle about the way I press her down on the table. She makes little begging sounds as I push aside her folds, press one finger in, then another. "This pussy," I grate. She angles up her hips as I press myself in. As I lose myself in her.

She cries out. I slide my hands all over her back. "I gotcha, baby."

I cover her, fucking her. I reach around and do her, lost in the sounds of her pleasure. Lost in her. Never have I lost myself in a woman so completely.

SOMETIME LATER, we're in the tub. I have her foot. She has the view. "Well-fucked is a good look on you," I say.

Her smile gets me in a way I can't describe. Her smile draws me to her, across the dark, bubbly water. I slide my hand up her calf, smooth and warm.

"You're just saying that because I'm naked," she says.

"So not true."

She reaches over the side and grabs one of the Italian chocolates a design house sent over. She closes her eyes and moans as she lets it melt in her mouth.

"I'll never get sick of watching you enjoy things."

"That works because I'll never get sick of enjoying things. Especially your things."

I massage the ball of her foot.

"You are spoiling me," she says. "You are ruining me..."

"For other guys? That's the plan."

The silence stretches long, punctuated by horns honking below. The ambient noise of Fifth Avenue. It's well after two in the morning, possibly after three.

"Have I modulated my mercenary carnivorous image with you yet?" I ask her.

She opens her eyes and gazes at me from across the steam. Like she has a thousand thoughts. What?

"We're actually working on it," I add. "Not to change the Max Hilton persona, but adding a corporate responsibility dimension."

"Yeah. I don't know if it'll help."

Something inside me twists. "What?"

"Well, the book. The pickup book."

"What? The book? It's ancient history. I don't think anybody even reads that book anymore." I move on to the next toe.

"Oh, people read the book. People take it to heart."

This gives me pause. The book has always had haters. I tend to ignore them. "It's designed to help awkward men have confidence."

"I don't know if it does that, but it definitely teaches guys who are stupid jerks how to be smart jerks. And they go out and royally mess with women."

I frown. What happened to her? Low and slow through gritted teeth, I ask, "Did somebody mess with you?"

"Not with me, but my roommate, Kelsey? Her boyfriend picked her up with your techniques. And they ended up living together and it turned out that the entire time, he was using your techniques to pick up a zillion other girls. While they were living together."

"Well, I'm sorry to hear that," I say. "It's an awful thing to discover something like that."

"She was devastated."

I don't know what to say. I stare out at the park, dark trees tipped with snow. "I have to say, though, he sounds like he would've been a bad boyfriend without the book."

"Yeah, but your book helped him *seem* like a good boyfriend. And my friend Jada? She went to bed with a guy who did the jungle-kissing move and it was like, false advertising. Those are two women I personally know. I know you wrote it when you were twenty, but seriously?"

I frown, confused. I think back on my state of mind when I wrote the book. The apartment above a grocer in Little Italy. *What the hell was she doing reading that book?* "So, your friends have a problem with me?"

"Some of my friends do. I'm honestly surprised you're surprised. Like you never get any blowback on the book?"

"I never pay attention to my critics. You can't get anywhere like that."

"So basically, everybody you deal with is in awe of you. You're surrounded by fans and yes-people and employees. Even in high school people were in awe of you."

"Not everyone," I say. I rub her foot, staring into the bubbly depths of the hot tub.

"Be serious. You've never had to deal with people who'd rather give your picture a magic marker moustache than wear Maximillion logo shit, but they're out there."

"I don't see how it's my fault they fell for some lines," I say.

She yanks her foot away. "Seriously?"

I frown. I don't feel like I did anything wrong. Is there something I'm not seeing? "Let me look into it. If I feel like there's a problem, I'll make a donation to something. The Harriet Tubman shelter, or..."

Mia's cheeks are rosy from the steam. She looks cherubic, but she's a cherub on the warpath. "You can't just throw money at it, Max. This isn't PR. These are real people in the real world."

I frown. If nothing else, I'm thinking I need to read that book again.

She narrows her eyes. "You better not be thinking of a Max Hilton line right now."

"I'm not."

"*Who needs the real world when there's hundred-year-old scotch? Or some shit like that? Is that what you were thinking?*"

"Oh, baby, you gotta do better than that for a Max Hilton line," I say. She snorts, but my mind is whirring. "I want to meet your friends. I want to talk to them."

"I don't know if that's a good idea," she says.

"Let me hear them out. I'm not that guy," I say. "You know I'm not."

"You can't do PR voodoo on them, Max. They're not stupid."

I frown. What does that mean? Does she think I can't win them over? Deep down, does she still think I'm *that guy*?

She gives me back her foot. "I don't want to talk about the book anymore."

The night goes on, but I'm not loving this. Being together feels right. I want to make it work. Instead we have problems with the press and her friends?

There's something that feels uncomfortably like high school about it. The hopelessness. The factions. Forces tearing us apart.

The idea that she doesn't entirely trust me.

We get takeout from the little Indian place down the street

and I press her for more details on the way back, but she doesn't want to talk about her friends anymore.

Why? Does she feel like there's no way to fix this? Is this just a one-time thing?

I want it to be more.

We spend the next day sprawled on the couch, watching musicals on the big-screen TV and singing along, something I can do with exactly zero other people.

We begin with the serious warhorses, starting with *HMS Pinafore*. We sing along to every song. She's such an amazing singer.

"How do you know all of this?" she asks me at one point. "Even when you came to the *Oklahoma!* practice that first day, you knew the songs backwards and forwards. I knew your family was musical, but god. I thought it was only classical."

"It's not my family. Not exactly."

She tilts her head. Interested. Caring.

I grab a bottle of wine and two glasses. I never talk about my late nanny, Annette, not even to Parker. I never wanted to. But I want to tell Mia.

So I pour the wine, and I tell her the story. What an important part of my life Annette was—more important than my parents. She was my mother in all the ways that counted. I didn't even know how to be playful until Annette came along.

"I didn't have any electronics or playmates or anything. It was just the music. Very stoic household. Cold. But Annette brought those fun songs. Show tunes. Beatles songs. Burt Bacharach. She had dyed blonde hair and huge rings on her wrinkly hands and an actual record player in her room. And when my parents went on tour, she'd bring it down to the living room and we'd sing and laugh. I suppose it gave her deniability. She could always report that we were working on music. But it was pop music, which was the devil in our house."

Mia threads her fingers into mine. Listening. Caring. I describe my childhood with Annette. I take my time. I paint the picture. Every new thing I tell her feels like a leap of faith, a risk, but then afterwards, when she's looking at me with all of that understanding and compassion, I wonder why I ever stopped sharing things.

When did I build this wall around myself? When did I stop letting people in? Always deflecting. Everything Max Hilton. Jokes and cocktail hour.

It's hard to explain about Annette to her, but I do it. Annette was the only sunshine in a grim childhood of scales and drills. The only bright spot for a little boy sitting on the bench until he dropped from fatigue.

I tell her how desperately I'd wait for my parents to go on another tour so that our home could be happy again. Me and Annette. Playing. It was the only time I could be a kid.

I see when the understanding dawns. "And when you were in *Oklahoma!* with me. I assumed it was like a punishment to you."

"It was the best thing that could've happened," I say.

"For me, too," she says.

"And then we took off to Europe that August," I say. "And I never saw Annette again."

"Wait..." Mia looks pale. "Annette's the one who died that summer?"

"Yes," I say.

"Oh my god," she says.

"She was dying of cancer. I didn't know. My parents took me away—I had important auditions coming up in fall, and they didn't want me to lose my stride. I never got to say goodbye to her. I never got to tell her what she meant."

"Oh my god," she says softly. "I'm so sorry."

"She brought so much joy to my empty childhood," I say, surprised at how even I keep my tone. "I never got to tell her."

She says, "I bet she knew."

"I don't think she did. It fucked me up. I was a shell for a long time."

"And I made it worse," she says.

"You didn't know," I say. "I didn't want you to. It felt good to just go cold."

We're silent for a long time.

"I hate that you couldn't say goodbye," she says.

"Me too," I say.

I break away and scrounge up desserts in the kitchen. I'm not used to this level of sharing. I go back with a plate of toffee somebody sent for Christmas.

"Your turn to pick," I say, setting it down. "Go ahead. Something fun. Surprise me."

She trolls through the streaming menu, looking for a new musical to watch.

I slide my fingers through her hair, thinking how there's nobody else I could do this with. Talk. Sing. Nobody else in the world. "We need to go to *Calle Corrientes*," I say. "We could fly down next weekend."

She widens her eyes. *Calle Corrientes* is the Broadway of Buenos Aires. "Just fly down? Just like that?"

"I've never been and I've always wanted to. Haven't you always wanted to go?"

"Of course I have. I'm surprised you haven't taken your jet down there if you wanted to go so bad."

I tuck her hair behind her ear. I rarely take trips for just pleasure. I lost the urge to do things for pleasure

Until Mia.

23

The last thing you want is a woman you can't walk away from.

~THE MAX HILTON PLAYBOOK: TEN GOLDEN RULES FOR LANDING THE HOTTEST GIRL IN THE ROOM

Mia

Max and I spend the whole weekend together. Reading in bed. Long walks. Hot tub. Music.

Kelsey's still sleeping when I get back that Tuesday morning, which I'm relieved about, because I don't know what I'm going to say to her.

But I need to say something.

What happened between Max and me feels beyond words, but he still wrote that book that screwed up Kelsey's life.

I shower and make coffee and scroll through my phone, finding an early yoga class. All the coffee in my belly hasn't helped me figure out what to say to Kelsey, but maybe yoga will center me, and the teacher today is a hard one.

I pull my winter coat over my yoga outfit and head out with my mat, walking the three blocks to class.

The teacher instructs us to leave the world behind and be on the four corners of our mats, but it's not easy. Every inch of me feels suffused with Max. I slide my finger over my bottom lip between poses, remembering how it felt when he nipped me there. The heaviness of his hands on my thighs. How he sounded when he came.

How it works is that I'm in your corner.

It's torture to put the Meow Squad uniform on. Drudgery to do my deliveries. I brace for Ryan to be upset once we're face-to-face, but as it happens, he's apologizing to me—he and the intern never got back to the party.

"Totally no big! It was fun, and I left early, too," I say.

"No prizes for either of us," he says.

"Sometimes the journey is the destination," I say.

He laughs. "You sure that's how it goes?"

I leave Max's office for last. I've chosen something delicious for him.

He sends everybody out and pulls me to him. "I missed you," he says.

"It's been six hours," I say.

"Have dinner with me tonight," he says.

"At your place?"

"Out. There's a place we won't get seen. Very dark and quiet."

I narrow my eyes. Jada and Tabitha might be having a gathering for after Jada's dress rehearsal, but it's not for sure.

Anyway, Tabitha and Jada are always having things. "You're on," I say.

I finally see Kelsey at home after work. She's already in her dance workout clothes. "Chop chop," she says. "Get in your leotard and you're going to give me the Ryan details on the way to the studio."

I go in and change, feeling like an asshole.

"Every last one," she calls out.

Five minutes later we're traipsing to her dance studio, and she has her arm in mine. "Well?"

I take a deep breath. "Ryan is out of the picture," I say.

Her dimples deepen. "Uh-oh, already?"

I take my arm from hers and stop, pulling her from the stream of pedestrian traffic.

"What?"

"Max," I say.

Her dimples disappear. "Max...w-what?"

"That's who I was with all yesterday. All the day before."

"Excuuuuuuse me?" she emotes. "No! Mia, no!"

"I know. I'm sorry. I didn't know what to do. I've been so torn and just...I don't know. You have this experience with his book—"

"—an experience with his book wrecking my life."

Nathan wrecked your life, I think, but is that me drinking the Max Kool-Aid?

"Max is not his book. He's not like his book at all. We have this history, and we've reconnected so powerfully. I fell for him so hard that summer, and it's all right there. You know how I fell for him."

"I know how hard he hurt you."

"It was high school. And we talked about everything that happened and it's amazing—"

"Nooooo!" She presses her palms to her eyes.

I grab her arms, pull them down. "I've felt like such a jerk. I want to be in solidarity with you, but I can't. It's so, so good with him. Like I never imagined..."

"Mia," she says.

"I want you to...at least keep an open mind?"

"Oh my god, Mia. Come on."

She's silent all the way to the next corner, thinking. But at least she's holding on to my arm.

"He was twenty when he wrote it. He didn't set out to ruin anybody's life."

She turns to me at the *Don't Walk*. "Look. Fine. I get that you could say that the book didn't ruin my life. Obviously I'm the one who decided to move in with that asshole. And the jungle kiss, guys have been using lines forever. Though, that's a diabolically good one. But the thing is, who writes that kind of book? I can get past it on behalf of me. I can't get past the book on behalf of you. Because you don't have a complete personality transplant between the ages of twenty and twenty-eight."

"I know what I'm doing. I know him. He's not that guy."

She rests her hand on my shoulder. "I don't want what happened to me to happen to you. What if Max is a player after all? He wrote the book."

"It's not like that," I say.

"He wrote the book. 'The last thing you want is a woman you can't walk away from.' Remember that little piece of wisdom? He literally *wrote the book* on being a jerky player."

"But he's not like that. Think of how you were at the age of twenty. Personally? I was a basket case."

"Excuses won't un-write the book for him." The light turns green and we're on the move again. "I'm officially registering my objection."

"This isn't a jury trial."

"I'm just saying. I'm not going to harp on this going forward.

I want you to be happy, and as your friend, I'll support you. But if he pulls a Nathan..."

"He makes me happy."

We go on in silence.

"Okay," I say, "and what if I told you he brought me to his secret yogic sex lair?"

She whips her gaze around to me. "To have sex?"

"It's not a sex lair, after all. He keeps his piano there."

"He goes there to play music?"

"It's a yoga school and a ballet school during the day."

"And he goes there every Tuesday to play? Why Tuesday? Did you ask him that?"

"I'm sure it's just his practice schedule. You have to schedule in your priorities, you know that. I didn't tell him that I followed him like a freak." I poke her arm. "So? Are you happy for that at least? To get the answer to our burning mystery?"

She puts on a grumpy face.

She sighs. "Okay, it makes one percent difference in how happy I am. Because I'm mostly worried on your behalf. That he's a player."

"Two percent," I say.

"You are such a dork. Okay."

"Thank you."

"He'd better be a good lay at least. Like amazing." She looks over and I'm just grinning.

"Jesus." She sniffs and takes my arm again.

I'M late to practice with Glen on Thursday afternoon. He plays "How Could I Ever Know?" unevenly. I want to cry. And the way Max did some of the parts was so much better.

"What's wrong?" he asks.

"Everything," I say.

"You're singing it fine."

Miserably I put my head down. I shouldn't say anything. Glen is wildly temperamental and this thing could go south fast.

But I can't help it. "Can you play the intro bar more like..." I hum the way that Max played.

"That's not in the score."

"Maybe it could be. Maybe try?" I shouldn't be asking. It's pushing it to be asking.

"If you have a problem with my playing, come out and say it," he says. "Or bring me a recording, but don't just pull things out of your ass for me to do."

"Sorry," I say. He would hate if he knew Max was playing it with me, and that my suggestions are Max-inspired.

He's silent for a long time.

"I'm just in a funk," I say.

He plays again, but kind of shitty this time. He's feeling unappreciated.

The next day, he quits.

By text.

He says he has a flare-up of carpal tunnel and sends me names of other guys. I know he's battled it before, but I also know that I pushed him.

I send him a get-well six-pack of beer to show I'm not mad or freaked out. I did this. Then I quick work my network and find a Columbia Conservatory grad student. He's never done the song but he insists he can be up with it next week.

I PayPal him half down and we make a date to meet.

24

Go ahead and make her compete for your approval.
Remember, you are in control.

~THE MAX HILTON PLAYBOOK: TEN
GOLDEN RULES FOR LANDING THE
HOTTEST GIRL IN THE ROOM

Mia

I meet Max at The Helvetica Room, a SoHo eatery that is
draped in blue velvet and it's all concrete walls and booths and
low lights. I make it there first. He comes in wearing a baseball
hat, and the waiter shows us to our table, a corner booth that's
very private.

"You know that hat doesn't disguise you any more than
glasses disguise Clark Kent," I say.

"Glasses do disguise Clark Kent," he says. "Nobody ever
guesses he's Superman."

I snort and pick up the menu, which has exactly five items on it, and no prices. "Magic 8-Ball says verrrrry fancy," I say.

"Everything's delicious," he says. "You still like seafood?"

"Love." I reach across the table and put my hand out.

He takes it. "Me too."

There's this silence where it's almost like we confessed our love for each other. I still love him. I loved him over the *Oklahoma!* summer. I thought he loved me.

"How was your day, honey?" he asks.

I grin, because he's thinking what I'm thinking—that things feel almost normal now. We're even at a restaurant! Yes, he's wearing a hat and we're in a dark booth, but still. "My day was good enough. How was yours?"

"Good. We did Vicious campaign stuff."

I'm smiling.

"What?" he protests.

"It's just fun to be out and ask each other about our days," I say. "Also, it's funny that you named your campaign Vicious, you must admit."

His smile is a small crinkle around the edges of his eyes.

The waiter brings wine. We order all the things, being that there are only five.

I go around to his side of the table as soon as the waiter leaves. I slide in close to him. I never had such an irresistible need to be close to somebody. "You love those arch names," I tease. Vicious. Mayhem.

"Somebody has been following somebody's career."

I straighten his lapel. "How can I not? Being that your picture is everywhere."

"That's not really my picture. It's so not me. It's a curated version of me."

"Well, it's your face."

He puts his arm around me. I snuggle in. How am I so

comfortable with him? It's not easy to drink wine from this position, but why would I even need it?

"I followed your career, too," he says. "I knew you were delivering sandwiches. I know you've been working steadily. Congratulations on the reviews for *Sir George and the Dragon*, by the way. That review in the *Times* that specifically pointed out your stage presence?"

"You read the reviews?"

"I went to the shows, Mia. You were the best thing in *Sir George*. I'm not just biased—you were. Everyone saw it."

I pull away. "You went to shows of mine?"

"Of course. I went to all of them. The ones I was in town for."

He was in the audience all that time? Out there in the dark? I'm reviewing every show in my mind. What did he think? "You've been going to my shows."

"Is it so hard to believe?"

"Well, I didn't hear about it."

"I wore a hat."

"Stop it. Seriously?"

He puts a finger over my lips. "You were amazing," he says. "And when you played Missy Bee in *Glenda Rayborne Girls*? That solo?"

I grin and pull away his finger. "God! Right? That solo!"

"I was on the edge of my seat for you," Max says. I can't believe he noticed. It was the least flashy solo, but the range it demanded was madness, and I was proud how I nailed it, night after night. Not a lot of people noticed. Only the musicians. "As soon as the progression started, I knew you were going to end up on a sustained high C. You made it sound easy."

I love that we have this language in common.

"You are so perfect for Reno Sweeney," he adds.

"I hope."

"Mia," he says. "It's so you. And I bet your dancing is right there with your singing and acting. You have the trifecta now."

"It'll be brutal choreography, but I've been working so hard on it. My roommate, Kelsey, is a dancer and we do trades. I'm helping her level up on her acting and singing, and she's helping me level up on dancing."

"You'll nail it," he says.

I nod, thinking about the grad student who's replacing Glen. I'll nail it if the student can halfway nail it.

The waiter brings the apps. Some sort of delicious-smelling bruschetta. I grab one without waiting for him. I crunch in and discover that it's beyond delicious.

"So what's the problem?" he asks.

"With what?"

"The dark cloud that passed over your face just now."

I sigh. "You remember Glen? Pianist, but he was also a guitarist, more on the popular music side—"

"Sure. Brown ponytail? Super high strung? Into jazz fusion?"

"Well, he lost the ponytail but he's every bit as high strung. And he was my accompanist but he quit on me. Just freaked out. I lined up somebody from Columbia, a grad student who should totally be able to handle it. But it's just, the unknown factor of somebody new so close to the audition."

"Glen was never cut out for collaboration," Max says.

"Hell no," I say. "He's mostly recording solo projects in his loft. That's more his area. Most groups won't work with him."

"But why not ask me?" Max says.

I blink. "Dude, for so many reasons. It would be a circus. And also, what about your brand? There's a reason you're playing pretty songs in secret, Max. You don't even keep a piano at your home."

"I'll wear a hat and sunglasses," he says. "A track suit. A wig. A full disguise."

"Seriously? You can't, Max!"

"You know I can. People won't know," he says.

"What if they do? I can't be a Max Hilton girl, and if you get busted, it'll make it look like your whole persona is fake."

"People don't see what they're not expecting. I know how to wear a disguise. It'll just be the music."

I press my thumb onto the plate, taking up every last crumb. *What if?*

He lowers his voice. "You know you want to."

I do want to. "Have you done it before? Full disguise?"

"Of course."

"And it's not weird? Like, there's a guy in disguise?" I ask.

"Gimme a little credit," he says. "I, too, attended the Shiz."

"I'm actually thinking about it," I say.

"You'd be a fool not to," he says. "We're good together. We nailed it already."

"It would be amazing."

"A grad student with a week to practice?" he says. "It might not suck, but it's just marginally better than handing your music to a house pianist."

"You think nobody would know?" I ask.

"I'd make sure of it," he says. "I have just as much to lose. Max Hilton doesn't hide things. He definitely can't be hiding a secret sappy side. It would be a nightmare for the press to have that."

"It's sad you can't play publicly. Why can't Max Hilton play? You could pull out that Ligeti," I say. Ligeti is a Hungarian composer whose etudes are among the most terrifying works for the piano. They're beautiful, but in a hard way. "Or Schoenberg? Max is remote and super cool. Not a man who skips through the park. I could see your persona whipping that out."

"I told you, I don't play those songs anymore," he says simply. "Only tunes that people would hum, now."

"Really."

"Remember how you said I attacked the keyboard like Terminator?"

"I'm sorry," I say.

"No. Don't be sorry. You were right. I was playing angry. I hated those pieces. You heard it and you were right. I was playing technically. This might sound a little strange, but it meant something that you saw it."

"You hated those pieces?"

"Yes. And you're the only one who noticed. You heard what was really inside that music. It made me feel less alone."

The admission hits me in the gut. I think back to him bent over that keyboard, jaw hard. I didn't know he hated the music he was known for. "You reached an elite level of musicianship in a type of music that you hated?"

"You're supposed to be miserable in high school, right?" he asks. "Isn't that a rule?"

"I kind of can't get over it. You were in a performing arts school and you hated performing."

"Not all performing."

I grin. "You liked *Oklahoma!*"

"I loved it. I mean, I never had the chops for doing it professionally, but I loved it. Maybe that's part of why I loved it. And then for them to put us together."

"Why didn't you just go over to the theater side anyway? Or the popular music side? They probably would've let you."

"My folks would've pulled me out of that school so fast— you don't know. I could've been snorting coke and making bombs, and they wouldn't have pulled me out as long as I was performing at an elite level, but show tunes? The seventh ring of hell. Popular pieces? Even Chopin would've been a bridge too far."

"Chopin is pretty far from what you were playing, I guess."

"Obscure classical music is the Miller family business." He picks up his silver butter knife this way and that, playing with the reflection. "If I'm honest, I liked what came with the child prodigy status. It was an instant place on top of the food chain. It feels good to be good at something, even if you hate it."

"Like being star quarterback," I say.

"In a way. When I'm in that studio, I'm playing just for me. Sometimes I don't even worry about technique."

I do a fake gasp.

"So what do you say? I'm your official accompanist. You can't say no."

I bite my lip. Am I going to do it? "Fine. Yes," I say. "Let's do it!" I'm just smiling. I can't stop.

The waiter brings another course.

He says, "You'd nail it without me, but..."

I nod. He doesn't have to finish the sentence. He knows how to play to show off my voice.

We linger long over dinner. I confess to him that I brought a condom to the cast party he never made it to. His family left for Europe by then.

We make each other tell who we lost our V-cards to. We bitch about the stadium traffic and United Nations building double-parkers.

Around dessert is when Max notices the commotion up front. "Crap," he says. "The press."

"Here? I thought they didn't bug you here!" I say.

"They usually don't. It's the profile guy. The *Times* guy." He pulls out a few hundreds and sets them on the table and sends a quick text. "Come on."

We slide out. He takes my hand and leads me toward the back of the restaurant.

We run into our waiter. "I left money on the table," he says. "Can you get us out the kitchen way?"

"Come on." The waiter leads the way through a swinging door. He seems unfazed—maybe he's used to celebrity exits.

We make our way through the bright bustle of the kitchen. A few cooks scowl at us. Seconds later we're out in the alley. Max's limo pulls up and we get in.

"I'm sorry," he says as we're back in traffic, safely ensconced behind the tinted windows. "This sucks. I wanted us to have a normal date and not just hide out at my place all the time."

"It was fun," I say. "But I'm glad we didn't get caught. With my audition."

"I know," he says. "Tarquin must've gotten tipped off. He smells that I'm keeping something from him."

"He's the reporter from New Year's Eve?"

"Yeah. He thinks I'm hiding something. Don't worry, I won't let him think you're a Max Hilton girl." He leans up and gives instructions to the driver to drive around.

"Where are we going?"

"I don't know. I'm figuring it out. I was thinking about a walk, but it's gonna rain. My place is out because Tarquin's people might be lurking if they're really on the warpath tonight. There's the studio, maybe..."

Impulsively, I turn to him. "Come to my place."

"Really?" he says. "Your place?"

"Why not? Kelsey's at a cast party. You can sit on our shabby couch, and if you behave, I'll let you see the view of your tower from my bedroom."

He smiles. "How can I say no to that? It sounds absolutely magnificent."

I snort.

We head out through the streets. I'm smiling stupidly. I feel happy with this man. Like we were meant to be together.

The limo draws up in front of our building.

"You are literally two blocks off Times Square," he grumbles.

"Oh, shut it." I press a finger to his lips. "Not all of us can be brilliantly rich."

We get out of the car. I step onto the sidewalk. Max ducks into the front window to say something. I look up at our window and see lights on. And people. "Looks like everybody is actually there," I say when he rejoins me. "The cast party must've ended. Or moved."

"I don't mind if your friends are there if you don't," he says. "I'd love to meet them. And will your friend with the jungle-kiss guy be there? It'll give me a chance to explain. To hear her out. I'd like to talk to them about the book."

It's then that I remember the chart. With the shoes. And his face on a dart board. And the words *Bring Max Hilton to his grovelly knees*...still up on the wall.

My blood races. Max wouldn't understand. And all the people would be there.

I swallow. "Umm, it might not be the perfect timing," I say.

Max frowns. "Why not?"

I don't know what to say. I'm a deer in the headlights. All I know is that I can't let him see that chart. "It just might be weird." I mumble something about crashing the cast party.

25

Always stay just a little bit out of her grasp.

~THE MAX HILTON PLAYBOOK: TEN
GOLDEN RULES FOR LANDING THE
HOTTEST GIRL IN THE ROOM

Max

I've always been able to tell when Mia's bullshitting, and she's bullshitting now. She doesn't want me to meet her friends. "Is this about the book?"

We move to the side to let people rush past.

"Can we just do something else?" she asks. "I feel like some preparation might be needed."

"What does that mean? They're that angry about the book?" I ask. Our friends hated each other in high school. I hate the idea of repeating that. "If they're pissed, I'd like to be able to hear them out and talk about it. Surely they can't hold me responsible for how people use the book."

"It's a timing thing," she says.

"Does that mean they *do* hold me responsible? Because it's just a book."

"Well, that might not be the attitude to take with them. It's more than just a book."

"No, actually, it's not more than just a book." My words sound harsher than I meant them to. "And what does that mean, exactly? Do *you* hold me responsible?"

"For *how* people use the book?" she asks. "That has nothing to do with anything."

"Do you?" I demand. It's unfair of me to press her. I don't know what's come over me.

"I think that's a weird question. If you recall, you do specifically tell people how to use the book, and encourage them to do as you say. So you would technically be responsible for *how* people use the book."

I straighten. Mia was always so fiercely loyal to her friends. She'd fight to the death for her friends. It's something I loved about her. But right now, it's messing me up. "That's ridiculous," I say.

"How is that ridiculous? The book teaches guys how to seem better than they are."

"It's just a form of coaching," I say, annoyed. "If you went and got coaching on how to say the right thing in a job interview, is that wrong? How is this different?"

"It would be wrong if the coach told me to pretend I was something I wasn't," Mia says. "And meeting in a bar isn't a job interview."

"Meeting in a bar is exactly like a job interview," I snap.

She's shaking her head. Is this our first fight? "It's so not."

"Meeting another person is about putting your best foot forward," I say. "And ideally you vet the person. Check the person out a bit before hiring them. Or definitely before sleeping with them."

"Excuse me? What are you trying to say? That my friends will just sleep with anybody?"

"That's not what I meant," I say, cringing at my own words. "That came out wrong."

"How are they supposed to confirm a fake heartwarming story about a dog? A story that shows they have a generous soul? Are they to demand family pictures? That's just not fair."

"The book was designed to inspire guys to have confidence," I say, trying to patch things over. "To be unique, let their personalities shine through."

"But it's not their personalities shining through, it's your personality. It's your stories. And, what do you call the thing where you're supposed to completely ignore the pretty girl and talk with everybody else? Emotional manipulation. Come on, Max, you have to at least admit that."

I should admit it, but I'm feeling defensive, now. "All performance is emotional manipulation. At the Shiz, you worked your ass off to wring emotion out of music. And the actors there? Method acting is emotional manipulation. The key of D minor is emotional manipulation. But I'm the bad guy here?"

"It's different," she says. "And the men are only supposed to choose girls they will never feel attached to, so they can't get hurt. Like, what the hell is that?"

"So you think there's no point in me going up there? Are we back to high school? To a thing where our friends hate each other? Because that's not where I want to be. You think I can't make it right?"

"It's not that—"

"What is it, then? I'm not that cold, heartless guy. I'm not that guy from the Shiz, and I'm not Max Hilton, that guy on the billboards. I'm not *that guy*, Mia." And then this icy feeling comes over me. "Or maybe you do think I'm that guy."

"No," she says. "I don't think you're that guy."

"I wrote the book, though, didn't I?" I say. "False advertising. Manipulating women."

"Just—let's go elsewhere."

"You think I'm that guy," I say, disheartened. "One bad day and I'm back to being the Terminator. Again."

"Are you talking about that summer? I didn't understand what was going on with you," she says. "That's not fair."

Maybe it's not fair. It's been so long since I've shown anyone my heart, I don't know how to do it. "And you assumed the worst."

"And apparently you haven't forgiven me," she says in a small voice.

I watch myself turn asshole. "Who knows, maybe I am that guy," I say smoothly. It's my Max Hilton attitude. I put him back on like a comfortable cashmere overcoat, a coat so plush and thick, it even protects my heart.

"Max—"

"Have fun at your party." I get in and shut the door. I tell the driver to go.

26

Never beg a woman for anything. She should be begging you.

~THE MAX HILTON PLAYBOOK: TEN GOLDEN RULES FOR LANDING THE HOTTEST GIRL IN THE ROOM

Max

Rehearsals for Catwalk for a Cause go as scheduled, bright and early the next morning. We can't control the skits and songs that contributing businesses come up with, but we control the context, and that's everything. I sit there with my PR team, making final decisions, but my heart isn't in it. I'm reeling from the argument. Twisted in knots.

I'm angry at her for not believing in me enough to let me talk to her friends. Assuming the worst.

I'm also angry at myself for overreacting. She clearly wanted to prepare her friends instead of having me burst in with no notice. But I had to be an asshole about it.

And when I'm really and truly honest with myself, I know that I'm angry because she has a lot of good points about the book. Maybe I'm even a little ashamed. I hadn't thought about that book in years. I didn't even remember what's in it—until I started to reread it.

It turns out that I did tell guys to pretend the dog story was their own. I coached them to lie.

But the rehearsal must go on.

It's a strange relief to inhabit Max Hilton again, to pretend not to care about anything except style and pleasure. It's easy to disappear into that persona. To laugh about stupid things. I could disappear into Max and never have to feel bad again.

I suppose, in a way, that's what I did.

So I'm going through chapter after chapter of the book at rehearsal, absorbed in the advice I was giving guys.

"Whatcha got there?"

I look up. It's Tarquin. I tuck away the book. "Who let *you* in?" I joke, because I'm the one who let him in. I gave him a pass to attend the rehearsals. The show is part of his profile.

"Is that the famous playbook?" Tarquin says. "I read that thing."

"You read it?"

"Everyone did." He sits down uninvited. "So I heard a rumor," he says. "I heard that you were out at the Helvetica room with Mia Corelli, the showgirl."

I want to correct him, to say she's an actor, not a showgirl, but that would reveal too much. It would reveal that I care. Max Hilton doesn't care about things. "You'd be wrong," I say simply.

"Is it possible that she's the delivery girl you partnered up with on New Year's Eve? The one who ran out of your office?

I'm smelling a new Max Hilton girl. Is this somebody you're taking an interest in? Maybe grooming her to replace Lana?"

Inwardly, I cringe. It's the last thing I'd want him thinking. God, Mia would never forgive me. I think about telling him we went to high school together, but that'll just get him more interested in our connection. "Honestly, why would I want a delivery girl as a Max Hilton girl?" I say, giving him the full Max Hilton ennui. "Am I doing a reality show now?"

"Is she the same person?" Tarquin says.

I sigh. "There are no new Max Hilton girl slots available, much as that disappoints women the world over. Many want to be. Few qualify. You can go ahead and print that."

"I'm not here to do your PR."

I bite back a smile at how much he hates that angle. I need something for him to latch on to now, something juicy to turn his attention from Mia. I get the idea to tell him about last year's product flop—loungewear we had in testing. It's embarrassing, but it won't kill us. I call Parker over.

"What's up?" Parker asks.

"I'm telling him about the at-home line. You still have those shots?"

Parker sits and cocks his head. "Really. The at-home line?"

"Yes, really." I give him a cool smile. Parker and I have told the at-home line flop story at parties, but it's not something I'd normally want printed.

I start the story the way we usually do, "So we were brainstorming for our work-at-home market," I say. "Techies, entrepreneurs." I describe how we went pretty far down the road to designing it and producing prototypes. It was a whole line before we realized people were considering the clothes to be sweats.

Parker chimes in right on cue, painting the picture of the first horrifying focus group. We couldn't get people to stop calling them sweatshirts, sweatpants. We had entire focus groups testing how to get people to stop calling them that. We'd get drunk and joke about naming the line "They're not fucking sweats!"

We have Tarquin laughing. It's the perfect anecdote to put into his piece—something embarrassing and behind the scenes. Something that shows the fallible, human side of Maximillion.

Parker has his phone. He's showing Tarquin the raw photos from the shoot.

I feel her before I see her.

I stand.

She's picking her way around lighting and camera equipment, heading toward our table. My heart pounds. How did she find me?

I LOVE SEEING HER, that's my first feeling. As fraught as we left things last night, I love seeing her. I want to tell her that I'm sorry about the way I acted. About being an asshole.

But I also hate that she's here, because I just got Tarquin off her scent, and here she is. And like all good journalists, he can figure out when he's been thrown a bone for the purposes of distraction, and that's what the at-home collection is—a big, juicy bone meant to distract him from the better meal.

I direct my gaze at Tarquin, who's still huddled with Parker. I need her to spot him, to see the danger and turn around and leave, but she just smiles at me. Uncertainly. Bravely. Coming to me, her dark curls barely tamed in a red hairband.

She stops in front of me. "What are you doing here?" I say under my breath, tipping my head at Tarquin.

She doesn't notice.

"I don't think you're that guy," she declares. "I never thought you were that guy. And I need to tell you something—"

She doesn't see him. This is a disaster. He'll know she's the woman from last night. He'll see I'm hiding something and conclude I'm grooming her or helping her with her career.

Mia would hate any implication that I'm helping her with her career. Or worse, that she's a Max Hilton girl I'm keeping under wraps.

I can feel Tarquin's attention perk up like a thousand Mia career-ruining prairie dogs peeking out of their holes, scanning for prey.

"Look," I say to her, widening my eyes. "Not every girl can be a Max Hilton girl. I'm sorry."

She looks at me aghast. "What?"

My gut twists. But I have to do it. "Not every girl can be a Max Hilton girl."

Now the whole table is watching us. She opens her mouth and closes it, horrified. Has she seen Tarquin? I can't tell.

"Like I would *ever*." With that, she turns and leaves.

"Persistent," Tarquin says.

"Not every girl can be a Max Hilton girl," I say again, softly.

Parker jumps right in there—we're in tune like that. "They all want to be. Every week," he says to Tarquin. "I'm not saying it gets old, but it does get old." He launches into some story. Parker knows just how to handle Tarquin. He's an amazing ally.

I text her under the table. I tell her that Tarquin was there, and I had to throw him off the scent. Nothing comes back. People are coming to me with questions. I answer them, trying to act unaffected.

I built an empire, but right now, it's feeling like a cage.

I step out into the alley and call her. It's a five-alarm fire, me actually calling somebody.

She picks up. "How could you say that in front of a reporter?" she demands. "How could you? Oh my god!"

"It was the perfect way to make you uninteresting," I say. "It was for the best—"

"For the best? Are you kidding me here? I was going there to apologize, and that's what you do? You paint me to look like a Max Hilton girl wannabe in front of a reporter? I can't believe you said that, Max! I have the most important audition of my life coming up."

"I was trying to throw him off the scent," I say. "Trust me, it made you uninteresting."

"I wanted to apologize, to you." She pauses. The pause is ominous.

"You think I *wanted* to say that?" I ask.

"No, I don't think you wanted to say it," she says finally. "But how does this thing with us even work? When that's the best option as a thing to say?"

"We make it work," I say.

"Says the guy who has so much less to lose," she says.

Voices in the background. "Where are you?" I ask.

"Does it matter? I have to go. I need to focus on this audition. And look, it turns out the grad student will be a fine accompanist. He'll be fine, and I'm going with him for the audition."

"Fine isn't good enough. Mia. You can't go with a grad student. With a week?" I say. "No. We have to talk. Where and when?"

"'*Not every girl can be a Max Hilton girl*'? You know how that felt?" I can hear the pain in her voice. It's the lunchroom all over again. It's her whole history of clawing herself up from nothing, fighting to be taken seriously.

"I'm sorry," I say.

It's not enough.

"Max." Her voice sounds so sad, my heart feels like it's cracking apart. "I don't know if this works. Do we leave the past in the past?"

"What are you talking about? No."

"I feel like this was my wake-up call," she says. "At least for now. Respect me enough to let me focus." And with that, she's gone.

I'm standing there leaning against the cold brick, feeling like my world has shattered.

Now I remember why I wrote the book.

27

Never buy her a drink. That's a move for losers.

~THE MAX HILTON PLAYBOOK: TEN
GOLDEN RULES FOR LANDING THE
HOTTEST GIRL IN THE ROOM

Mia

I tear down the chart and stuff it in the recycling bin.

When I showed up at his rehearsal, I was going to tell him about the chart, to confess all. I wanted him to know that not inviting him up wasn't about my being embarrassed of his book, or about being unsure of him.

It was my embarrassment over that stupid chart.

I pull the darts off the dartboard, one by one, and free the book flap with his picture. I stick that in the recycling, too. I lift the dartboard off the wall.

When I think back to how it felt to stand there in that cavernous space, his handful of minions looking at me like I'm some sort of desperate loser, I feel physically ill. Literally nauseated.

And in front of a reporter!

I tell myself it's for the best. This isn't working. And he never did take responsibility for the book. For the fact that he outright encouraged dudes to lie. He doesn't deserve darts in the face, but, seriously?

That afternoon, I start working with the grad student from Columbia.

Unlike Glen, this guy is okay with my managing him, but he makes a zillion errors. He's so young. He promises to practice, but the next day he's at practice and he's still not getting the hard passage that works alongside my voice. I try to be encouraging, but I'm getting nervous.

I call my girl squad together a day later.

Shy mail carrier Noelle is the first to arrive. "Should I come back?" she squeaks.

"No, come in!" I say, pulling her in. "Now I get to eat all your caramel popcorn."

She grins and puts the bowl on my coffee table. The caramel corn is her own small-town-voodoo recipe that she makes on the stove. She waits expectantly.

I grab a handful of caramel corn. "Yum."

"Do you think it's true about Malcolm Blackberg?" she asks me nervously.

"Who's that?" I ask.

"The new owner of the building. Who might tear it down in spring?"

"What? No. I heard no such thing," I say. "Are you sure? That sounds like a rumor."

"Well, it's not confirmed," she says. "But I think it's more than a rumor."

She's scared. We're really her only family. I hope it's not true. I grab another handful. "We'll figure it out," I tell her, trying not to talk with my mouth full. "We're all together in this," I add.

"Thanks for saying that," she says.

"It's true. And also, I mean, this is a valuable old building. It's practically historical—I bet there's a law against it." I'm hoping there is. Tear it down?

Tabitha and Jada arrive next. Jada has a twelve-pack of hard cider. She hands a few out and starts stocking the fridge.

Tabitha's wearing an arm brace. "What happened?" Noelle asks her.

"Carpel tunnel maybe? And this is my hair cutting hand," Tabitha says. "I need to lay off, but I don't think my clients want me cutting their hair with my left hand."

"That sucks!" I say. How long can Tabitha pay her rent without cutting hair? But I don't want to pry. It's worrying, though—no way is her roomie Jada rich enough to carry their whole rent.

"Hey, did you and Jada hear about some Malcolm guy buying the building?" I ask.

"Everybody's heard about it," Tabitha says. "He's our new landlord."

Apparently I haven't been reading my mail. Kelsey gets home and even she's heard about it, but she doesn't think the city would let him demolish the building. Most people agree—no way can he knock it down. But then again, he does own it.

Vicky arrives with Smuckers and three more theatrical neighbors, including Antonio. A bunch of us pet Smuckers at once—there's barely any room on his little white body for another petting hand. That all ends when Lizzie arrives with cookies. It's a party.

Jada and Noelle decide they want to teach Smuckers to jump through a hoop over Vicky's protests, and I have to scold people to stop paying attention to Smuckers, because I have a dilemma. I have gathered them for an audition dilemma.

"Hey, where's the chart?" Francine asks.

"I'm not doing that anymore," I say. "And you're all getting your challenge money back."

"Oh, god, no!" Jada says. "You're not falling for him."

"And be the next Max Hilton girl? Please," I say, even as a pang of grief stabs me. I'd hoped having my girl crew around me would lessen the pain, but it's not working.

I loved being with Max.

Did I mess up? I tell myself to focus on the audition problem.

I stand up in front of them and describe the dilemma. I tell them the songs I was originally thinking of: "Wonderful" from *Olympus on My Mind* for my comic one and "How Could I Ever Know?" for my serious one.

"'Wonderful' is a go, but 'How Could I Ever Know?' is the tricky one. It's not something a pianist sight reads."

Most pianists, anyway.

Should I go for a different song for the audition? A boring but safer one that doesn't show off my range? Something that the house pianist could handle.

I sing a bit of "How." I have a recording of what the grad student sounds like—not pretty. I play a YouTube version of it.

Francine winces. "If you use an unprepared pianist, the casting director might wonder if you're the kind of person who does things at the last minute."

"Right?" I say.

Antonio thinks I should shoot for it anyway. "Go big," he says, and I kind of love him for that. Francine argues with him.

Jada thinks I should go with the house pianist for "How Could I Ever Know?" Using the house pianist is what's expected. Yes, the house person will be unfamiliar with the music, but I'll get a break if they make mistakes, and I can show how well I ride them out.

Kelsey thinks I should prepare a different song totally for my serious one. Tabitha thinks I should try "How" with the house pianist, and if the song is going shitty, switch to a backup song.

"Something easy like 'The Impossible Dream,'" Kelsey suggests. "That could be your backup."

In the end, that's what I decide. I sing bits of three songs and let people vote. Most of them are in the theater or connected to the theater, so their opinions are trustworthy.

We decide on "The Impossible Dream" for my backup serious one.

28

Remember, you're the alpha. You're the pursued. Let your reality be stronger than hers.

~THE MAX HILTON PLAYBOOK: TEN
GOLDEN RULES FOR LANDING THE
HOTTEST GIRL IN THE ROOM

Mia

The show's pianist is a bull of a man, maybe fifty, and clearly very experienced. I sit through one audition after another, and the hopefuls who don't bring their own players get excellent quality accompaniment. In some cases, the actor would've been better off with the show's pianist than the one they brought.

I'm starting to feel hopeful. Maybe he can pull this off.

Suddenly it's my turn. I go up and hand my packet with my

head shot and bio to the casting director, who looks annoyed and a bit sleepy. Then I head over to the pianist, who is on the far side of the stage. Apologetically I hand him the music.

"How Could I Ever Know?" is on top. He gives me a side eye. "Seriously?"

Because coming in with this piece, I should've brought my own accompanist.

"I know. My guy..." I wave my hand, indicating that I had a guy and he won't be showing. Hopefully it looks like a *we-got-this!* wave and not an *I-want-to-curl-up-and-die!* wave.

He frowns at the music, annoyed. Well, it's a lot to ask. "No guarantees. A lotta ink," he adds, meaning all of the quarter-notes and key changes.

"Fair enough. And here's my backup." I direct his attention to "The Impossible Dream." "And for my comic song..." I pull out "Wonderful."

"That works," he says. "You want to start with 'Wonderful'?"

"If we could," I whisper with a smile. I walk up onto the stage, stand under the bright lights. I want to cry. He's more worried about "How" than I am.

God, all the hours of work. All my hopes piled onto that song.

I force myself to smile. I do the acting and dancing portion. It goes great. I'm ecstatic. Then it's time for the singing.

I remind myself that this is the role I was born for. They might already see that.

"Wonderful" goes off without a hitch. I make it big and brassy, but then, it's easy to do that one well.

I exchange a glance with the pianist. Time for the hard one. Sweat trickles down my spine. He starts in strong.

I launch into the first bars, but then he gets the timing wrong. It screws me up for where I'm supposed to come back in.

I gloss over it, singing my heart out there on the bright stage, pulse whooshing in my ears.

And then he stops altogether. "Wait," he says. "Hold up."

The air seems to brighten and buzz with static. Moments buzz by. It feels like hours but maybe it's seconds.

I tried so hard.

I turn to him. I want to try again. I don't want to sing "Impossible Dream." Other people have sung it. "Back up from..." My voice sounds tinny, like it's from another planet. "Up from..." I hum a trio of notes, a proposed starting place.

I glance nervously over at the casting director.

He looks annoyed. I smile, trying to look like I'm having fun, like this is going to be amazing, but my heart is crumbling.

I make eye contact with the pianist, trying to look friendly, to relax him. He starts in. He's doing it right this time, but he's playing tentatively, more slowly than I'm used to.

I sing the beginning, keeping him buoyed. He heads over the hard part without incident, but I'm overly careful now, because I'm taking care of him instead of focusing on this amazing song.

It doesn't help that the casting director has already put down my bio and head shot.

No!

He consults his clipboard, ready for the next one. Already moving on. I'm coming up on the impressive high run, but then the pianist stumbles the refrain. Screwups can spread like infections, one creating another.

He stops. "Okay, maybe the other."

I feel like a sense of hush all around us. Not a nice hush. It's the hush after an explosion. Boom. Damage done. Painfully obvious.

The casting director glances at his underling. Are they about to thank me? The singing was my strong suit!

"Hah!" I bark happily.

It's a crazy *hah!* A boisterous *hah!* The complete opposite of how I feel, but it's very Reno Sweeney.

Everyone's looking at me like I'm crazy.

I march to the center of the stage. I thrust out my arms, a great ringmaster. If I go down, I'll go down in a blaze. "We're going to do it amazingly this time!"

I look around like everything is magical. I can feel his attention. I channel all of the brightness of the world into my smile. I make my energy big—big enough to fill the room. I make it commanding.

I step to the forwardmost edge of the stage. One more time.

There's commotion by the piano. I'm not even looking. I'll make this song the best thing I ever sang. I'll show the casting director he can't do this show without me. I'll carry that pianist. I'll sing it acapella if I have to—that's my decision. If he stops, I'll keep going, even if he says for me not to.

No matter what. That's what I repeat to myself. *No matter what.*

I make a dramatic hand signal, like I'm tracing an upward tornado. "From the top!"

He starts in...no, launches in, a player transformed. Like he was born to play the song.

The first run crashes over me.

My heart splits open.

He's playing like Max. And then I realize it's because he is Max.

Max is here.

Playing.

His notes feel like bravery. And love.

I slide into the song like I'm coming home. Singing all the way up to the high notes. The upper atmosphere, crystal bright and true, and then on down into the emotional middle, full of drama and color and warm resolution. Then back on up, tension and release. I make the hard parts sound easy, the easy parts feel like a dream.

I don't care about anything outside the song. It's just Max and me, creating something beautiful and fleeting while the world falls away.

We live and die in that song. It's the best, most heart-breaking version we've ever done.

And then it's over.

And the fog clears from my mind. And the casting director is standing, holding a sheaf of papers down at his side. Just standing.

Out of the corner of my eye, I see Max head to the exit. He's wearing a ball cap. How do people not see it's him? But they don't. People are staring at me instead of staring at him.

"Okay," the casting director finally says. "That was..." He seems to realize he's standing, seems to be confused by that, like some unseen force pulled him from his seat, marionette-style. He sits, still looking startled. "Thank you."

"Thank you," I say, heading down the stage left steps, very nearly floating down them. I go back to the seats, passing the next hopeful on her way up. She gives me a shell-shocked look, like she's thinking, *what the freaking hell?!?!? I have to follow THAT?*

Shivers go over me. Rain over me like a deluge. Because I nailed it. I want to say sorry, but I'm not sorry. I grab my bag and my coat.

The assistant to the assistant rushes over and confirms my contact info. She grabs my arm and whispers, "It was amazing!"

I smile a shaky smile and burst out the side stage door, bursting into the cold January sunshine. Max is nowhere.

I text him. Where are you?

He texts back: Did it go okay? I thought it went okay.

Me: It was amazing.

Max: I wanted to make up for the other day.

Me: I need to see you.

Max: Maybe we leave it.

I stare at the words, unsure how to reply. I type a "but," then backspace it. Am I three dots on his end? Three dots, starting and stopping?

Max: In the past. Like you said.

Me: What if we don't leave it in the past?

Max: I hope you get the part.

His text takes my breath away. Not in a good way. It's more like I feel empty, because it's such a finalistic communication.

Also, I can feel the pain right through it.

He's hurting—I can feel it through the blocks of concrete and metal that separate us. For once, Max opened his heart to somebody. He opened his heart to me. And it's been a disaster.

Twice.

I get in a taxi and take it to his tower. It's rush hour. It takes forever. Finally I'm there. I go to the security station. They don't let me in. They won't even say if he's in there, as if I'm just another fan in a legion of fans.

I go across the street and find his window, but I can't tell if anybody's in his office. I stare up at the tower that I so impudently gave him three stars for.

And it's here I get it. It's here I understand everything.

He didn't play like a robot because he feels nothing. He didn't create the cold, careless Max Hilton persona because he feels nothing.

He did those things because he feels too much.

∼

MEOW SQUAD MAY BE BARRED from the building, but I still have allies there.

I take the day off from work the next day, and just before lunchtime, I buy him an amazing lobster roll sandwich. I put cheesy puffs in the bag along with it. I include a note. A picture of a heart. Underneath I write, *I'm outside the building. Waiting. We need to talk.*

I see a woman from the seventh floor I used to deliver to; she's heading in with a coffee. I beg her to deliver my bag to Max's assistant. She seems a little bit bewildered, but she agrees.

I wait outside on a bus bench. I don't even scroll my phone. I'm waiting for him. I want him to see that.

People come and sit by me, waiting for busses, and then they're gone. Three hours into it, the same busses come by again. I wonder if the drivers recognize me. Some of the busses have Max's face on them, ironically.

At around six, the lights in his twenty-fifth-floor office blink off. I sit up.

He never comes down to see me.

29

Go ahead and make her compete for your approval. Remember, you are in control.

~THE MAX HILTON PLAYBOOK: TEN GOLDEN RULES FOR LANDING THE HOTTEST GIRL IN THE ROOM

Mia

A week later I get the news: I landed the part of Reno. And Kelsey got in as one of my backup singers.

My friends and I celebrate like crazy, hitting different dance clubs. I want most of all to tell Max, though. He was a big part of getting the role. I feel sad he won't respond to my texts or my sandwich note.

A day later, I'm pissed off. Because really?

I stop going near his building.

If he won't reply, maybe it's not worth it after all. Maybe he meant it when he wrote, "never go after a girl you can't walk away from."

Still, I miss him.

I take my vacation days. I'll be quitting my job soon and I'll lose them if I don't take them. I head out to Sadler for a long weekend. Maybe that will stop me from missing Max.

My parents can't believe I've landed a normal paying gig on Broadway that even has health insurance like a regular job. I'm sitting at our old cracked Formica kitchen table eating a bowl of ice cream with jimmies sprinkled all over the top telling the story of the call for the second time.

My mom puts down a stack of napkins and hands one to me. "You're gonna ruin your appetite for dinner."

"Lasagna? No chance," I say, grabbing a napkin. They're still using napkins printed with the logo of the failed donut shop from when I was in ninth grade. There are boxes and boxes of them in the garage—*boxes of shame,* my mom used to say sometimes.

"I can't believe you still have these," I say.

"I always want to throw them out, I hate looking at them, but your father says they're perfectly good napkins. You always need napkins, he says." She sits down across from me and pops open a can of fizzy water. "Five more minutes."

"Smells amazing," I say.

"You did it," she says. "Here, we worried you were shooting too high, but you did it."

"Yeah, I know you thought that," I say, trying to keep the annoyance out of my voice. "You only said it all the time. Shooting too high."

"We didn't want you to be disappointed," she says.

"You couldn't have tried a saying like, *do your best?* Maybe, *follow your bliss?* Something positive?"

She stares out the window. I look at the lines in her face, more lines than last year, and I feel bad for saying it suddenly.

"Never mind, it's okay, Ma," I say.

"No, it's not. We could've been more encouraging. But you know. It's hard to work at something and have your heart broken," she says. "We wanted to spare you."

I sit back. I felt like they were trying to hold me back with that saying. I never imagined they were being protective. Trying to protect me from all of the heartbreak they had with their endless failed businesses.

"I appreciate it," I say.

"No, it was negative."

"Well, all's well that ends well." I trace the old familiar donut. "How do you know when to throw in the towel?" I ask. "How do you know you're just throwing good after bad? How do you know?"

My mother wipes some condensation off the side of her can. "You mean like the donut shop?"

"All of them. The businesses you built and loved and lost. Do you ever look back and say, I quit too soon? We should've kept hammering away?"

"Usually we held on to those businesses too long," she says. "You think things should work out. You put all your heart in. It's hard, emotionally, to look at facts, when your heart and your sweat is in a thing."

I nod. Is that what I've been doing with Max? Texting and sitting outside his office like an idiot? Not wanting to look at the facts?

"Have you ever quit when you shouldn't have? Have you ever looked back and said, *if only I'd stuck with that one?*"

She sighs and stares at her can, fat red letters up the side. "Do you remember the millinery shop?" she asks. "You were pretty young at the time."

I narrow my eyes. "The millinery shop? You mean the hat store?"

"Yes, the hat store! It was a little hole in the wall. You were just a baby and I'd bring you there and I made these beautiful hats. People didn't really want them for the most part. The sales barely covered the rent. It was before Etsy was a thing, of course, so I only had the storefront, and a few local people to outsource fabric cutting to. But making those hats, with you in your little playpen, that was the best time of my life."

"I didn't know," I say. I love hearing that one of her businesses brought her joy.

She shrugs. "Oh, I suppose my hourly probably worked out to five bucks an hour on a good day, so it really wasn't a get-rich store, but when I look back, I wish I'd stayed. Because I loved that work. I loved making those hats. We wanted a deal with Bloomingdale's and we thought we were going to get it, but when it didn't materialize, we gave up. But I like to think that if we hadn't given up, maybe it would've been something humble but doable. A small dream that we could love."

"You wish you would've stayed with it? You think you would've made it with the hats?"

"The point is, it doesn't matter. You can never know the outcome of a thing, Mia. The only thing that you have is how it feels. We were always so focused on schemes to build our wealth, move to the other side of the tracks, get a pie-in-the-sky moment, we didn't concentrate on what made us happy. All of the other concerns beyond that, you just have to be bigger than those concerns."

She's up at the stove, pulling out the pan. I grab out the bread and slice it, start slathering on the butter and garlic powder.

Ma turns to me. "It's something that we admire about you. I

know we haven't been so supportive, but you're out there doing what you love. Even if you hadn't landed this amazing part."

Dad comes in, followed by my brother, who grabs beers.

Mom's signature lasagna is loaded up with cheese and carbs and there's tiramisu in the fridge. We're feasting our faces off, but I can't stop thinking about what Mom said.

I don't know the outcome with Max. I don't know what will happen with us. I know it feels good.

And maybe I need to keep trying.

30

Guys are oblivious as a rule. You don't have to do much
to rise above the competition.

~THE MAX HILTON PLAYBOOK: TEN
GOLDEN RULES FOR LANDING THE
HOTTEST GIRL IN THE ROOM

Max

Parker and I head to the auditorium at seven. We've put a
lot into this; I really want it to be a success. It's not just about
image. The city's best designers have gone all out donating
clothes. The models have donated their time. Maximillion
employees have solicited donations from businesses and vendors
for the raffle. We've got some surprise models lined up for turns
on the catwalk—comedians and musicians, mostly. Some
companies are doing skits.

I go back to check on the Maximillion team of models.
We're trotting out the Vicious line tonight.

The designers have things under control. I'm not surprised; I've built my business by putting good people in place and letting them run with their ideas; checking on them is really just a formality, a way of showing them I'm right there with them.

A way of trying to get my mind off of Mia, even though everything makes me think of her.

I head back through the front, past the catering staff, thinking about her little note. I gave Parker the sandwich. Like enjoying it might be dangerous, somehow.

I check on the team of event planners, whose base of operations is off to the side of the giant space. Everything's running like clockwork just when I could use a disaster to distract me. Guests in tuxedos and gowns are starting to arrive, moving through like exotic fish.

Parker comes up and hands me a drink. "We gotta get over to the captain's table—the show's gonna start."

It won't start for twenty minutes, but there are lots of dressed-up people between here and there, which means photos. It's easier to say no to photos when it's somebody else's event.

I make my way over, posing for pictures and saying Max Hilton things, being the carefree playboy who exists in the glittering dimensions of screens and billboards and camera lenses.

It was almost enough for a while.

Lana comes up and hugs me. She's with her real boyfriend, a man who's allergic to public events. I shake his hand, thank him for making it. Everybody looks amazing.

That, too, makes me think about Mia, declaring herself more beautiful and fascinating than the models in my pictures.

So Mia.

Fifteen more minutes, and we're finally home free, heading for the four empty chairs at the table at the end of the runway. Our fashion industry co-hosts are already there, next to Henry Locke and Vicky Nelson, who I know is a friend of Mia's.

I go over and shake hands with her. She's pleasant but cool. Does she think I'm being reckless with Mia's career? Does she hate the book, too? I clap a hand onto Henry's shoulder.

"So good to see you," Henry says. Henry and I became friends while we worked together on rehabbing the studio complex. His foundation is involved in a big way with this night. In fact, the Lockes' favorite animal shelter is this year's charity.

Parker leans across the table and says something to Henry.

I feel something brush against my leg—once, then again, with more deliberation.

A wave of surprise comes over me; it can only be Vicky, who's seated directly on my right. Is she rubbing my leg by accident? It has to be by accident. She's crazy about Henry.

I angle away, but there it is again.

"I'm sorry, that must've been my leg," I say to her.

"What do you mean?" she asks.

"I think...our legs."

"Oh!" She ducks under the table, bringing up a little white dog wearing a bejeweled bow tie. "Smuckers! What are you doing?" She gives me an apologetic look. "I hope it's okay that he's here."

"Of course!" I ruffle his furry little head.

"We're raffling off his diamond bow tie collar," she says. "He'll be modeling it later on. He's the spokes-dog for this charity."

"Spokes-dog," I say. "A vital role." It's a little bit silly, because, really? Spokes-dog? But Henry Locke beams at Vicky.

She grins back over at him, and I'm blown away by the affection they have for each other. The sense of their mutual acceptance and support. Something dark ripples through my chest.

The music starts up. The lights go down. The models come walking out. Everybody's showing their playful collections—this isn't a hugely serious show. A few rounds in, Lana has bicycle messengers riding around the catwalk with her bags.

I order another drink. The night is going to be endless.

Love ruins a man. Just walk away.

Mia

Kelsey lines up my Meow Squad co-workers and friends by height. She hands out the squares. Jada adjusts our sequined ears. Sienna complains about her letter. "Can't I be the 'L'?"

"You're the 'Y,'" Kelsey says. "The 'Y' is important."

I give some last-minute instructions. The same ones I've given a dozen times already.

I've been in a lot of shows, done countless auditions, but I've never felt so nervous, never felt like so much was at stake.

"Flip over the squares when I give the signal," I say.

"Breathe." Jada loops an arm over my shoulder. "You got this."

I'm not so sure. "What if he's just...annoyed? There's a good chance of it."

"I promise you, he won't be annoyed," Kelsey says.

"Angry, then."

"You don't know until you try," Noelle says. "You're scared right now, but you thought up this scheme when you weren't scared. Your bravest self thought up this scheme. Trust that girl who's brave."

"That girl wasn't thinking about the downside. Max hating it. What have I done?" I wrap my arms around myself. "This could be the high school lunchroom all over again," I say.

"We can still pull out," Jada says.

"What?" Sienna complains. "Are you shitting me?"

"Nobody's pulling out." Kelsey claps three times. "Walk-out positions."

"What if I created this just to punish myself?" I say to her.

"Then I'll get you a year's supply of Peanut Butter Kandy Kakes. Okay? And we'll dance it all off in *Anything Goes*."

I barely hear her. I'm back in that lunchroom, flat on my face with spaghetti all over me. "I seriously think I might throw up," I say. "What if I've recreated my worst nightmare?" And I close my eyes, worried about the Max Hilton girl thing again.

I remind myself for the hundredth time—I need to go bigger than that.

Max and I can go bigger than all of it.

The last thing you want is a woman you can't walk away from.

~THE MAX HILTON PLAYBOOK: TEN
GOLDEN RULES FOR LANDING THE
HOTTEST GIRL IN THE ROOM

Max

The show really is interminable.

And then the strangest thing. A pair of women come down the runway, arms linked. They're wearing cat suits. Matching sparkly ears. Aprons.

It takes a while to process that this is the Meow Squad uniform—sort of.

I turn to Parker. "What is Meow Squad doing up there?"

Parker shrugs.

Only businesses that donate get to do a turn, and they're supposed to be modeling clothes.

"Meow Squad made a huge last-minute donation to the shelter," Vicky says. "Well, it makes sense. Meow Squad, cats, right?" Her eyes sparkle.

Another pair of women walk out. And then another pair. They stop in a clump at the center of the catwalk.

And then Mia strolls out, boldly owning the catwalk in the uniform she despises. Her cheeks glow pink with high emotion, a fighter to the end.

"She hates that uniform," I mumble to nobody in particular. "What is she doing? She hates being seen in it."

As if that's the issue.

The women have squares with letters on them. They run around and get into formation, spelling L-O-V-E Y-O-U.

"How sweet is that!" Vicky exclaims.

I stand, heart thundering.

The women hoist Mia up above them, cheerleader-style, holding her feet.

She holds up a lone letter— "I"—and gazes down at me. I can barely process it. Her up there, hanging her heart out. Opening herself up.

I love you.

Waiting.

And no way will I leave her standing there. I'm moving before I can even think about it. I jump up onto the stage.

I nearly have a heart attack as she begins to free-fall backwards, but her friends catch her neatly and bounce her to the floor in front of them.

Dancers.

I go to her. "Mia, what are you doing?"

"I wasn't sure if you were getting the letters. Or my texts," she says.

My heart feels like it's bursting. "So this is what you came up with?"

"I was an idiot. I love you—that will never stop. I need you to know."

A hush falls over the room—people are straining to listen, but the only sound I can hear is my pulse, banging in my ears. "What about the Max Hilton girl thing?"

"I decided we can be bigger than that," she says.

God, this woman.

"Be bigger." I cup her cheeks, only vaguely aware of the applause this seems to spark. "You just went for broke. You shot for the stars."

"Ummm..."

And then I kiss her. The applause turns deafening.

I pick her up and whirl her around. I don't care that everybody's watching.

The music changes and she laughs into the kiss. "Let me down, the next group needs to come out," she says.

"You're not going anywhere," I say, kissing her again. "I love you."

"You do?"

"Like I ever stopped," I say. "Look at you."

"You never know how a thing will turn out," she says. "But you just have to go forward."

"Hey," I say. "How about a number?"

"You want me to sing?"

I grin. "Stay right there." I grab the microphone from the MC. "Are you ready for our surprise musical guest?" I ask the crowd.

There's clapping. I'm heading over to the pit. I lean down and confer with them. IPads come out. People are finding music. The song I'm asking them to play isn't hugely hard. A lot of them probably played it in high school or college.

The catwalk is clear aside from Mia. Her eyes widen when

a couple of stagehands bring up two chairs. That's what we'd always use for props for the wagon when I sang "The Surrey with the Fringe on Top."

"No!" She grabs my lapels. "What about your brand?" she whispers. "You don't have to do this!"

"If my brand can't handle cowboy songs, what the hell good is it?" I whisper. "Frankly, I think this'll be an improvement." And I want to meet her on this stage. Her bravery. Her passion. It's not a sacrifice when it's love.

One of the orchestra players comes up, tablet in hand, having volunteered to take Aunt Eller's parts.

Mia's laughing as the first strains start up. She takes her place, standing just to the side of the chairs, pantomiming hanging clothes on a clothesline. I peel off my jacket and toss it over the back. I stick my thumbs in my waistband. The first chords strike up.

The crowd goes wild, clapping and roaring as soon as I begin to sing, describing how I'll take her out in my surrey with the fringe on top.

Nobody has ever heard Max Hilton sing.

She remembers the whole thing, of course. All of her lines, and so do I. They say emotion helps to imprint things into your brain. These are songs we'll never forget.

Mia beams at me as I sit on one of the chairs and pretend to be driving a team of snow-white horses. She's skeptical as Laurey. But I win her over, describing all the places we'll go. Eventually she sits. This is how we work together. This is how our worlds work together. With us being brave.

The number ends, and somehow we're off the stage. People are crowding around. Everybody loved it.

Parker comes up to me. "That was fucking diabolical. It was so stupid, it was cool."

Mia rolls her eyes.

I pull her to me. Somebody's scrounged up an extra chair for her at our table. I'm a little disappointed; I would've preferred her on my lap.

She sits and says hi to Vicky.

The show continues on. I remember nothing. There's just the feel of Mia's hand in mine. The wonder that I feel when I look at her. The way I never want to let her go.

Tarquin comes over later. "So this is what you were up to. The Max Hilton girl thing—that was all to not spoil the surprise?"

"Something like that," I say, slinging an arm around Mia. "And no, she's not a Max Hilton girl." I kiss her on the forehead and give him a pointed look.

"Please," she says. "I'm the *only* Max Hilton girl."

"No, I'm the Mia Corelli guy," I say.

Tarquin groans. "I got it," he says. "Maybe you'll keep me in the loop if there's any more news?"

I nod. I don't know if Mia caught it, but he means, if there's an engagement.

She comes over that night after the show ends. We fall into bed and make love by the moonlight, with the music of the show still ringing in my ears.

"It was such a crazy success," she says after. "Only you could pull that off." And then she frowns.

I brush a dark curl from her forehead. "Is something up?"

"I have to confess something. The night you almost came up? I have to tell you what happened." She goes on to tell me a crazy story about her friends reading the book after she was assigned to deliver sandwiches to me. She was trying to do the rules from my book on me. And something about darts on my face. I act like I'm mad, but how could I be? I wrestle her under me. "I'm planning on getting a lot of mileage out of this, I hope you know," I say. And then I kiss her.

She sighs.

"I still want to talk to them and try to make this right," I say.

And I kiss her again.

33

Believe in yourself. Shoot for the stars.

~THE MAX HILTON PLAYBOOK: TEN
GOLDEN RULES FOR LANDING THE
HOTTEST GIRL IN THE ROOM

Mia

The Wilder Club is hopping. I can tell where my group is just from the laughter in the far booth. I take Max's hand, feeling jittery about having him meet my friends, but he really wants to. "You good?"

"Yeah. I've always wanted to meet the people who draw moustaches on me," he says.

I snort and drag him around a group of bright-haired neighborhood people and up to the bar. Sweat beads on my forehead underneath my hat, and it's not just because it's hot inside.

Several sets of eyes follow us. People have recognized him. "Two local brews," I say to the bartender.

"Is that the drink here?"

"Yup." I turn and watch him look around. It's strange seeing The Wilder Club through Max's eyes. It always struck me as wonderfully old school, full of aged woodwork and plants and vintage maps. Tiny brass lamps on thick, plain tables. I love the coziness of it, but Max's habitat is made up of limos and places of airy glamour that are lit by chandeliers.

And he looks larger than life in here, a sleek, magnificent hawk at a gathering of colorful songbirds.

"A little different from what you're used to," I say.

He pulls me to him by my scarf. "I love seeing your life." He kisses me, and my nerves ratchet down. We're together. We can handle this together.

A couple of women come up and ask Max to do a selfie. He's fun about it—he makes the selfies good, and my chest just swells to watch it. I've never felt so right with a man.

"For the love of god, don't put the location," I say to them while Max is paying for the beers.

"Don't worry," the one says. "The place would be mobbed."

An angry, booming voice. "You." I spin around and Antonio's giving Max his best Scarface meets Blue Steel. "Nobody puts their hands on my flower," he growls.

"Except maybe Kelsey?" I say to him, grinning. "Can Kelsey put a hand on your...*flower*?"

Antonio gives me outrage. Then, "It is in no way like a flower." He turns to Max. "And you!"

"Dude." I loop my arm in Max's arm. "Max, this is my cousin Antonio. He's awesome and studying to be an actor. Antonio, Max is with me. And you're not a murderous gigolo anymore."

Antonio frowns. He liked being a murderous gigolo.

I make them shake hands.

"You had that poor boy shaken," Max informs Antonio. He tells us what Rollins said about him. Antonio is excited that Rollins was so convinced. Something unwinds in my belly, seeing them get along. It's Kelsey and Jada I'm worried about, but this is a nice first step.

"Have you ever thought about modeling?" Max asks Antonio. "I mean, if the acting doesn't work out."

Antonio likes that. He's been thinking about it, though his experience is all in Milano, he says to Max. "And for the record," Antonio says, "I was kissing my thumb."

"He was kissing his thumb, it's true," I tell Max. "So was I."

Meanwhile, my gang has spotted us. We make our way over to the big corner booth. Lizzie and Jada and Tabitha are there. Antonio slides in next to Kelsey.

I introduce him around. Kelsey smiles as she says *hello*. Jada is gracious when he congratulates her on the show, but it's not okay. The fun has stopped and people are stiff now. I feel like it might never be okay. Is politeness between Max and my friends the best I can ever hope for?

There's more small talk, which is bad enough, but then he takes a book from his pocket and sets it on the table.

The Hilton Playbook.

And that really stops the conversation in its tracks.

"Oh, look," Kelsey says unhappily.

Despair spreads through my gut like acid. He wrote the book. He can't unwrite it.

Jada folds her arms. "You carry it around?"

"I've been re-reading it. I want to know your experience with it," he says. "You don't have to tell me, but I want to know."

"How I ended up with a jungle-kissing reverse-chaser?" Jada asks. "How Kelsey lived with one?"

My mouth goes dry.

"I don't know." Kelsey drains her beer.

Except Max really is interested, and I think that Kelsey senses it, because she launches into her story. What it felt like to have Nathan take the center stage, and be all scintillating, but ignoring her. "He seemed so funny and unique, but it was all your lines!"

He nods. Some protective instinct seems to be telling him not to use the interview-coaching analogy. "I didn't...think it through from that angle."

"It's not an angle," Jada says. "It's a freaking ruse. I specifically gave a guy the benefit of the doubt because of that cute dog story and it wasn't real. I felt deceived, and I feel like your book encourages that."

He nods. They don't want excuses, and he's not giving them.

"It was wrong to suggest they memorize it," he says simply. "They should have their own unique thing."

"Yeah, that's a start." Jada tells him her friend Gracie's story.

"I didn't mean for it to be used that way," he says. "I'm sorry."

"Thank you for saying that," Kelsey says. "I do appreciate it." The way she says it, though, there is a *but* in there. She appreciates it, *but...*

Sweat prickles along my spine.

"I mean it," Max says. "And I think sorry isn't enough. I'm thinking about doing a new edition. I talked to my publisher and they'll go for it if I write it. I can encourage guys to be confident and interesting without being fake."

"You're thinking about doing a new edition?" Jada sounds intrigued.

Kelsey's not so sure. She turns to her most hated section. More beers come.

I want more. I want my friends to see the vulnerable,

passionate, brilliant guy I see. I want them to see the Max who knows every word to every song of *Hair*. I want them to see the creative, thoughtful man, not the Max Hilton of Ferraris and zillion-dollar watches and devil-may-care liquor carts.

"There's something you're not saying," he says.

Kelsey gives me an apologetic look, then turns to Max. "Look, I'll own right now that I had a part in what happened with Nathan—your book helped get him in the door, but it was on me to see him for what he was. To not be blinded by his looks. But here's the thing—I got burned by a guy who read your book. He only read it. You wrote it. You put down every single one of those words. How can I trust you to be good to Mia when this is the way you were directing guys to behave? People change, but do they really? Or do they just get better at hiding shit? So if you think I'm not saying something...that's what I'm not saying."

"He's not that guy," I protest. "You need to give me a little credit here, Kelsey."

Max settles his hand over mine. "I'm going to prove you guys wrong," he says.

"I want you to," Kelsey says, raising her beer. "To you, proving me wrong."

"He's gonna," I say.

We all clink glasses, but it doesn't break the tension. I'm staring down the barrel of a reality where my friends tolerate my boyfriend, but they don't trust him with my heart.

How will this ever work?

I drink my beer, but I barely taste it. I give Max a nervous smile.

The talk turns to Tabitha's hurt wrist. She's been so worried about not being able to make rent, being that her injury prevents her from cutting hair, but tonight she's back to her sunshiny self, as if she'll make rent without a problem. "I've got a plan B," she says simply.

"Is it a secret plan B?" Lizzie asks. "Or can you tell us?"

She and Jada exchange mysterious glances.

"Oh my god, you have a secret plan B!" Lizzie says. "You have to tell! Tabitha, what is it?"

"I hope it's not illegal," I say.

"We're not supposed to tell. We signed a thing," Jada says.

"We're not even supposed to tell we signed a thing," Tabitha says.

"But we didn't sign a thing saying we wouldn't say we signed a thing," Jada says.

"I think it was in the thing we signed?" Tabitha says. "But I don't think it's technically illegal, Mia."

"Wait, what?" I say. "Not technically illegal? Okay, we need to order a few more rounds and get it out of you two."

"Erp! Don't even!" Jada swings her glance to Max. "Let's talk about you some more, Max. I'm curious about your pickup system," she says. "How did you develop it? How did you know what would work? You were twenty years old without much experience dating from the sound of it. Was there some sort of testing protocol, or what?"

I try not to stare daggers at Jada. I really, really wanted this topic to be over.

Max is toying with his napkin. Like he doesn't want to say something. So of course, everybody's attention is riveted on him. "I was...on the other end of it, in a way," he says.

I sit up. "You were on the other end of the pickup system?"

"What does that mean?" Kelsey asks. "A woman did a system on you?"

"It wasn't a system, not anything anybody was consciously doing. It was just...me observing the effect that this woman had on me."

I frown. Who the hell is he talking about? "I've had enough of this topic," I say.

"I haven't!" Tabitha says. "I want to know."

My cheeks heat. I want everyone to stop talking.

"She was playful and outrageous," Max says. "A little bit bossy. And so goddamn beautiful, it killed me."

Antonio frowns, not loving the sound of this. I grit my teeth. What is Max doing? He would talk about some past crush at a time like this?

"She was a force of nature," Max continues. "And the outrageous things she'd do. With every little thing she did, I'd just want her more. She dressed so brightly when I first met her. Loud colors and metallics."

Kelsey listens, rapt. "The alpha-signaling."

Jada exchanges glances with Lizzie.

"Yup," Max said. "Like she was anointing herself. Choosing herself." Max looks over at me. "Freshman year of high school. That's when she came into my life."

Something in my belly turns upside down. *What?*

"She was the bravest, boldest woman I'd ever met," he continues. "She came up poor; she wasn't supposed to even leave her tiny town, but she set her sights high, believed in herself when nobody else would. She'd literally bulldoze you with her reality. And god, the stories she would tell!"

I stare at him, stunned. The book describes me? In my mind, I run through his rules: Alpha-signaling. Surrounding yourself with interesting people. Boss people and tell them what they want. Be playful and outrageous. "What are you saying?"

"We started out enemies, but one summer we did this musical together, and it was the best summer of my life. But I screwed it up, and we were enemies again. Even so, I'd sneak into Miedlow Hall and listen to her sing. I couldn't stay away from her. I loved her."

"What?" My voice sounds hoarse, like it's coming from somewhere else. I feel like everything I ever knew has been turned upside down.

"When I left high school, I was sure I'd lost my chance at love. She's why I wrote the book."

"Love ruins a man. Just walk away," Antonio quotes.

I'm trembling inside. "Max?"

"It was easy to go hard." The way he looks at me, I think his entire soul is there in his eyes. "They say cynics are just disillusioned idealists. You should know that writers of pickup books are just heartbroken romantics."

I'm blindsided.

"Jesus Christ!" Kelsey says. "It was about Mia."

Antonio gazes into the middle distance. "He wrote it because he couldn't have Mia. His heart was broken in pieces. Never pursue a woman you can't walk away from. Never fall in love."

"Max," I whisper hoarsely.

Max presses his hand over mine. "I just love you, that's all. I couldn't get over you."

There's no sound at the table. Everybody's staring at me now—I feel their eyes on me, but all I can see is him.

"Excuse me, Max Hilton?"

I look over. It's a couple of college kids, phones in hand.

"Sorry to interrupt," the one says, "but it's my friend's birthday...would you mind..."

Max kisses me on the cheek and stands to do a selfie with the strangers. "As long as you don't give the location," he says.

"God, right?" Jada says, eyes shining with emotion.

I exchange glances with Kelsey while they're doing the selfies. She's smiling huge, her dimples deep. "Okay, okay," she says. "That works."

The night goes on. Some more friends come by and things

get raucous. People are surprised that Max is in our group, but the novelty wears off and he blends in easily. I sit back, watching my friends. It's easy to forget how we all have the same performing arts roots.

The book was about me.

Around midnight everybody wants to play eighties songs on the old-fashioned jukebox, and Kelsey and Antonio are sexy dancing on the tables. The bartender does his usual scolding, then turns back to serve more beers.

Lizzie announces she's hungry, and we hatch a plan to order ten of our official apartment pizzas. Snow has started to fall in huge, pretty flakes. We run to our place in a group, laughing and screaming, desperate to arrive before the pizzas.

A few minutes later, we're all crowded into the elevator, rosy-cheeked and out of breath.

I find his hand and squeeze.

EPILOGUE

Six Months later

MIA

I'm touching up my makeup one last time while a guy from wardrobe reinforces a hem on my Reno Sweeney pants.

"Bad luck to wear something that's being sewn on me," I say. "And I don't even care. I feel lucky."

"You are lucky," Kelsey says. "We are lucky."

She and I slap pinkies.

It's like a dream, being in the show together. We're pretty sure it's going to get extended, too. Ticket sales have been through the roof.

The stage manager calls out the ten-minute warning.

Kelsey sees something over my shoulder and her eyes crinkle with glee. "Don't look now."

Of course I look. It's Max, coming through the crowded dressing room with an armful of roses.

I stand. "How'd you get in here?"

"I'm Max freaking Hilton, baby."

"He's Max freaking Hilton," Kelsey says.

I snicker. It's an inside joke with our group to say that and tease him about it.

But the truth is, when we're all hanging out together, we get the real Max Hilton—not the one who drives a Ferrari and spends his days looking pensively over Mediterranean cliffs.

We get the Max who plays piano and does laundry and remembers people's birthdays. And is a great friend.

And an even better boyfriend.

"No kissing Reno," the stage manager says, pointing at Max. "No, no, no."

"You'll muss my makeup." I breathe in the scent of the flowers, so rich and sweet. "Thank you."

"Nervous?" he asks.

"It's opening night," I say.

He leans in. "But are you really?"

I bring my lips close to his, wishing so badly that I could kiss him. "I've been training for this all my life."

He kisses the top of my head, and I'm sure he gets a face full of hairspray. "I'll be out there," he says.

THE SHOW IS AN ABSOLUTE HIGH—THERE'S no other way to describe it.

I can feel the audience soaring during the peaks. I can feel them swooning when the romance story takes off. Their cheers after our first big tap number fill my chest to the absolute brim.

Most of all, I can feel Max out there, true north in the darkness.

I wait in the wings after the big final dance number as the members of the cast go out to receive applause, starting with the small roles—the sailors and passengers—and working up to the leads.

I catch sight of my parents in the front, right next to Max. It's beyond thrilling to have them in on opening night.

Finally it's my turn. I go out with my co-stars. We grab hands and bow as a foursome. The applause feels like starlight.

Max and I take my parents out to dinner at The Four Seasons. The two of us tend to prefer low-key restaurants these days, and he'll even indulge my passion for diners, but it's special for my folks.

After an amazing time, we drop my folks at their hotel and head to The Wilder Club.

Kelsey and Antonio have gotten there early; they've staked out our gang's favorite booth. They're snuggled together in the corner of it.

"You sure you want company?" Max asks as we walk up.

"Sit," Kelsey says.

Max and I slide in. The guys start talking about how great we are, retelling the high points of the show from the perspective of the seats. Just shamelessly stroking our egos.

Drinks come and they keep on.

I catch Kelsey's gaze and grin. She puts up her pinky, and I put up mine.

The four of us double-date a lot. It's been a total blast. We're planning a picnic in the park on Monday, and it's supposed to be perfect weather. I'm bringing the sandwiches.

I'll be throwing in the cheesy puffs.

Max knits his fingers into mine. "Seriously killed it," he says.

"And anybody who says otherwise will find the end of my blade," Antonio jokes.

Tabitha and Jada arrive in full sparkle mode with a couple of other friends. They all shove in. "Are you talking dirty, Antonio?" Jada asks.

Antonio snorts.

Parker comes by; the booth gets so crowded that I have to sit on Max's lap. Which I don't mind at all.

When Max and I get back to his place, there are vases of roses everywhere, and champagne on ice on the table.

"What is this?" I ask.

"I wanted to celebrate."

"I didn't know! We could've left Wilder hours ago."

He comes to me, begins unbuttoning my shirt. "I wanted to stay. We have a lifetime to celebrate."

My belly flip-flops. *A lifetime.* "If you think you're going to get some action, you're right."

He already has my shirt off. "You really were so amazing."

I'm pushing off his suit jacket. "Action getting more likely."

Eventually, we're ripping off each other's clothes and throwing them everywhere. Maybe it's the adrenaline, but I've never wanted him so badly.

I scream and laugh when he hauls me over his shoulder and carries me to his bed.

Later we're just lying there, looking out over the city. He wraps his arms around me and kisses the top of my head. "What are you thinking?"

"I'm thinking about amending the grade for your tower to five stars."

"I want ten stars. What do I have to do for ten?"

"Hmmm," I say with a mysterious smile. "Good question."

He growls and flips me over on my back and looms over me with that half grin.

Then he kisses me.

And there are not enough stars.

∿

THANK you for reading Breaking the Billionaire's Rules! I hope you enjoyed your time with Max and Mia as much as I did!

~

ARE you ready for more of the gang? Have you been wondering how Tabitha is going to pay her rent? What is her mysterious secret? What in the world did she sign?

Find the answer in Tabitha's book, ***The Billionaire's Fake Fiancée***, out now!

ACKNOWLEDGMENTS

There is a strong theme of friends lifting each other woven through *Breaking the Billionaire's Rules*. And whoa, that was *definitely* a theme when it came to writing this book and getting the details right.

So many of my book loving/reading/writing/word-nerding friends came through for me! You guys! What would I do without you?

The following list runs in semi-chronological order of appearance in the process. You guys helped me to reach higher than I could've alone.

Mira Lyn Kelly, kisses to you for that coffee shop discussion on the lunch-cart girl concept. Courtenay Bennett, thanks for discussing the pick-up-book-writer-guy concept with me and for being so supportive of the whole thing, plus your amazing read-through and thoughts on Max!!!

Skye Warren and Molly O'Keefe, you guys are such brilliant critique partners! Thank you for seeing so clearly when I couldn't. Joanna Chambers, thank you for spending hours on Skype with me—all of your insights were pure gold to me. You so pulled me out of the fire! Deepest gratitude to my generous and talented writing group—Elizabeth Andrews, Terri Whitman, Mark Powell, and Marcia Peck—thank you for the thoughtful read and the incredible ideas and discussion of all things Max and Mia. You guys so came through! Thank you to Becca Mysoor for the mind-blowingly important feedback. OMG, you slay!

A wildly grateful shout-out to Sadye Scott-Hainchek for the amazing edits; to Judy Zweifel for the world-class proofread; and to Peggy Schnurr and Hilary Suppes for the late-breaking proofreading—you guys are angels to this writer who could not stop changing the book! Thanks also to Joan Lai and Courtenay Bennett for some eagle-eye last-minute catches.

At this point, if there are typos, it's because I can't stop changing the book like, ever.

Hugs to the lovely Molly O'Hare for expert assistance in the theatrical department, and Michele Catalano of Catalano Creative for the gorgeous cover.

And to you, Nina Grinstead—you keep me sane with your sweet friendship and crazy smarts! Thank you to the whole Social Butterfly gang—Brooke, Sarah, Chanpreet, Shannon, Hilary and Jen and the rest—love you guys!

Huge love also to Melissa Gaston – I seriously don't know what I'd do without your savvy and professionalism and your fun attitude. Pinky slap!

I'm wildly grateful to all of you book-loving bloggers who support my work with your kind words and tireless passion. I see you, and I so appreciate the time you take to read and to craft those reviews.

Major kisses and love to the Annika Martin Fabulous Gang. You guys inspire me and lift me in a ways you can never know. And total tackle-hug love to my ARC Gang – your support and kind words and fun attitude is everything to me. Like really!

In summation, heart eyes at you all.

ALSO BY ANNIKA MARTIN (AKA CAROLYN CRANE)

Enemies to lovers Romantic Comedy

Most Eligible Billionaire

The Billionaire's Wake-up Call Girl

Breaking the Billionaire's Rules

The Billionaire's Fake Fiancée

Return Billionaire to Sender (fall 2020)

Dark Mafia

Dark Mafia Prince

Wicked Mafia Prince

Savage Mafia Prince

Romantic Suspense standalones

Against the Dark

Off the Edge

Into the Shadows

Behind the Mask

MM Spies (with Joanna Chambers)

Enemies like You

Criminals & Captives (with Skye Warren)

Prisoner

Hostage

Ultra dirty romantic comedy series

The Hostage Bargain

The Wrong Turn

The Deeper Game

The Most Wanted

The Hard Way

www.annikamartinbooks.com

ALL THE ANNIKA DEETS!

I love reading fun, steamy books, doing yoga, taking pictures of my cats, rocking out to 90's music, taking long baths, consuming See's chocolate suckers, mooning over heroes' hands, and helping animals. I also love connecting with readers and reviewers.

newsletter:
http://annikamartinbooks.com/newletter

Facebook:
www.facebook.com/AnnikaMartinBooks

The Annika Martin Fabulous Gang:
www.facebook.com/groups/AnnikaMartinFabulousGang/

Instagram:
instagram.com/annikamartinauthor

website:
www.annikamartinbooks.com

annika@annikamartinbooks.com

Printed in Great Britain
by Amazon